### *"Didn't I ever say that I was proud of the way you look?"*

Celine asked huskily. "That I like to watch you walk? That your smile gives me a thrill? And your hands, so strong and gentle, made me feel cared for?" She caught a quick breath. "Haven't I ever told you how much pleasure your body gave me, in bed and out of it?"

"No." Max's voice was hoarse, his jaw rigid, his cheeks dusky. His eyes met hers with somber fire.

Celine moistened her lips with the tip of her tongue. "Perhaps," she said hesitantly, "it's too late now. I should have. I'm sorry."

She had moved Max, she could see. "I wish I had," she said softly. And, willing her fingers not to tremble, she took one of his hands in hers and laid it against her cheek. "I wish it wasn't too late."

Dear Reader,

This month marks the advent of something very special in Intimate Moments. We call it "Intimate Moments Extra," and books bearing this flash will be coming your way on an occasional basis in the future. These are books we think are a bit different from our usual, a bit longer or grittier perhaps. And our lead-off "extra" title is one terrific read. It's called *Into Thin Air*, and it's written by Karen Leabo, making her debut in the line. It's a tough look at a tough subject, but it's also a top-notch romance. Read it and you'll see what I mean.

The rest of the month's books are also terrific. We're bringing you Doreen Owens Malek's newest, *Marriage in Name Only*, as well as Laurey Bright's *A Perfect Marriage*, a very realistic look at how a marriage can go wrong before finally going very, very right. Then there's Kylie Brant's *An Irresistible Man*, a sequel to her first-ever book, *McLain's Law*, as well as Barbara Faith's sensuous and suspenseful *Moonlight Lady*. Finally, welcome Kay David to the line with *Desperate*. Some of you may have seen her earlier titles, written elsewhere as Cay David.

Six wonderful authors and six wonderful books. I hope you enjoy them all.

Yours,

Leslie Wainger
Senior Editor and Editorial Coordinator

Please address questions and book requests to:
Silhouette Reader Service
U.S.: 3010 Walden Ave., P.O. Box 1325, Buffalo, NY 14269
Canadian: P.O. Box 609, Fort Erie, Ont. L2A 5X3

# A PERFECT MARRIAGE

## LAUREY BRIGHT

FROM THE LIBRARY OF
CARMEN LOPEZ BUSTOS

*Silhouette*
INTIMATE™ MOMENTS®
Published by Silhouette Books
America's Publisher of Contemporary Romance

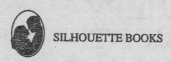

SILHOUETTE BOOKS

ISBN 0-373-07621-5

A PERFECT MARRIAGE

Copyright © 1995 by Daphne Clair de Jong

This edition published by arrangement with Harlequin Enterprises B.V.

® and TM are trademarks of Harlequin Enterprises B.V., used under
license. Trademarks indicated with ® are registered in the United States
Patent and Trademark Office, the Canadian Trade Marks Office and in
other countries.

**Printed in U.S.A.**

**Books by Laurey Bright**

**Silhouette Intimate Moments**

*Summers Past* #470
*A Perfect Marriage* #621

**Silhouette Special Edition**

*Deep Waters* #62
*When Morning Comes* #143
*Fetters of the Past* #213
*A Sudden Sunlight* #516
*Games of Chance* #564
*A Guilty Passion* #586
*The Older Man* #761
*The Kindness of Strangers* #820
*An Interrupted Marriage* #916

**Silhouette Romance**

*Tears of Morning* #107
*Sweet Vengeance* #125
*Long Way From Home* #356
*The Rainbow Way* #525
*Jacinth* #568

## LAUREY BRIGHT

has held a number of different jobs, but has never wanted to be anything but a writer. She lives in New Zealand, where she creates the stories of contemporary people in love that have won her a following all over the world.

# Chapter 1

Max Archer sat absently twirling a glass of whisky on the table before him while his four male companions tossed quips among themselves and chuckled at each other's rejoinders. The New Zealand Legal Practitioners' annual conference was officially over, and all that remained was the final dinner in a couple of hours' time.

Max was tempted to give that a miss and drive home to Auckland. He wondered if Celine would be there. Was this her night class evening? Or a bridge or badminton night? He couldn't remember.

His idle gaze was caught by one of the younger women lawyers, seated at a nearby table. Katie something, he recalled. Bright and keen. Her blond mane of curls framing a heart-shaped face, combined with a lusciously curved figure, would ensure that she was favourably viewed by some of those whose favour counted, and vastly underestimated by most of her opponents.

She was a treat to the eyes, anyway, and Max let his linger. Her attention seemed to be on the silver-haired veteran barrister next to her, but she looked up, meeting Max's gaze for a second, and smiled. A hand lifted to her hair, pushing it back, her eyes half closing. Then she smiled at him again and returned her attention to her elderly companion.

Max pulled his gaze away and raised the whisky glass to his lips. He shifted uncomfortably in his chair, wondering if the coquetry had been unconscious or deliberate. Not that he was about to find out. He was, he reminded himself, a happily married man.

"Hello, darling. That looks nice."

At the sound of Max's voice, Celine turned from the vase she was filling as he came through the door from the garage into the utility room. The pigskin briefcase she'd given him last Christmas was tucked under his arm, one hand holding his overnight bag, the other a suit bag that he'd slung across his shoulder.

She smiled at him, pausing with a long-stemmed, salmon pink carnation in her fingers. Not for the first time, she thought what a good-looking man her husband was, with his lean, dark, male elegance. She'd once heard a courtroom opponent refer to his "glacial blue eyes," but for her they were more often warmed by affection.

She inserted the carnation into the vase and picked up a piece of ladder fern, considering where to put it. "How was the conference?"

Max came over to drop a quick kiss on her cheek. "Not bad. A couple of useful sessions. You didn't mind that I went straight to the office this morning?"

"No. Of course not." She glanced at him with mild surprise and returned to contemplating the floral arrangement. "I was out most of the morning, anyway." She slotted in the fern, and gave a couple of carnations a final twitch. "You haven't forgotten the Hardings are coming to dinner, have you?"

"I had, actually. I brought some work home, too, but maybe I can put a couple of hours in later. Are you using a new perfume?"

Celine gave a little laugh. "It's the flowers."

He bent closer to her and breathed in. "No, it's you."

She half turned, raising a hand to tuck a glossy strand of dark brown hair behind her ear. "Shampoo," she said. "I washed my hair." He was closer than she'd realised, and her eyelids automatically lowered a little as she tipped her head back.

For a second Max's eyes had a strangely unfocused look, before he stepped back. "Why don't you let it grow?" he asked her. It swung in a sleek, straight cut just below her ears, the ends curving gently.

Confused, she said, "I've had it this way for years. Don't you like it?"

"It was long when we got married."

"I was twenty-four when we got married."

"So?"

Celine shook her head, smiling. "I'd have to pin it up all the time." She turned to pick up the vase. "Are you going to stand there all day? I have to put this in the hallway."

He stood back, then followed her to the spacious entry hall, where she placed the flowers on a polished antique table with cabriole legs.

Late sunlight glowed through the fanlight over the front door, making a petal-like pattern on the gold Italian marble floor. The fanlight and the heavy kauri door had been rescued from a demolition site by the architect who designed the house. Celine had worked closely with him to plan a home that was a blend of new and old, aiming for comfort, functionality and style. Max thought they'd done a good job. He liked living in the house and he enjoyed entertaining his friends and professional acquaintances here.

Celine had chosen the furniture and interior decor herself. So successfully that other people had come to her for help. A few years ago she'd converted the third bedroom into a workroom and embarked on a course of study to improve her skills, and what had begun as a favour for friends had evolved into a part-time occupation for which she was paid, Max deduced, quite substantially. He had never inquired exactly how much she had in her personal bank account, nor queried what she spent from either her own or their joint account.

"Will I have time to shower and change?" he asked, heading for the curved staircase.

"Plenty. I told them six-thirty to sevenish. And you know Honoria. They're bound to be late."

Max was never late unless delayed by fire, flood or acts of God. Without commenting on Honoria Harding's notorious inability to be on time for anything, he went upstairs to the circular gallery from which the bedrooms opened, his footsteps soundless on the thick mushroom carpet.

Celine returned to the utility room to clean up discarded leaves and bits of stem, then went to the kitchen, making sure the braised lamb shanks were simmering nicely in the oven, and the passionfruit mousse in the refrigerator had set. She opened a bottle of Grove Mill Black Birch to go with the lamb, and left it to breathe, then checked the table settings in the dining room. Alice, her home help, had fixed the table before she left.

The sliding glass doors were open to the wide terrace outside, where an outdoor table and chairs waited invitingly under a canopy of flame-red bougainvillea sprawled over the pergola, and the tubbed frangipani, one pink and one white, gave off their sweet, exotic scent. Three broad, shallow steps led to the tiled area around the swimming pool.

Celine glanced at the slim gold watch that had been her tenth anniversary present from Max, made a small adjustment to the table napkins, and left the room to go upstairs.

Max had unpacked his clothes and hung up the suit. The door to his wardrobe was ajar, the empty overnight bag tucked into a corner. When her friends complained that their husbands left their socks under the bed and never hung up wet towels, Celine sat silently counting her blessings. She knew used socks, shirts and underwear would be in the laundry basket where they belonged, and the only evidence of Max's presence in the bathroom would be a residue of warm steam from the shower and a lingering smell of the rather expensive after-shave that he liked. Tidying up after himself seemed second nature to Max, part of his personal code of good manners.

Celine opened her wardrobe and took out a champagne-gold dress, one of her favourites. The classic crossover bodice and narrow skirt suited her and the style was timeless. She laid the dress on the bed, kicked off her shoes and went to get clean undies from her drawer.

Max opened the bathroom door as she dropped the undies on the bed. He strode into the room, naked and unhurried, giving her an absent smile as he went to his dressing table and pulled out underpants and socks. Max had always been unselfconscious about his body, and even now he had no reason beyond the bounds of public modesty to hide it. He was tall and lean, his flanks taut, his legs and arms trim and lightly muscled, and his stomach flat. He played squash and tennis, and for his thirty-fifth birthday she had bought him the latest in exercise machines, which he had looked a bit quizzical over but used generally a couple of times a week. He said if nothing else it was a good stress reliever.

"Have you finished with the bathroom?" Celine asked as he turned.

"It's all yours." He pulled on sleek-fitting underpants, his mouth quirking as she took a turquoise satin wrapper from the inner door of her wardrobe and made for the bathroom. He was often amused at her need to cover herself even on her way to and from the bedroom to the en suite bathroom, but he'd given up teasing her about it.

When she came back, her face already lightly made-up, the satin wrapper belted around her waist, Max, dressed in grey slacks and an open-necked shirt, was standing in front of his dressing table, combing his hair.

Celine went to the bed and stepped into lace-trimmed primrose satin panties before shedding the wrapper and picking up the matching bra. She leaned forward to ease her breasts into the cups and fasten the hooks, then straightened and reached for the dress. A strand of hair had floated across her mouth and she automatically tossed her head to flick it away. It was then she realised that Max had put down the comb and was just standing in front of the mirror.

"What are you doing?" she asked as his eyes met hers in the glass. She held the dress in front of her. "Max!" She knew what he'd been doing—watching her dress, in the mirror.

As Max turned, she expected him to make some bantering comment. Instead he said irritably, "For pity's sake, Celine! We've been married for twelve years, and you're still hung up about me seeing you naked?"

"I'm not," she said stiffly. "Not when—the circumstances are right."

"You mean when we're in bed, and you're sufficiently turned on that it doesn't matter."

"Well, what do you want? Am I supposed to parade around naked for your benefit?"

"It would make a change... No, of course not, if it makes you uncomfortable. I'm sorry I snapped." He smiled at her and then deliberately looked away as she lifted the dress over her head.

Pulling a gold leather belt about her waist, she said with a hint of acid in her voice, "Did they have a stripper jumping out of a cake at this conference?"

Max laughed. "No such luck, I'm afraid. Even without the possible repercussions on the Society's reputation, the women members wouldn't stand for it."

Celine bent to put on her sandals, one hand on the bed to steady herself. "Were there many women?"

"About a third. And some of the men brought their wives to the dinner last night." As Celine crossed to her dressing table and took a pair of pearl drop earrings from a drawer, he leaned back with folded arms and said, "There was one girl there that I bet a few of the old codgers wouldn't have minded bursting out of a cake."

"Young woman," Celine said, inserting an earring, her head on one side. "It's sexist to call them girls."

"She looked like a girl to me," he said, grinning. "Any female younger than twenty-five does, these days."

Celine cast him a smiling glance and turned her head the other way for the second earring. "It's a sign of middle age. What was her name?"

"Katie something-or-other. Looks like a cross between Marilyn Monroe and Bo Peep, and specialises in industrial law. Are we middle-aged?"

"Something like it. I see forty looming on the horizon." She peered into the mirror, looking for lines.

He strolled over and hooked an arm about her waist. "It's looming faster for me. You're a very attractive woman. And you still will be when you're ninety. All the old gents in the nursing home will be making passes at you." He bent his head to kiss her.

Laughing, she turned her face so that the kiss landed on her cheek. "Don't, you'll smudge my lipstick. Anyway, I've got stuff on to make it last through dinner, and it tastes horrid."

Releasing her, he said, "Do you think we could nip down for a quick drink before Tom and Honoria arrive?"

She smiled at him. "You pour them while I put the finishing touches to the hors d'oeuvres."

They were on the deck, companionably sipping at their aperitifs when the doorbell pealed.

"You go." Celine swiftly finished her gin and tonic and picked up Max's empty glass. "I'll take these away."

When she came back bearing the hors d'oeuvres, he had their guests seated on the terrace. Tom stood up to kiss her cheek. "Celine! Lovely as ever." He was a thick-set man with sandy hair retreating in good order from his forehead, and friendly brown eyes.

"Thank you, Tom." She bent to put the plate on the table. "Hello, Honoria. Is Max looking after you?"

"Beautifully, thank you." Honoria wore her blond hair sleeked back into a chignon spiked with glittering combs. An apricot silk jumpsuit clung to a cat-thin figure, and a row of bracelets jangled down one arm. Max had once said that whatever Honoria wore, somehow he always saw her in form-fitting leopardskin and six-inch heels.

Max was filling champagne flutes with sparkling wine. "The latest vintage of Pelorus," he was telling Tom. "See what you think."

While they discussed wines, Celine asked Honoria about the Harding children, a boy and a girl of high school age. The subject occupied Honoria happily for twenty minutes, and when Celine excused herself to attend to the meal, Honoria picked up what remained of her second glass of Pelorus and followed, propping herself against the kitchen counter as Celine, declining the token offer of help, warmed bread rolls, removed the casserole from the oven, and placed the vegetables in serving dishes.

"It smells divine," Honoria told her. "And looks wonderful, too. I don't know how you do it. I can never have everything ready at the same time. The vegetables get cold while I'm fixing the meat, or the meat overcooks while I deal with the vegetables. Or the sauce goes lumpy, or I forget to serve the potatoes."

"If I had a family I'd probably find the same," Celine told her. "There always seems to be a child around with some urgent need when their mother's entertaining."

"I think it's an attention thing. They're afraid you'll get distracted and not remember them or something. Mine still do it, and they're teenagers! Here, can I carry something?" Honoria gulped the last of her wine and picked up the two dishes that Celine indicated.

Max and Celine had been on their honeymoon in the Cook Islands when they met Tom and Honoria. The Hardings had been married longer, but were only a year or two older, and the four of them had spent several evenings together watching island dancers or dining out at the various restaurants, and shared the expenses of boat trips and taxi rides. Fortunately the islands were well suited to Honoria's flexible notions of time. Even Max, after the first couple of days, had become quite relaxed about it.

After returning to New Zealand they had seen one another two or three times a year. Max and Tom enjoyed a casual male comradeship and while Max derived a good deal of what he deemed innocent amusement from Honoria's flamboyance and her ingenuous conversation, Celine appreciated her warm-heartedness and the shrewd judgement concealed behind an artlessly breathless manner.

Sometimes they talked in a vague way of sharing another holiday, but it had never got beyond talk. Perhaps all of them were secretly afraid of spoiling the memory.

When they'd seen Tom and Honoria off and shut the door, Max dropped the arm he had draped about Celine's shoulders, and rubbed a hand on the back of his neck. "Do you need any help to clear up?"

"Honoria and I have done most of it, and Alice will be here in the morning. You go and read your brief, or whatever it is you brought home."

"You're a wife in a million, you know that?" he said lazily. "Actually, I could probably be persuaded to leave it for tonight, if you're interested." Fractionally, he raised an eyebrow.

Celine laughed. "You," she said, "are full of wine and nostalgia. I'm not going to be responsible for seducing you from your work." She walked away from him across the hall.

Max looked after her, his expression pensive, and after a moment turned and went upstairs to his study.

In the bedroom Celine put on a pair of rose silk pyjamas before going into the bathroom and dropping her undies into the laundry basket. Max had given the primrose set to her, she recalled. He quite often gave her frivolous, sexy lingerie that she would seldom buy for herself. Unlike some men, he knew her size and didn't seem to mind shopping for intimate female apparel.

Perhaps when he'd watched her put on his gift earlier this evening, he'd fancied removing it himself. The first time he'd given her a nightgown—red nylon with black lace frills smothering the minimalist bodice and circling the hem—and told her to put it on because he intended to take it off later, she'd laughingly accused him of wanting to own his woman, buying and controlling what she wore.

"You've been reading feminist literature," he guessed.

"And what have *you* been reading?" she'd retorted. *"Playboy?"*

"For the articles," he told her solemnly. "Actually, I haven't opened one since I was a teenager. I just saw this in a shop window and I thought you'd look good in it."

Celine had thought she looked like a tart, but hadn't said so. If he really wanted her to wear it, she didn't mind. No one else was going to see her in it.

Over the years his taste had refined, or perhaps he'd realised that she wasn't the black-lace type. He still liked low-cut gowns with lots of lace, but he was more likely to buy satin than nylon, and choose muted or pastel shades. He had never given her pyjamas.

She had, of course, provided herself with some specially glamorous nightwear for their honeymoon. Some had been bought earlier, for the long weekend that they'd spent together, which they had both tacitly known was a trial run to test their sexual compatibility before they committed themselves to marriage.

She'd found Max a very satisfactory lover, neither hurried nor selfish, and plainly she'd satisfied him, too. There were few awkward moments, and on their way home he'd said to her, "Would you like to choose an engagement ring tomorrow?" From that point on they had never doubted their commitment to each other.

Celine got into bed and picked up her book from the bedside table. It was a sex-and-shopping saga that had been pressed on her by a member of her bridge club. She got through a chapter and a half before turning off the light.

"Do you fancy a few days away?" Max was putting on his tie in front of the mirror the next morning, while Celine straightened the bed.

"You don't have another conference, do you?"

Max pulled the knot up to his collar and adjusted the tie. "I meant just you and me. A holiday." He turned to face her.

"Do you have time?"

"One of my clients has decided to plead guilty after all, so I could leave early on Friday, and take Monday off, too. Maybe we could go to the Bay of Islands, or Taupo."

"You've just been to Taupo."

"Hardly had time to appreciate the lake or the views, we were kept so busy with seminars. The hotel where we had the conference was quite good, and right on the lakeside. We could stay there if you like. Or we could just drive until we find somewhere we want to stop."

Tempted, Celine gave it a moment's thought. "*This* weekend? Oh, I can't, Max."

"Why not?"

"I'm collecting for the Pacific Hurricane Relief Fund on Saturday afternoon."

"I see. Right."

"If I'd known sooner—" Celine left the bed and took her wrap from the wardrobe. "But they've had enough trouble finding volunteers, and at short notice—"

"Yes. Well, it was just an idea." He shrugged. "Maybe we can do it some other time."

"If another client has a change of heart I'll let you know. It's about the only chance I'm likely to get."

Fancying he sounded ever so slightly grumpy, Celine said reasonably, "I have a fairly full schedule, myself. I can't just drop everything whenever you happen to have a free day or two."

"I don't expect you to," he answered. "Forget it. I'll see you downstairs."

When she got to the kitchen he'd had his cold cereal and two pieces of toast and marmalade, and was finishing his coffee. She took the crumb-dusted plate and put it on the counter ready to be stacked in the dishwasher, and poured herself some coffee.

Max got to his feet, saying, "I'd better get going." He came round the table to drop a kiss on her cheek. "'Bye."

Briefcase in hand, he headed out the door, turning to close it. Celine was standing with one hand on a chairback, putting the coffee cup down on the table, and he paused, then came back to her, sliding his arms about her.

He pulled her close and kissed her properly, taking his time. Celine put her hands on his arms, kissing him in return.

Easing reluctantly away, his eyes lazy and lustrous, he murmured, "See you tonight." And then he went and picked up the briefcase, this time closing the door firmly behind him.

At five o'clock Celine was in the bath. She'd filled the tub to halfway before getting in, and used a generous dollop of scented bath foam. She'd spent the morning shopping for groceries and getting her legs waxed, and the afternoon in the garden. Then she'd had a refreshing swim in the pool and come upstairs. At intermittent intervals through the day she'd recalled with pleasant expectation Max's kiss and his parting words.

She soaked in the bath for half an hour, feeling wonderfully decadent and pushing the faucet with her toes every so often for more hot water.

After drying herself off, she used body lotion and a matching spray perfume before she smoothed on a light, creamy makeup and pink lipstick, and made up her eyes with a subtle hint of violet shadow, finishing with the charcoal grey mascara she favoured, softer than black but less obvious than blue.

She was humming as she took from its hanger a cool, sleeveless, lavender silk fastened on the shoulders with thin ties, the graceful skirt flowing from the hipline. "It suits you," Max had approved the first time she'd worn it. "Makes your eyes look like pansies."

Her eyes were neither blue nor brown, the inner irises dark gold, the outer part a deep but indeterminate colour that changed subtly with what she wore. Looking in the mirror, she supposed that for a woman in her thirties she looked really quite good. Her figure had scarcely changed since the day she had married.

If she'd had children, her bust, which she'd always felt was on the meagre side, might have become fuller, her trim hips wider. Honoria complained that it had taken a vicious regime of dieting and exercise to regain her figure after she'd had her babies. Celine wondered if she'd have minded so much.

She'd probably never know. She and Max had both had tests after she'd been off the pill for two years. "No apparent abnormality," they'd been told. The middle-aged doctor had worn half-glasses and a beard that made him look like a Victorian schoolteacher. "Go home and try to relax," he'd ordered them, as though giving them a hundred lines. "Give it time."

They'd left relieved that they'd been pronounced normal, and for a while every time they made love they'd sternly advise each other to relax, and then dissolve into mutual laughter.

But after a time the joke wore thin.

They'd made tentative enquiries about the possibility of a medically assisted pregnancy.

"Even if we were accepted for the programme," Celine confessed, after studying the available information, "I'd feel like a laboratory specimen. Is it very important to you... ?"

"No," Max had said promptly. "I was afraid it was to you. I'd go along with it if you wanted to, but..."

They'd decided that while other people might find the numerous tests and procedures worthwhile, it wasn't for them.

"We could enquire about adoption," Max suggested; but hesitantly he confessed, "Only I'm not sure how I'd feel about a child that wasn't really mine."

"If you couldn't feel it was yours, it wouldn't be fair to the child." Smiling a little sadly, Celine added, "I guess we're stuck with each other."

Max had reached across the bit of the sofa lying between them, and taken her hand, drawing her to him. "That's fine with me," he told her, and put his arm about her so that she could rest against his shoulder.

Celine had closed her eyes on a couple of small tears that she hadn't allowed to fall, and said goodbye to the shadowy child who had haunted the recesses of her mind.

Neither she nor Max believed in hankering for what might have been. You could say, she supposed, that their marriage was built on that very foundation.

There had, of course, been occasional setbacks and doubts and the odd argument. But they were both mature, self-aware people. They liked each other a great deal, and from that liking and their determination to make a good marriage, they had built a loving and faithful relationship, envied by many of their friends whose marriages or long-term love affairs had broken up amid shards of bitterness and recrimination.

# Chapter 2

A cotton apron tied over the lavender dress, Celine opened the doors from the dining room and spread a cloth on the small table outside. The weather was balmy and there was no wind. She set silver cutlery and placed a tiny crystal bowl of pansies in the centre of the table before returning to the kitchen.

She was drizzling Cointreau over a bowl of pears when the telephone rang.

"Darling, I'm going to be late, I'm afraid," Max said. "Andrew's asked me to help out with a tricky case of his, as my workload's a bit lighter this week. Don't wait dinner for me. We're not having anything special, are we?"

"I found a nice piece of smoked kingfish that I thought we'd have with salad."

"That'll keep, then," he said cheerfully. "Don't you have a night class or something, anyway?"

"Tonight it's the badminton club. I wasn't planning to go, actually."

"You're all right, aren't you? Not off-colour?"

"Just feeling a bit lazy. I've been gardening all after-noon."

"Have an early night," he advised her. "I won't disturb you if you're sleeping when I get home."

Celine put the phone down with a little bang. She stood uncertainly by it for a moment, sighed and went quickly out to the terrace, carried the pansies inside and placed them on the dining table, then returned to gather up the silver and whip off the dainty tablecloth, dragging the doors shut with one hand as she retreated inside.

In the kitchen she put away the two varieties of lettuce, the firm, rosy tomatoes, the slender fresh cucumber and the jar of black olives. The pears, she supposed, would do just as well tomorrow.

There was still plenty of time to go to her badminton, but somehow the idea had no appeal. After making herself a salad sandwich, she carried the plate into the lounge to eat sitting in front of the television.

She went upstairs early as Max had suggested, spent an hour skim-reading the remainder of her book so that she could discuss it with its owner, and turned off the light. She didn't even hear Max come in.

On Saturday Celine came home tired, hot and footsore after collecting house-to-house for the Hurricane Relief Fund. She'd dealt with barking dogs, reluctant givers, and people who peeked through the curtains pretending not to be home, and one man who had lectured her on the iniq-uity of taking good money out of New Zealand to assist is-land communities that he seemed to think had called down the wrath of God upon themselves. But they were balanced by children who had emptied their money boxes and el-derly people who gave generously and apologised for not being able to donate more.

Max was in the swimming pool, and she went upstairs to change into a swimsuit and join him. But by the time she arrived on the terrace he was coming into the house, a towel wrapped about his waist.

"Hello," he said. "I didn't know you were home. My mother phoned to say Michelle and Tony are here for the weekend, with the kids. I said we'd go over for lunch tomorrow. Okay?"

"Fine." She smiled at him. Max's sister and her family ran a dairy farm near the pleasant coastal town of Tauranga, and didn't visit Auckland very often.

In the morning they lay in bed for an extra hour before breakfast, Max listening to the bedside radio while he filled in the cryptic crossword in the Saturday paper, and Celine reading a historical romance from the library.

"Did you know that a woman was artificially inseminated in 1785?" she asked him.

"Really?"

"According to this book."

Max glanced at the cover. "It's fiction, isn't it?"

"But the author has obviously researched it well. A Frenchman called Thouret performed the procedure on his wife."

"With another man's—?"

"No, I don't think so."

"So, what was wrong with him?"

Celine shrugged. "Maybe he was just experimenting."

"Was he a scientist?"

"A doctor, I think."

"Hmm." Max frowned over the paper in his hand. "Do you know many birds?"

"As in females or wildlife?"

"Wildlife, probably. I'm sure the second bit's bird. 'The girl's forgotten the words?'"

"Hummingbird."

"Of course. Thanks." He filled in the clue. "Are we going to church this morning?"

"Mmm. We could go straight on to your parents' afterwards."

"Better get up then."

"When I finish this chapter. You can have the bathroom first."

* * *

"Auntie Celine! Uncle Max!"

Two olive-skinned little girls came running across the lawn, the older one dark-eyed and dark-haired like her part-Maori father, the younger with striking green eyes and fair hair inherited from her mother. Max swung four-year-old Susan up into his arms, and six-year-old Maxine clung to Celine's hand, pulling her along to the house and into the big lounge, announcing, "Uncle Max and Auntie Celine are here."

They were Maxine's godparents, and she took a proprietary attitude to them.

Michelle, her two-year-old son on her knee, waved a hand. "Hi!"

Her husband was talking to his father-in-law by the big empty fireplace. Max crossed the room to kiss his sister, and Michelle's husband gave Celine a hug before she turned to the tall, grey-headed older man and kissed his cheek.

"You're looking well, my dear." He held her hand in both of his as he smiled warmly down at her. "Nice to see you."

"You, too." She released herself and said, "I'll just take these muffins into the kitchen. I suppose Nancy's there?"

In the kitchen, Max's mother was turning over a couple of roasted chickens before replacing them in the oven. She presented a cheek to Celine and said, "Lovely to see you!"

"What can I do to help?"

Celine knew her way around this kitchen almost as well as she knew her own. For years her family had lived across the street from the Archers. Nancy Archer and Beth Pentland, both recently married, had moved into the neighbourhood at about the same time, and become firm friends. Their children had been thrown together almost from birth.

Celine's older brother had been Max's closest friend and his best man at their wedding, but he'd met a Dunedin girl while studying medicine at the university there, and remained in the South Island. Her younger brother had gone off to see the world when he was twenty-two, and settled in

America, where he had a highly paid job in the automobile industry, but no family.

It was not until after her own marriage that Celine had stopped calling her mother-in-law "Auntie Nancy" and been invited to use her name without the prefix.

"I don't suppose you want to call me Mum," Nancy had said pragmatically. "You remember your own mother too well for that."

Beth Pentland had died only a few years before Celine married Max. Nancy had been totally delighted with her son's marriage to the daughter of her dearest friend.

After lunch the two younger men went for a stroll while Max's father, pretending to watch the Sunday sports programme on the TV, dozed in his favourite armchair and his mother read the Sunday paper. Michelle put the baby down for a nap, and she and Celine sat on the back steps, watching the girls play on the lawn. A swing dangled from one of the trees and Maxine was pushing her sister, who clung grimly to the ropes.

"Remember when it was us out there?" Michelle said. "I'm beginning to feel old. Tony and I had our tenth anniversary the other day."

Celine smiled. "We can beat you there."

"Mmm. That's right. D'you ever regret it?"

"Getting married? No. I regret—a bit—not having children. But we've learned to live with that."

"You and Max would have made good parents. You two never fight, do you?"

"We've had disagreements. What couple doesn't?" Celine looked at her sister-in-law curiously, finding her expression pensive. "Do you have a problem?"

Michelle made an odd little grimace, half smiling. "Do you remember David Dryden?"

"Dreamboat Dryden?" Celine laughed briefly. "Of course. Who could forget?" David Dryden had for a few months been Michelle's boyfriend when she and Celine were still in their teens. Besides being spectacularly good-looking, he was endowed with brains and personality. All of the girls had envied Michelle.

"He happened to be in Tauranga the other day. We bumped into each other and had a cup of coffee together. It was nice. Only we got talking, and I didn't notice the time, and I'd forgotten to pick up Tony's suit from the drycleaner. He needed it that night."

"So what happened?"

"He was annoyed and...I was going to tell him about meeting David, but...somehow I didn't. I started yelling at him instead about him thinking I was his household slave and brood mare, and...well, a lot of stuff that I didn't even know I felt until I let it out, and—" Michelle clenched her fists and raised her eyes heavenward "—it felt so *good.*"

Celine laughed, and Michelle grinned wryly at her. "We had a fearful row. Only afterwards I was ashamed, because most of the time I don't really feel like that, and by then it was too late to tell him about David, and it's become this big guilty secret! Which it wasn't. You see what I mean?"

"Mmm. I think so."

"I mean, I just happened to meet an old friend, you know—I had Timmy in the pushchair, for heaven's sake!— so why am I feeling so guilty?"

"Maybe because he can still make your heart flutter a bit?"

Michelle looked about to deny it, then smiled sheepishly. "Yes, a bit," she acknowledged. "And I suppose I was flattered that he still thought me attractive. Not that he tried to come on to me, but you know, you can tell. He was really nice, and I told him I was happily married, because it's *true!* He's divorced, and he said he envied me."

"And then you went home and Tony said, 'Where's my suit?' and you were suddenly Mrs. Housewife again."

Michelle nodded. "That's it."

"Would you have felt bound to tell him if you'd run into an old female friend and had coffee with her?"

"I probably would have mentioned it."

"But the time for mentioning it wasn't in the middle of a row, so the moment passed. Let it go. You've done nothing you're obliged to confess about."

"You're right. It would only upset Tony. And I don't want to start another row!"

On the way home Celine asked Max, "Would you be upset if I told you that a few weeks back I'd run into an old flame and had a coffee with him?"

Max glanced at her, his brows raised. "Upset? No. Did you?"

Celine shook her head. "Actually, no. Would you think it odd that I hadn't mentioned it the day it happened?"

This time he looked at her for a bit longer. "Not particularly. Why all these hypothetical questions?"

"I just...wondered. I mean, some men are insanely jealous, aren't they?"

"You don't think I'm one of them?" He sounded mildly shocked.

"Good heavens, no! Thank goodness. No, it was just...I was reading a magazine," she said hastily. "You know, problem pages."

"I see."

She had an idea he knew that wasn't where the question had arisen, but he made no further comment.

Only, when he had put away the car and followed her to the house door, he said suddenly, "Have you ever seen Mike Parrish again?"

Surprised, she answered, "Not since you and I got engaged." Not since one incongruously sunny day nearly fourteen years ago, when she'd been young enough to have her fledgling heart broken by an unscrupulous married man. "He went to Australia," she said. Along with the wife he had assured her he was separated from, in the process of divorcing, and the two children he'd never mentioned.

The door swung open, and they stepped into the utility room. She turned to him with the key in her hand. "I told you it wasn't me I was talking about."

"Okay." He closed the door and put a hand on her waist as they moved towards the front of the house and the stairs. "I believe you."

That night after he'd switched off the light, Max reached for her and drew her into his arms, finding her mouth unerringly in the darkness, and they made love with the ease of long familiarity, attaining a climax together. Afterwards she lay relaxed against his shoulder, her hand resting on his chest, until she was nearly asleep. Max gently eased his arm away and lowered her head to the pillow before shifting to his side of the bed.

Celine's father phoned two days later, sounding confused and agitated.

Five years after Celine's mother died, Ted Pentland had married a pleasant, middle-aged widow and moved to Rotorua, where Dora hoped her arthritis would benefit from the hot mineral springs.

"Dora's in hospital," he said. "I think it's serious."

Celine tried to phone Max. Told he was in court, she left a message with his secretary. Then she cancelled a couple of appointments, packed an overnight bag and drove her car south to Rotorua.

Apart from supporting her father, who was obviously very concerned, she would be useful to provide transport. Dora had a car but Ted hadn't driven since he'd suffered a haemorrhage behind one eye and had lost some of his vision. The other eye was weak, needing a strong lens in his glasses, and although he might have scraped through a driving eyesight test he didn't feel confident at the wheel of a car.

Max phoned that evening after he'd got home.

"We don't really know anything yet," she told him. "They're doing tests. I'll stay until they have some results."

"Sure," Max said easily. "Tell Ted I hope everything's going to be all right."

It was a week before Celine arrived back home, in the late afternoon.

She unpacked quickly and inspected the food supplies. Alice had kept the place vacuumed and dusted, and probably left Max casseroles or salads for his dinner. He was no cook.

Tonight she'd make him a proper meal.

She was stirring a sauce when he came in. "That smells good," he said, and came over to put his arm about her waist as she lifted her face to him.

He kissed her mouth, but after a second she pulled her head away to watch the sauce, which was on the point of boiling. As she lifted the pot from the heat, Max dropped his arm and said, "Isn't it a bit hot for cooking?" There were several pots on the stove.

"How long is it since you had a decent meal?" she asked him.

"Last night, actually. Andrew and his wife took pity on me and invited me to dinner. How's Dora?"

"They want to operate, but they're not sure it will be a cure."

"That's rough. When?"

"Maybe next week, if they can fit her in. They've sent her home, meantime, and she seems okay except she's a bit tired, but Dad's worried sick." Celine leaned over the pot, frowning. Did she see lumps? She stirred furiously with the wire whisk, turned off the hot ring and replaced the pot to keep the sauce warm. "This'll be ready in about ten minutes," she said, peering at the potatoes.

"Okay." On his way out of the room, he turned in the doorway. "Are you going back next week?"

"I think I'd better, at least until they know if the operation is a success."

"I guess so." He hesitated, and then turned to go upstairs.

Over dinner she told him about the tension of waiting for tests and of her father's pessimistic outlook that he'd tried to hide from Dora.

"Poor old Ted," Max commiserated. "After losing your mother, this seems unfair." He pushed his plate away and said, "Will you be back for Stephen's retirement party?"

"Oh—the twenty-fifth, isn't it? I'll try. Who gets to take his place?"

"Actually, I do."

"Oh, Max! Why didn't you *say?*"

"I didn't want to tell you on the phone."

"Well, congratulations." Smiling, she picked up her half glass of red wine and raised it in a toast to him, then came round the table with it in her hand and bent to kiss his cheek.

Max curved an arm about her to drag her onto his knee.

"Careful! You'll spill my wine!" She held it away from them.

"I missed you," he said. There was an unusual note of tension in his voice.

"You missed my cooking?" she teased.

He didn't smile. "No—"

A bell began to ring in the kitchen. "That's the apricot soufflé," Celine said. "Let go, Max. I don't want to over-cook it."

"Damn the apricot soufflé!"

But she had put her glass down on the table and was struggling up.

"It took ages to make," she told him, "and I don't want it to go rubbery in the oven."

The soufflé was perfect, and Max had a second helping. As they packed the dishes afterwards, he said, "Like to go for a walk?"

"That would be nice." Before they built the house they used to walk a lot, looking at homes that they admired, de-ciding which features they'd like to have in their own. Later they'd enjoyed peeking into other people's gardens, occa-sionally taking home a cutting or root given away by some gardening enthusiast they'd met trimming a hedge or weed-ing a verge.

Outside Celine tucked her hand into Max's arm, and they set off at a fairly brisk pace. The suburban houses sat well back on their sections, surrounded by lawns and gardens. On the wide verandas of many older homes, fragrant roses or fading mauve wistaria climbed the supporting posts. Newer houses echoing the Colonial style stood cheek-by-jowl with architects' contemporary fantasies.

Now and then a dog woofed warningly from behind a wrought-iron fence or a closed wooden gate, and once a fat tabby cat emerged from under a hedge and wound itself briefly about Celine's ankles as she stooped to stroke it before walking on.

Brilliant scarlet bougainvillea surmounting a white-painted concrete wall drew their eyes, and a few yards further on a slender clematis vine with starry white blooms clung to a wooden trellis. A sweet, wafting scent made Max look up appreciatively as they passed under a tall, yellow-blossomed Australian frangipani, and a high hedge smothered in pink-tinged jasmine stopped them for a few moments to enjoy its beauty and inhale its perfume.

When they regained their own front door and stepped inside, the house seemed very warm and a bit stuffy. Celine yawned as she slipped off her light jacket.

"Tired?" Max enquired sympathetically. "It's been quite a strain, helping your father through all this, hasn't it?"

"Mmm. I think I'll go straight up to bed." Celine turned to the stairs.

"Shall I come with you?"

"It's early." She glanced back at him. "I'll have a leisurely bath and read for a while."

By the time Max came upstairs, she was fast asleep.

Max's new position as a senior partner entailed a good deal of extra time while he took over Stephen Chatswood's workload. He seemed to be working late, either at home or at the office, nearly every night. Celine had her night class, badminton and a committee meeting to keep her occupied, and that week it was her turn to host the book discussion group. She was glad she hadn't had to cancel that.

When Ted rang to say the hospital was sending Dora to the operating theatre the next morning for exploratory surgery, Celine left a note for Max and drove back to Rotorua.

It was late when he phoned. "We seem to have hardly seen each other while you were home," he said ruefully, after enquiring about Dora and being told they'd taken her into the hospital that afternoon.

"I know. Did Alice leave you something to eat?"

"Yes. You both spoil me, you know. I could buy something, or eat out. Or learn to cook."

"You don't need to—I *like* cooking!"

"But you're not here," he pointed out.

"Max—?" Her father was in the room, rustling the newspaper laid on the dining table before him. She half turned away. "You don't mind, do you?"

"It wasn't a complaint," he said with a hint of impatience, "just an observation. Don't worry about it. I know you're needed there."

After a week of post-operative care in the hospital, Dora was recovering quite well. A malignant growth had been found, and there was still a question mark over her prognosis, but the doctors were cautiously hopeful. Celine stayed until Dora was home, and left a few days later, when she was getting up and pottering round the house. "We'll manage," Ted told Celine. "We'll just make the most of whatever time is left us."

So Celine was home in time to go to Stephen Chatswood's retirement party with Max.

The Chatswood home, a large, Mediterranean-style house, overlooked Mission Bay, where a narrow strip of sand fronting the Waitemata Harbour inflated the price of real estate, and in summer drew the suburb's residents to enjoy the beach.

The house was crowded and there was a lavish amount of food and drink, but Celine partook sparingly of the wine so that she could drive home, allowing Max to imbibe freely if he liked. Not that Max ever overindulged.

She was talking to Stephen's wife and another of the partners when she noticed Max with a very pretty young woman, his head close to her long blond curls as he bent to hear what she was saying. At this distance, with a smile on his face, Max looked younger, almost the same as he had been when he and Celine were newly married—or even earlier, perhaps. When he'd been engaged to a girl he'd met at university, planning to marry at Christmas.

The girl with him had her head tipped slightly to one side, and began winding a strand of hair about her finger as she talked. She wore a slim-fitting dress that was low enough for generous, creamy breasts to peek above it, and short enough to draw attention to her long, bare legs, sleek and honey-tanned.

Max altered his stance, placing one hand on the wall beside him and shifting his feet. The girl changed position, too, leaning against the wall. The small, casual movements had the effect of bringing them closer together, almost as if they were trying to shut themselves off from the crowd about them.

"—Don't you think, Celine?" Mrs. Chatswood was saying.

Celine dragged her eyes back to her hostess. "Absolutely," she said firmly, wondering what it was she was agreeing to.

"Well, I wondered, you know, if you would help us," Mrs. Chatswood said.

"Er, I'd be pleased to if I can," Celine said more cautiously, hoping for further enlightenment.

"Stephen says you do it professionally. We'd pay, of course."

Something about redecorating the house, then. "When did you want to start?"

"Oh, we're planning a bit of a holiday first, but perhaps I could phone you when we get back?"

"Yes, do."

"I want to involve Stephen, you know. Give him plenty to think about. I won't have him sinking into old age, the way some men do when they retire."

The next time Celine saw Max he was talking to the middle-aged office receptionist, mother of a large adult family. Later in the evening she caught a glimpse of the blond girl, this time with one of the other senior partners, her expression sweetly attentive but her eyes slightly glazed as she twirled a glass of wine in her fingers.

On the way home Max sat beside her with his arms folded over his safety belt, whistling softly.

"You sound happy," Celine said as she drew to a halt for a red light. "How much did you drink tonight?"

"I don't need to be drunk to be happy," he protested.

The light changed and she pressed her foot down on the accelerator. "Who was the blond girl? One of Stephen's granddaughters?"

"Which blond girl?"

"The one you were talking to."

"When?"

"What do you mean, *when?*" She glanced at him, wondering if he had, for once, overindulged. "At the party, of course."

"When at the party?" he said with exaggerated patience. "There were about sixty people there."

"Most of them our age or older. You certainly can't have forgotten her—she was gorgeous! All legs and curls and big blue eyes."

"Oh—her," he said. "You must be talking about Kate. Kathryn Payne. Didn't anyone introduce you? She's our new junior partner."

Surprised, she turned to him. "You didn't tell me they'd appointed a woman. She's very young."

"Twenty-five. Her looks are deceptive. She's extremely well qualified."

"When was the appointment made?"

"A few weeks ago. With the reshuffle on Stephen's retirement, we wanted her to settle into the job with time to spare."

"You didn't mention it."

"Didn't I? You haven't been home much, lately. I started to tell you that she was at Andrew's the night they asked me to dinner, but we got talking about something else."

It was true Celine had been away or out rather often lately, and they'd had few opportunities to talk. "Is she good?"

"She got the job over about a dozen other candidates. She's quick and smart—I've been handing over some of my caseload to her so I can cope with the extra from Stephen's."

"She seems to have settled in all right," Celine said thoughtfully.

"How do you know?"

"Well, you and she were having a cosy little tête-à- tête at one stage." She cast him an amused sideways look.

"What do you mean?"

Teasing, she said, "You had her nicely backed into a corner—not that she seemed to be minding. If you ask me, she's a bit of a minx. Did you see her hanging on old Charlie's every word later on?"

Max said coldly, "I was not backing her into any corner, and she's a highly trained professional lawyer with a great future."

"Max, I was joking!" Astonished, she turned her head for an instant, seeing him scowling and sitting very straight in his seat. "I'm sure you were just making the new partner feel at home in the firm. And so was Charlie." Her tone turned mock-soothing. "*Of course* it has nothing to do with her happening to be an extremely attractive blonde, and young enough to be . . . well, *Charlie's* daughter, anyway."

She expected him to laugh and relax. Instead he sat immobile and unspeaking, the silence prickling between them.

It was silly, she thought. Of course she didn't suspect Max of philandering. She trusted him completely. He'd never given her reason to do otherwise.

"Kate," she mused, something tantalising the back of her mind. "Didn't you meet a Kate—or Katie—at the conference in Taupo? Is she the same one?"

"She prefers Kate."

*"Bo Peep?"* With a ripple of laughter, she recalled what he'd said. "The one you wanted to see jump out of a cake?"

"I didn't say *I* wanted her to. Anyway, it was a stupid remark."

"Well, I don't suppose you'd have said it in public."

"You haven't repeated it to anyone, have you?"

"Of course not! I'd forgotten all about it until you mentioned her name. A cross between Bo Peep and Marilyn Monroe—I can see what you meant."

Max flexed his long legs and readjusted them as though the car had become too small for him. "I only said she *looked* like that. I didn't know her then."

"Oh?" Celine flicked another teasing glance at him, laughter hovering at her mouth. "How well do you know her now?"

His smile was a trifle forced. "I mean, she's a partner in our firm. She's entitled to some . . . respect. It isn't her fault she looks—well, the way she does, that people think she's a bimbo. She's a bit sensitive about it."

Celine privately thought that Kate or Katie might very well look rather different if she pulled the mane of rioting curls back in a more mature style, or wore a little less makeup and a bit more dress.

Being fair, she reminded herself that tonight the girl had been at a party. Surely she didn't wear that kind of thing at the office. And supposing she did? If she liked to dress that way, there was no law against it. "Does she put her hair up at work?" she asked idly.

Seeming disconcerted at the question, Max took a second to answer. "No. She pulls it back sometimes in a sort of clip thing, or one of those coloured bows. Keeps it out of her eyes, I suppose."

"Does she have a boyfriend or anything?"

Max turned to look at her. "I've no idea." He sounded irritated, perhaps bored. "Why?"

"She didn't seem to be with anyone tonight. I just wondered. I mean, it can't be for lack of choice, can it?"

He shrugged. "Maybe she does. I hadn't thought about it."

# Chapter 3

Celine went to Rotorua several times in the next few weeks, usually staying overnight. Dora seemed well, though frail-looking, and the third time Celine decided on impulse to drive back to Auckland after the evening meal, which Dora and Ted ate quite early.

On her arrival the house was dark and empty. She switched on some lights and made herself a cup of tea, read the paper, which she hadn't had time to do all day, and went up to bed.

She was fast asleep when Max came in, but she stirred when he opened the bedroom door.

He murmured, "Celine? I thought you weren't coming home tonight."

"Mmph." She heard vaguely the sounds of him entering the bathroom and a little later coming out again, felt him bump into the bed with a stifled curse, then the mattress depressing under his weight as he climbed in beside her.

Sleepily she inched closer to him, sliding an arm over his chest and nestling into his side. In the summer he wore only the bottom half of his pyjamas. He felt warm, and she rubbed her cheek briefly against his chest, the wiry hair tickling her skin.

"Are you awake?" he whispered.

"Mm-mm," she grunted in denial.

His chest rose and fell briefly beneath her cheek, in laughter or a sigh, as she slipped back into sleep.

Brushing her hair in the morning, she asked him, "What time did you get in last night?"

"I didn't look." He had his back to her, contemplating the contents of his wardrobe. "When did *you* get in? I thought you were staying in Rotorua."

"After nine. Dora seems okay for now, and I think Dad's quite enjoying looking after her. It must have been past midnight before you came in, wasn't it?"

Max pulled a shirt from its hanger. "Probably. Sorry I disturbed you." He shrugged into the shirt and started buttoning it.

"Only for a minute."

He glanced at her. "Yes, you dropped off again pretty fast."

Celine put down the hairbrush and turned to go downstairs.

"Celine?"

Her hand on the doorknob, she looked back enquiringly. He was tucking the shirt into his pants. "Would you like to go out to dinner tonight?"

"Who's invited us?"

"No one." He did up the zip without looking, and felt for his belt buckle. "I thought you might like a night out. We could go to a show or a film afterwards, maybe. Just the two of us."

"Sounds nice," she said doubtfully. "Only I promised Sharon and Stephen I'd go round this evening to talk about their redecorating. I've already put them off once because of Dora."

"You're going to do some work for them?"

"Didn't I tell you?" As he shook his head, she said, "Sharon asked me at Stephen's retirement party if I'd help her redesign the interior of their home."

But on their way home he'd been in a strange mood, and somehow the subject of Sharon's plans had never come up.

"Can we go out tomorrow—or, no, that's tournament night at badminton—another time?"

"Sure." He jerked the belt closed about his waist, looking down to fasten the buckle. "Let me know when you have a free evening."

Celine frowned slightly, not sure if she detected a hint of sarcasm in his tone. But he had turned away from her and was stooping to get his shoes out of the wardrobe. Mentally shrugging, she opened the door and went on downstairs.

Their social calendar became even more crowded as Christmas approached. Together or separately they attended several pre-Christmas functions, both business and private, and as the newest senior partner of the firm, Max thought they should invite his colleagues and their spouses around one evening for drinks and snacks.

"What about the Chatswoods?" Celine suggested. "I think Sharon is a bit worried that Stephen will drop out of everything, now he's retired."

"Yes, ask them, that's a good idea."

"I might have a chance to talk to Sharon again about their house."

It was an informal gathering, with everyone appearing relaxed as they sat or stood chatting on the terrace and around the pool outside. Celine circulated with trays of titbits and Max made sure everyone had a glass of wine or fruit juice or a soft drink.

There was no real need to watch for people who had no one to talk to or looked uncomfortable, because they all knew one another anyway. But Celine sensed a tension in Max that was unusual for him.

As he handed her a glass of wine for herself, she said, "Your new junior partner isn't here, is she?"

"No, she isn't," Max said shortly, picking up a glass for himself from the table nearby.

"Did she say she wasn't coming?"

He shrugged. "Not that I recall." He lifted his glass and sipped at it. "*Damn,* this is too sweet. I thought I had dry."

Surprised at his vehemence, Celine said mildly, "Get another, then."

He shook his head, looking thoroughly out of temper. "It doesn't matter," he muttered. "Andrew and Lisa aren't here, either. Their kids' school has a Santa party tonight." He tilted his head suddenly. "Was that the doorbell?"

"Yes, I think so."

She made to put down her glass, but he was already on his way, saying over his shoulder, "I'll go."

She was talking to one of the other partners when Max returned with Kate Payne and a handsome, fair-haired young man. Celine excused herself and went over to them.

"I've been looking forward to meeting you." She smiled at Kate as Max, with an oddly tight look on his face, made the introduction. "I didn't have a chance at Stephen's retirement party."

"And this is Dave—er—Robards?" Max looked interrogatively at Kate's escort.

The young man smiled, showing excellent teeth, and held out his hand. "That's right, Mr. Archer. How do you do, Mrs. Archer?" His accent was North American, and his tone held a hint of deference.

"Celine," she corrected him. "The States or Canada?"

"Canada," he answered. "I'm just spending a few months in your beautiful country."

"Can I get you two something to drink?" Max offered, his expression relaxing a little. "Medium white for you?" he asked Kate, obviously anticipating her affirmative.

"I'll have a beer, if you have it," her companion requested.

As Max strode away to get the drinks, Kate said, "Sorry we're late. I've been showing Dave around a bit. We went up to the summit of Mount Eden. It was lovely there—cool."

"Wonderful view!" the young man said. "The harbour and the city look just great from there at sunset. I was blown away!"

"Not literally, I hope." Celine smiled. The wind could get fierce on the summit.

Kate said, "Actually it was quite lovely, hardly any breeze at all. Dave insisted on going down into the crater." She smiled up at him.

"I've never got the chance to walk inside a volcano before. Even a dead one," he told Celine.

"Dormant, not dead," Kate informed him. "It could blow again at any time."

He looked from her to Celine. "Is she pulling my leg?"

Celine said, "No, she isn't. They only look dead. Scientists say that several of the volcanic cones about Auckland might erupt again. We hope there'll be plenty of warning."

"It seems so peaceful!"

"What does?" Max asked, returning with the drinks. "There you are, Kate." He smiled at her as she took the glass from him. "And here's your beer." He offered a frothing glass tumbler to Dave.

While the young couple explained, Celine looked about covertly, noticing that most of the food on the plates placed at strategic points about the terrace had gone. Murmuring an excuse, she slipped off to the kitchen to replenish the supplies.

Later, when everyone had left, Celine and Max walked around picking up glasses, leftovers and empty plates. "That went off all right, didn't it?" Celine said cheerfully.

"Mmm." Max sounded slightly absent. "I suppose everyone enjoyed themselves."

"Except you?"

"What makes you think that?"

Stacking several plates with care, she said vaguely, "I thought you seemed ... distracted."

"Just feeling my duties as the host," he said.

She smiled automatically, not convinced. "Are you all right, Max?"

"Why shouldn't I be?"

"Oh, I don't know. Lately you've been . . . different."

"In what way?" He stooped to fish out a paper napkin floating on the surface of the pool, holding it away from him as it dripped. Without waiting for an answer, he said, "I need a holiday. We should go away at Christmas."

"Where?"

"Anywhere." He squeezed the napkin in his hand and threw the sodden ball accurately and rather forcefully into the plastic bin she'd brought out for the rubbish. "Do you have any preferences?"

"We may not have much choice. A lot of places will be booked out over Christmas and New Year. And we can't leave till after Christmas Day, anyway."

"Why not?"

Celine stared at him with surprise. They always went to his parents' home for lunch that day, with other members of the family including the grandchildren. And on Boxing Day they drove down to Rotorua to see her father and stepmother. Ted and Dora would have spent Christmas with Dora's daughter and her family. "Your mother will be expecting us."

"My mother might be thankful for two less to cater for," Max suggested. "Maybe she'd like to go away herself, if she had the chance."

"We all help," Celine said, puzzled at his tone. "It's not as though she has to do everything herself. I always thought she and your dad enjoyed having the family there."

Max put a hand up and shoved it through his hair, uncharacteristically ruffling its smooth cut. "I suppose they do," he admitted. "I just thought we might do something different for a change. But if you think she'll be hurt..." He shrugged and went over to pick up the rubbish container. "I suppose you'll want to go to your dad's the next day, too."

"I think we should, especially the way things are. Maybe we could book a hotel somewhere down south, and call in to see Dad and Dora on the way," she said helpfully.

Max gave her a glimmer of a smile. "Sure. I'll see what I can do." On his way through the door, he paused. "Don't forget the staff party's on Friday night, at the office."

"Most of them were here tonight," Celine said. "Would you mind if I don't go this time? I've got the bridge club final the night before and I haven't finished my Christmas shopping. I'm running a bit late this year—I don't want to leave it until Christmas Eve."

Max's blue eyes looked curiously opaque. "Please yourself. There's no need to be there if you'd rather not."

When Max arrived home late on Friday night, she was sitting on the floor of the bedroom dressed in a nightgown and wrap and surrounded by parcels and boxes, rolls of Christmas wrapping paper, gift cards, coloured ribbons and bows.

He leaned on the doorjamb, his arms folded, and she looked up. "How was the party?"

"The same as usual," he shrugged. His eyes were bright and his hair less sleek than usual. She thought there was a faint flush on his cheeks, too. Staring a little, she asked, "How much have you had to drink, Max?"

"Not so very much." He was examining her with an unfamiliar, dispassionate look, as though she were a painting he was trying to assess. He straightened, jerked his tie undone, and came away from the door, strolling over to her. Celine moved a roll of bright printed paper away from his feet, afraid he would step on it.

"Come to bed," Max said abruptly.

She looked up, a small, puzzled smile on her face.

"Come on," he said, bending down to take her hand as she reached for the scissors.

"I haven't finished," she protested, looking at the strewn paper, the neat pile of assorted gaily packaged parcels in one corner, the several items in plain paper waiting to join them. "It won't take long."

"Never mind." Impatiently, he tightened his grip, hauling her willy-nilly to her feet. "Do it tomorrow." His other hand pulled undone the neatly tied bow at her waist so that her wrap fell open, revealing the thin nightdress underneath.

"Max!" Half laughing, half bewildered, she demanded, "How much *have* you drunk?"

His diction was perfect as he said, "I don't need to have been drinking to want to make love to my wife." His hand still imprisoned hers, drawing her purposefully closer.

"No, but—" She stopped as he shot her a strange look, not just a glance into her eyes but a comprehensive, lightning survey of her entire body.

"You're a beautiful woman," he said, his voice deepening. "I," he added with calculated deliberation, "am a very lucky man." He tugged her into his arms with inexorable strength, looked down at her face and then lowered his eyelids and kissed her, his mouth hungry and seeking, almost aggressive in its demands on her.

She could taste whisky on his lips, in his mouth, but she soon forgot that in the shock of the kiss. He overcame her resistant stillness with the sheer force of his embrace, perhaps not even noticing her hesitancy in his singleminded onslaught. She felt the growing heat of his body, and was faintly surprised at an answering warmth in her own as his mouth continued its insistent assault, and his hand swept down her back to her thighs, almost roughly pushing up the satin wrap and the gown beneath it as he found her warm skin.

Celine tried to step back, her foot crunching down on a festive ribbon bow, and instinctively she pulled away to look down at what damage she'd done.

But as her mouth left his, Max stooped and swung her up into his arms, striding straight to the bed.

He fell onto it with her, and his hands went to the shoulders of the wrap, shoving it aside, while his mouth found the hollow of her throat. He wrenched at the garment, momentarily lifting his head, a heavy frown on his face, and Celine moved her arms, slipping them free of the sleeves. He seemed likely to tear something if she didn't help.

Max grunted and bent to return to her mouth, while his hands roved over her shoulders and arms, then found the straps of the nightgown and lowered them with a swift jerk, raising his head so that he could see her breasts.

She felt them tingle and peak at the look in his eyes, the tight buds hardening instantly under the quick, almost rough caress of his palm across them before he lowered his hand to unfasten his belt.

Celine gasped as the buckle came free and she heard the slide of the zip. "What are you doing?" Max always took his time, he was slow and tender and considerate, not like this—hasty, importunate, impatient.

He looked at her, his eyes alight, his cheeks darkened with colour. "I'm making love to my wife," he said, pausing to get his shoes off. She'd never before known him to lie down with them on. The shoes were flung to the ground, and his navy socks, followed immediately by his pants and underpants. He knelt over her, his hands gliding up her thighs, rucking up the flimsy gown. "Undo my shirt, will you?"

It sounded more like an order than a request. Not knowing whether to be shocked or amused, she found herself complying. Max dealt with the sleeve buttons himself, and shucked off the shirt, his loosened tie going with it. "Good," he said with satisfaction, and lowered himself between her thighs as he nudged them apart.

Her eyes widened. In a voice high with surprised indignation, she asked, "Are you going to *rape* me?"

He looked very intent, and rather ferocious, but his expression changed as he placed both his hands on her breasts. His fingers closing on them, he said softly, "Would I need to?" Then he brought his mouth down to them, and took one with his lips, circling the pouting centre with his tongue, worrying it gently with his teeth while his hand teased the other, until she gasped, and a pulsating wave of heat shot from her breast to her belly and down her thighs.

Max's head lifted, his eyes glittering with passion. "Would I need to?" he demanded again. His hands squeezed and kneaded, creating a strange, erotic pain.

Celine swallowed. It was extraordinary. She'd never been so aroused so fast. It was scarcely five minutes since he'd first taken her by the hand. She shook her head, definitely shocked now, but also incredibly stimulated.

Max didn't smile, he looked quite relentless as he moved swiftly and surely, so that she caught chokingly at her breath when she felt the hot length of him, so deep and inexorable. She saw him close his eyes, his mouth tight with fierce control, and his fingers suddenly raked into her hair, lifting her to him as he kissed her with blind, primitive passion.

She felt him drive into the centre of her again and again, and she arched her body, opened her mouth in brazen invitation, so that his tongue plunged into her throat, thrusting, thrusting, and then he shuddered, and she felt the heat flow from his body to hers, spreading like liquid fire through her limbs, and a dark starburst exploded about her, until her eyes were blinded and her ears sang and her entire being became molten and weightless.

His mouth finally left hers, drawing back, but he still had his eyes tightly closed, and a great unsteady breath made his body tremble. His lips were parted, and there was a faint shiny film of sweat on his forehead. The centre light blazed down on them from the ceiling.

Gradually Max's breathing slowed and steadied. He rolled away from her and lay prone with his face in the pillow next to hers. His voice muffled, he said, "I'm sorry."

Celine pulled the nightdress down over her thighs and wriggled up the shoulder straps, then searched for the tumbled, twisted sheet. "It's all right," she said. "I enjoyed it, too." In fact she felt, if still somewhat surprised, quite mellow and sated.

A ripple seemed to pass over his skin, as though he'd shivered. She smiled and arranged the sheet over his naked body, covering him to the waist.

Alcohol might have had more than something to do with Max's mood, but he'd admired her, even called her beautiful, and acted as though he literally couldn't wait another second to get her into bed with him. And she'd responded with an unwonted speed and passion. Sex that good after twelve years must indicate a healthy marriage, she thought. She reached into the drawer of the bedside table for a box of tissues. Maybe she wouldn't bother to finish wrapping the presents. It would be quite nice to snuggle up to her husband and go to sleep.

But someone had to turn out the light—at the switch by the door. She sighed, and Max stirred, throwing himself over onto his back, staring at the ceiling. Perhaps the light was too bright, because almost immediately he threw a forearm up over his eyes.

"I'll turn it off," Celine said, folding back the sheet.

"What?" He didn't move his arm.

"I'll turn the light off." She got out of bed, treading on Max's discarded clothes. She picked them up and laid them on the blanket box at the foot of the bed, and crossed the room to the light switch.

With her finger on it she was already turning to go back to bed. In the instant before the room went abruptly black, she saw that Max had lowered his arm and was watching her with a concentrated, yet almost bleak expression. The image of his face remained imprinted on her retina for seconds afterwards, and she didn't move straight away, but waited until it had faded before moving cautiously back across the carpet, avoiding the wrappings and ribbons.

She lay down on the bed, finding the edge of the sheet again and shifting sideways until she felt Max's warm skin against her own. She laid her hand on his chest, waiting for his arm to encircle her.

It was a moment or two before he moved to do it, but when he did he held her quite tightly. "Are you all right?" he asked, his voice low and troubled.

Celine gave a small laugh. "Of course I am. I didn't *really* think you'd rape me!"

"No," he said on a rather odd note. "I wouldn't."

"Well, then . . ." She adjusted herself more comfortably against him. "Go to sleep." He might not have been drunk, but he was certainly affected, she thought, by the alcohol he'd had. She hoped he hadn't driven himself home.

It seemed he had, though. His car was in the garage beside hers when she went out the next morning. Max had shut himself up in his study after breakfast, saying that if he wanted to have a real holiday at Christmas, he had to bring a few things up to date first. And after an early phone call from her mother-in-law, Celine had promised to go to a nearby shopping centre to see if she could get a particular brand of cigars that Nancy bought for her husband every Christmas, but which was inexplicably difficult to obtain this year.

Christmas shopping was in full swing, the shops seething with people and the staff stretched thin. After exhausting every likely possibility, and succumbing to one or two extra stocking fillers for nieces and nephews, Celine made her way back to the car and set off for another suburban mall that she guessed Nancy might not have tried.

By the time she had found the cigars and arrived triumphantly with them at the Archer home, it was after twelve o'clock. She ended up staying for lunch and helping Nancy afterwards to hang streamers and decorations and trim the Christmas tree.

"The children used to do this when they were at home," Nancy said. "Remember how you kids used to compare presents every Christmas, and all of you would end up at either your place or ours?"

"Not only the kids," Celine reminded her, smiling.

"No. That's right." By teatime the two families would have drifted in one direction or the other, and usually finished the day by pooling lunch leftovers for the evening meal.

Nancy sat back, untangling coloured lights from the insulated wire that held them. "These darned things always get in a mess, and we put them away so carefully every year! I still haven't got used to only having you and Max, and Michelle's and David's families for Christmas. There's always heaps of food left over." The Archers and the Pentlands between them had mustered eight children, but some now lived too far away to make it home every year.

"Max thought perhaps you'd like to have Christmas off—not be bothered with having us all for the day."

"Not be bothered? We love having you all here! Of course, if any of you wanted to do something else—I thought we'd only have Michelle every second year when she got married, but Tony's family celebrates for two days and it's very fluid, people just come and go all the time. So we're lucky, they come to us and then go on to his parents afterwards. And it's lovely to have the children."

Celine smiled. "Yes, Christmas wouldn't be the same without children around."

Nancy looked at her quickly, and then away. "There!" she said, holding up a tangle-free string of lights. "At last."

On her way home Celine found herself humming Christmas carols and remembering childhood Christmases. There had been the time that she and Michelle were both given their first bicycles, ending the day with identical skinned knees. The year that Max got a chemistry set, and had found it hilarious to ask the girls to sniff the pretty green "perfume" he'd made, nearly knocking them out with the vile stink of it.

And the time Celine's older brother had been caught kissing Michelle behind the big Christmas tree. Michelle, who already had a bust, and wore a bra while Celine despaired of ever needing one, had confided later that the kiss had made her toes tingle. Celine had thought it incomprehensible that any girl could have found her gangling, be-spectacled big brother attractive. Then Michelle asked, "What about Max, then? He doesn't wear glasses, anyway."

Celine had tried to imagine kissing Max, and burst into uncontrollable giggles. *"Max!"* she gasped finally. "You've got to be joking!" At thirteen Max suffered from acne, and had desperately tried to hide the height that had outstripped his classmates by hunching his bony adolescent shoulders. Blinded by familiarity, she had been naively unaware of the potential for dark, stern good looks in the gawky teenager.

Smiling at the memory, Celine touched the remote control and drove into the garage. Max was doing something at the workbench, and he turned and came to open the car door for her.

"You look happy," he said. "I wondered where you'd got to when you didn't come home for lunch."

"Sorry." She reached up and kissed his cheek. "I had it with your mum and dad. I was just thinking about when we were kids. I bet you never imagined you'd end up married to Michelle's skinny friend. What are you doing?"

He had a screwdriver in one hand. "The spare bathroom lock isn't working. If I can't fix it we'll have to get a new one. Did *you* ever think you'd end up married to Michelle's brother?"

"Not when you were thirteen or fourteen." She reached into the car to scoop up her parcels. "Fortunately, at twenty-six, you'd vastly improved."

"Most of us do." He made to take the parcels and she gave him the heaviest one. "You girls are luckier," he said as they walked to the house.

"Luckier?"

"Males go through an agonising period of not knowing when their voice or their body is going to betray them. They grow hairy and sweaty and seem to have extra hands and feet that keep getting in the way. And while they're turning into great ugly, hairy, smelly brutes, the girls they know are becoming these lovely mystical, unattainable creatures who are only interested in men several years older.''

"What, girls you'd known all your life?" Celine asked sceptically.

He grinned. "All girls. Even sisters, to some extent. At thirteen *you* were like a long-stemmed flower. I remember suddenly noticing that you had legs—not just useful things for scoring runs at beach rounders, but real dinkum female legs. And...other things.''

"I didn't have anything else." Celine started up the stairs.

"You did so. I remember when you started getting a figure.''

"I don't believe it. I was fifteen before I developed a respectable bust. And you hardly ever looked at me, you were in love with some girl in your class at high school. Angeline, wasn't it?''

"How do you know about Angeline?" he asked curiously, shouldering the bedroom door wider to allow her to precede him.

"Michelle told me. She said you had a picture of her hidden in your sock drawer with 'I love you Angeline' on the back in your handwriting.''

"The little sneak!" Max said wrathfully. "What was she doing going through my sock drawer?''

"*I* don't know!" Thinking back, Celine added, "She needed some rugby socks, I think, for a fancy dress party we were going to. She was a bee, if I remember correctly.''

"A bee? In *rugby socks?*" Max deposited the parcel he carried on to the bed and turned to her with raised brows.

"Stripes," Celine explained. "The school colours were yellow and black, remember? Anyway, she swore me to secrecy about Angeline. And then, of course, there was Tracee—with two e's—and Patty—with a y—and Melissa—''

"I had no idea you took such an interest in my adolescent love-life.''

"I didn't. Michelle did. She felt it was important, in case you ended up saddling her with an unsuitable sister-in-law.''

He gave her a rather peculiar look at that. "From the time I was—what, fourteen?"

"Some men marry their very first girlfriend. She said you couldn't be too careful."

He shook his head bemusedly. "What on earth did she think she could do about it?"

Celine laughed. "If you looked like you were getting too serious about anyone she didn't approve of, she'd have thought of something. You know Michelle."

"Indeed I do." He tossed the screwdriver gently in his hand. "I know she was over the moon when we announced our engagement. Did my sister take the credit for that?"

"I don't think so. As I remember she was rather surprised, though she certainly took to the idea."

As if the thought had just struck him, he added, "You two don't still tell each other *everything,* do you?"

"Not quite. No secrets of the marital bed," she assured him.

"I'm relieved to hear it. Well, I'll go and have a look at this lock."

Celine wondered if she'd been tactless. Michelle had liked Juliet, Max's fiancée. She had done nothing to break that up, but certainly she had done her best to further things when Max turned to Celine and began taking her out. Both of them had been through disastrous love affairs, and afterwards had drifted in and out of several superficial, temporary relationships. "You'll be good for each other," she'd said. "The two of you were always alike, even as kids. Sometimes what you need is a friend who understands."

Celine had thought they might have problems explaining their decision to marry to Michelle, but her fears were groundless. Michelle, incurably romantic, had simply taken it for granted that in their own quiet, understated way, Celine and Max had fallen in love. Her congratulations contained enough exuberance for all of them.

When Celine left the bedroom after putting away her bag and stowing the presents in her wardrobe, Max was squatting at the door of the other bathroom, manipulating the lock with the screwdriver, the brass face-plate lying on the floor. Celine went to lean on the wall nearby, her arms folded. "Can you fix it?"

"I think so. There's a worn shaft, but I've managed to turn the damaged bit. Might last a bit longer." He picked up the face-plate and began screwing it back on.

"You didn't *really* notice when I started developing a bust," Celine accused him, returning to their earlier conversation.

"Oh, no?" He cast her a brilliant, laughing look before returning his attention to the lock. "Remember that swimsuit you used to have with the sort of rainbow thing in front?"

"I wouldn't have expected *you* to remember it!" It had been white and featured multicoloured curved strips running diagonally from one leg opening to the neck edge. At twelve, bordering on being a teenager, she'd thought it extremely glamorous. "It was very modest!" she said. "A one-piece."

Max grunted as a screw fell from his fingers to the carpet and he had to grope for it. "Modest, she says!" He found the screw and placed it carefully, holding it while he fitted the end of the screwdriver into the groove. "When it was wet and clinging it didn't leave a lot to the imagination."

"I didn't *have* a lot," she reminded him, half laughing. "You *must* have had an overactive imagination!"

"Huh! There I was in the pool, minding my own business, and you and Michelle came along, disturbing me with your giggling and splashing—"

"I suppose we did giggle—girls do," she admitted.

"And when you got out to dive—" he gave a final, decisive twist to the screw "—there *you* were with that wet suit clinging to you, and I realised you'd grown bumps in front, and the cold water had—well . . ."

Amused, Celine nevertheless felt her cheeks grow warm. If she'd known then what he was seeing, she'd have died of embarrassment.

Max picked up another screw and began fastening it. "I couldn't get out of the pool for half an hour."

"What—? Oh!" Celine began to laugh.

Max tightened the screw and stood up. He was grinning, but she could see behind the adult humour the abashed teenager he'd been. "It was bloody embarrassing," he told her sternly. "I was scared stiff—and that wasn't meant to be a pun—that someone would notice. No wonder I hardly dared look at you for ages after that. I'd known you so long it was almost like lusting after my sister."

"Oh, poor Max!" Still laughing, she put a hand on his chest near his shoulder, and moved close to him. "Never mind. We're not teenagers anymore, thank goodness." There were definitely some advantages to growing older, she thought as she briefly, teasingly, kissed his mouth.

Christmas was, as usual, a happy blend of childish excitement, timeless ritual and family cheer. Crackers were pulled, and presents were opened before the meal of turkey, ham and several salads, with new potatoes and freshly shelled peas. Nancy's homemade pudding was set alight with brandy and ceremoniously set on the laden table. And the men had a cigar after the meal just as they always did, although neither Tony nor Max was really a smoker. His father normally used a pipe, but for Christmas and special occasions like the birth of his grandchildren he liked to offer cigars. The Christmas pack Nancy tucked in with his presents usually lasted the entire year.

When Michelle and Tony and the children had gone, Celine and Max helped to pick up the scattered Christmas wrappings and cake crumbs, and went home with leftovers pressed on them by Nancy to have for their evening meal. They had a swim, watched television for a while and went upstairs.

As Celine climbed into the bed, fumbled for the bedside light and switched it off, Max leaned over and brushed a kiss on her cheek. "Tired?" he enquired softly.

"Mmm, nicely so." She turned her face to him, smiling in the darkness. Then the telephone by the bed shrilled, making her start, and Max, with a muttered curse, leaned over and picked it up to answer.

"It's your father," he said, switching on the light and handing her the receiver.

"Dad?" Celine sat up, knowing it was bad news.

"Dora's taken a turn for the worse," he said. She could hear that he was making a heroic effort to keep his voice steady. "I think this time she's going, Celine."

# Chapter 4

Max drove with Celine to her father's home early next day, stayed for one night in the cramped second bedroom with its twin beds, and then left by bus for Auckland.

He had cancelled their holiday plans. Ted was in a state of near collapse, and Celine said simply, "I'm sorry, I can't leave him."

"No, I can see that," Max agreed resignedly. "Do you want me to stay? I was going to be on holiday, anyway."

"There isn't much you can do," Celine told him. He hated being idle, and she knew he'd find plenty to do at home. "I'll phone if we need you."

Dora died five days later. Max arrived for the funeral, and between them they persuaded Ted to come back to Auckland with Celine. He seemed so shattered that she didn't think he would look after himself.

"He's suddenly become an old man," she said worriedly to Max as they got ready for bed after settling Ted in the guest room. "He wasn't as bad as this when my mother died."

"He's older now, not so resilient. And maybe the second time is worse. Dora was younger than he is, wasn't she?"

"Yes, I suppose he wasn't prepared for her to go before him, too." She yawned as she got into bed. "He doesn't seem to know what to do. He said he can't see himself living in that house without her."

"When he's got over it a bit maybe he'll change his mind." Max slid in beside her, drawing her into the circle of his arm.

"Rotorua's so far away, though. I don't like the idea of him being there on his own. Dora's family can't be expected to take him over." Celine yawned again. She'd spent long hours keeping a bedside watch at the hospital, while trying to make sure that her father got sufficient food and rest. And the funeral had been difficult. Dora's family had expressed definite ideas about how it should be conducted, not always in accord with what Ted wanted. Somehow Celine had adopted the role of go-between and conciliator. "Sorry," she said, "I'm bushed."

"I realise that." Max kissed her forehead and withdrew his arm. "Good night."

"Mmm," she murmured gratefully, and hunched down into the blankets. "Good night."

Max lay on his back, one arm behind his head, his eyes open, until she had dropped off to sleep. Looking towards her in the darkness, he couldn't see her face except as a pale blur. Along the circular gallery, a door opened and shut softly, and a few minutes later he heard the toilet in the spare bathroom flush and the door open again, Ted returning to his bed. Max sighed, turned on his side and gave his pillow a punch. Then he closed his eyes, willing himself to sleep.

Max would never have believed that one extra person in the house could make such a difference to his comfort. Ted had been an early riser all his life, and at six sharp he was up and using the bathroom. Max was thankful that he didn't have to share theirs. Celine got up at seven now, even at the weekend, and went down to make breakfast for her father, who would be waiting at the kitchen table.

"Shouldn't he be getting used to doing things for himself?" Max queried once as Celine left their bed. "He won't have Dora to make his breakfast when he gets home."

"It's more to keep him company," she explained. "At least while he's here I can give him that."

"How long *is* he here for?" It had been ten days now.

"Until he's sorted out what he wants to do, I suppose." Celine headed for the bathroom.

That evening Max, as usual, found Celine preparing dinner while Ted read the newspaper in the lounge. He wondered what on earth Ted did for the rest of the day, that he had to read the morning paper in the evening, when Max himself would have liked to have a look at it. To give him his due, Ted always offered instantly to hand it over, but courtesy demanded that Max invite him to finish reading, first.

Celine, busy washing a lettuce at the sink, said, "Dad's talking about going back to Rotorua in a few days. But he thinks he'd like to sell up and move to Auckland."

"Shouldn't he give himself some time before he makes a decision?" Max felt slightly guilty about his morning irritability.

"It's not as though he has family there." Celine shook the lettuce leaves and placed them in a basket to drain.

"You're the only family he has here," Max pointed out.

"That's better than nothing. I still don't like the idea of him being on his own. Max . . . ?"

He had a sinking premonition, even as he said, "What is it?"

"This is a big house for the two of us. Would you mind if Dad moved in with us for a while?"

Yes, he would mind, Max knew. He minded that he could never read his own newspaper when he wanted to, that he was woken each morning by stealthy door-closings and unaccustomed stirrings and the sound of the plumbing working. He minded that last Sunday evening his father-in-law had sat in a corner alternately grumbling because he didn't understand the plot of the TV play they were watching, and noisily shaking and folding the pages of the Sunday paper.

There were a lot of things that he minded. And he knew that every one of them was trivial, that he was a selfish human being to be minding at all when Ted had so recently lost his loved wife, when the older man had so much more to complain about.

"How long?" he asked Celine cautiously.

"Well, until he settles on something. If he does sell the house, I thought he might buy a flat in Auckland, but this afternoon he mentioned something about a retirement home."

"Is he ready for that? What about one of those villages where you can buy a flat, and later progress from one stage to the other?"

"Maybe. I don't know, though. We'd need to go into what's involved. And I don't want him to feel we're pushing him into anything."

"Well, if you think it's best, of course he can stay... for a while. You're not seeing it as a permanent solution, are you?"

Celine shook her head. "Not if you wouldn't like it."

"I wouldn't!"

She looked away from him, and wiped her hands on a paper towel.

"Look," he said, going to her and touching her shoulder, "I'm sorry, I know he's your dad. But I just don't think it would work."

"I thought you liked him."

"Of course I like him! It isn't that. But—I guess I'm used to just the two of us being in the house. I find it a bit... unsettling."

She turned her head to give him a pained smile. "It's just as well we don't have children, then, isn't it?"

"You know that would be quite different!"

Celine shrugged. "Anyway, half the time you're working late, and even when you are here, most nights you're shut away in your study. It's not as though we're together that much."

Nettled, he retorted, "Well, you know, when I'm home you're just as likely to be out at your bridge or badminton, or your night class or your book club. Although I notice you've stayed around for your father more than usual."

Celine threw down the crumpled paper towel on the bench. "What am I supposed to do, wait around every night twiddling my thumbs in case you come home and want my company? I thought you were pleased that I had interests of my own. You said so!"

"That was years ago, when I was still a struggling junior partner." He had been at least relieved that Celine was self-sufficient enough to find plenty to do when he was busy forging his career. "We ought to have more time for each other now," he said.

"I see. Now that you have time for me, I'm supposed to give up my own interests to cater to your whims!"

"I don't mean that!" Max flushed angrily.

"What *do* you mean, then?" Her chin was thrust forward, her eyes bright with annoyance.

He opened his mouth and then clamped it shut, controlling his temper. "We seem to have lost the point," he said finally. "Of course your father's welcome to stay as long as he needs to. But not forever, I'm sorry."

Celine swallowed her own anger. "Thank you. I understand. You're entitled to say how you feel."

Offering an olive branch, he said, "Would you like me to set the table?" They had been eating most meals in the dining room since Ted had been with them, because the cosy kitchen table was only big enough for two to sit there in comfort.

"Thanks, I've already done it." Celine picked up the basket of lettuce and shook it over the sink. "You go on up and get changed. Dinner will be about twenty minutes."

*I suppose,* Max thought, resigned, *I can buy another newspaper to bring home.*

*  *  *

Max and Celine spent a weekend helping Ted to pack up the furniture and effects that he wanted to keep. Some went into storage, and Celine and Ted stayed to dispose of the rest. Dora's family took charge of her personal belongings and clothes.

When they returned after emptying the house and leaving it in the hands of an estate agent, Ted looked gaunt and grim, and Max felt intensely sorry for him. "It's really taken it out of the poor old fellow," he said to Celine.

"Yes. It's been hard for him." She put her hands on her back at the waist and flexed her shoulders.

"Are you all right?" It hadn't been exactly easy for her, either, Max thought.

"Mmm, just a bit stiff." She'd spent days packing things into labelled boxes and clearing cupboards and drawers, not to mention the final clean-up.

He came to stand behind her, massaging her shoulders. "Better?" he asked after a while.

"A bit. Thanks." She stretched and said, "I think I'll have a nice, long, hot soak and go to bed."

"Good idea. I'll see you later."

She smiled at him and went on upstairs.

Her hair felt dusty and gritty, and she fancied it smelled of the sulphur that permeated the air of Rotorua, so she washed that first in the basin. Head wrapped in a towel, she emptied a generous amount of bath salts into the tub before lowering herself into the steaming water.

Half an hour later she tucked another towel about her and used the electric dryer on her hair, then slipped into one of her more glamorous nightgowns. Getting into bed, she picked up a book and began to read. When her eyelids drooped, she looked at the bedside clock and wondered how long Max would be, contemplating going to find him. She heard her father climb the stairs, use the bathroom, and close his bedroom door, but still Max didn't come. In the end she put the book down and switched off the light, falling almost instantly asleep.

* * *

As the weeks slid by, Ted took a mild interest in the real estate columns of the classified ads, but seemed unimpressed with the very attractively laid-out villages that Celine took him to see. He began pottering around the garden, advising Max on what sprays to use for black spot and aphids and how to prune the shrubs. Max thanked him politely and later asked Celine if Ted had decided yet where he was going to live.

"Give him time," she said. "It's a big decision."

"How much time does he need?" Max sounded unusually irritable.

Although, Celine reflected, it wasn't so unusual these days. In fact, he'd been uncharacteristically moody lately. "What's the matter?" she said. "Are you feeling all right?"

"There's nothing wrong with me. You're looking a bit strained, though. Do you want me to speak to your father, try to get him to make up his mind?"

"No. If you want him to go—"

"I didn't say that!"

"It's what you meant, though."

"Oh, for God's sake!"

It was the kind of tense, unconstructive argument that they'd been having too often lately. As always, it ended in them both stiffly apologising, but with nothing really resolved. Sometimes Celine wondered if it would be better to have a real, loud, shouting quarrel, rather than these low-key exchanges of barbed remarks. But, that had never been their style.

And neither had ever harboured grudges or nursed resentments. Their differences had been quickly resolved by a gracious admission of fault, a smile exchanged, or a compromise that satisfied both of them. And sometimes by a wry remark that set them both laughing and dissolved any bitter aftermath.

They seemed somehow to be losing their capacity for laughter. Max was spending less and less time at home; his hours at work appeared to have escalated back to the level of when he'd been in his twenties and fighting for a permanent place in the firm.

Celine found herself tied as she hadn't been before, by a reluctance to leave her father alone for long. Accustomed to snacking at lunchtime on fruit or a tomato sandwich, she now had to think about giving him a nutritious meal, because he seemed thin and almost frail. Also, he was in the habit of sitting down for morning and afternoon teas, and taking a hot drink with a biscuit before going to bed. She knew he was quite capable of making a cup of tea himself, but if she was around he assumed that she would have one, too. And then he'd talk about Dora, about Celine's mother, about the past. Thinking that he probably needed a sympathetic ear as part of the grieving process, she sat patiently listening.

Somehow, exercising patience with him left her a little short of it for Max. Often she found herself profoundly irritated with both of them, as when Ted, following a lifelong habit, cast the newspaper on the floor with its pages sliding into disorder, and Max picked it up and precisely realigned their edges before folding it into a perfect rectangle and placing it in the magazine rack by the sofa.

But what troubled her most was that Max seemed to have lost interest in their sex life. They hadn't made love for ages.

She'd thought at first it was out of consideration for her, because she had been tired when she'd first brought Ted home, and was still finding that one extra person in the house made an amazing amount of added washing, cleaning and cooking—and she didn't like to ask Alice to work extra time, as the home help had other employers and a carefully worked out schedule.

There were nights that Max didn't leave his study until after midnight, and others when he stayed at the office until nearly that hour. A couple of times she'd given him an unspoken invitation, normally enough to make his eyes kindle into desire, his mouth curve in promise.

Instead he'd turned away, his eyes blank and cool, as though he hadn't seen.

One night, long after her father had gone to bed, she went along to Max's study. She'd washed her hair, put on a specially pretty nightgown that he had given her for her last birthday, sprayed her body with a floral perfume, and pulled on a long, transparent peignoir that she seldom wore.

When she tapped on the door and went in, closing it behind her, he looked up from the papers strewn on the big old oak desk that she'd found in an antique shop when she was furnishing the room, and regarded her with a peculiarly empty expression.

She smiled at him, and walked slowly across the Persian rug towards him. "You're working too late," she reproved him.

Max sat very straight in his chair as his eyes involuntarily took in the seductive garment floating about her over the satin gown that skimmed her slim figure. "Celine—" His voice was low, slightly unsteady.

She smiled again, and went round the desk, put her hand on the swivel chair and turned it a little towards her. "Max," she said, the other hand tugging at the satin ribbons that tied the peignoir at her throat, "I miss you." The ribbon parted, and the edges fell back, further revealing the satin nightdress, low-necked with a front slit from ankle to thigh.

She curved her arms about his neck and sank onto his knee. The chair moved of its own accord, and his arms came round her waist to steady her. She lifted her bare feet from the ground, rubbing them against his trousered legs. Her lips pressed on his jawline, his cheek, then his mouth.

She felt him take a breath, fast and uneven, and smiled against his mouth. Drawing back her head a fraction, she defined the contour of his ear with a finger, traced the heavy, straight brows, and ran her thumb over the outline of his mouth. "Kiss me, Max," she whispered, and offered him her lips.

His hands on her waist tensed, and his lips touched hers almost tentatively. She opened her mouth for him, encouraging him, and the kiss gradually became erotic, impassioned, as she stroked his hair and his nape. She found one of his hands and brought it up to her breast, over the satin that barely covered it. She felt the hand convulse on her soft flesh, and then his palm closed over the centre, and she knew he could feel the small, sudden pebble of hardness under the flimsy fabric.

Nestling down into his lap, she was reassured by the answering surge of his body, and her arms tightened about him, her tongue sliding along his, inviting him to further intimacies.

His abrupt movement startled her as he stood up out of the chair, bringing her to her feet. She tilted her head back to look at him, her hands still linked behind him, her pelvis snug against his. "Come to bed," she urged, making a subtle, seductive movement.

Max was breathing quickly, his face flushed. His hands were on either side of her waist. She edged closer, leaning up to kiss him again. But he raised his hands, pulled her arms down, and said hoarsely, "No!"

Celine blinked. Disappointed and offended, she stepped back a pace, and glanced at the work on the desk. "Is it that important?"

"Yes." He dragged a harsh breath into his lungs. "No. It isn't that."

Looking at him again, she instinctively pulled the edges of the inadequate peignoir together. "What, then?"

"I'm sorry," he said. "You're very...sweet and—I don't mean to be a boor, but—the fact is, I can't."

*"Can't?"* Her gaze dropped momentarily to the front of his trousers and swept up again. "What on earth are you talking about? Do you think I didn't feel it?"

The dark flush that had receded from his cheekbones briefly returned. "I don't mean I'm physically incapacitated—" He raised one hand to rub his forehead with a thumb and forefinger, and then swung away so that he wasn't looking at her. He picked a pen up off the desk and dropped it. "I mean I can't...I can't sleep with you. I can't make love to you."

For long seconds Celine's mind was totally blank. Then several wild and disjointed thoughts clashed together, from the unlikely to the unthinkable. Momentarily she felt that the room—maybe the entire world—had tilted, so that everything was off-centre, unbalanced. She took a deep breath and let it out. With determined calm, she said, "Look at me."

She saw him brace his shoulders, then he turned slowly and faced her, his blue eyes cool and resolutely steady.

"I think," she said, "I have a right to know why."

His throat worked as he swallowed. "I know. I'm sorry if it hurts you. But it was inevitable that you'd have to know sometime." He paused, and the silence stretched. "You and I have never lied to each other, Celine. I'm...I've been . . . seeing someone else."

*I don't believe it!* was her first thought. She stared at his unwavering eyes, and told herself it couldn't be true. But, as Max said, they'd never lied to each other. And this was not something that he would make up, for any reason.

"You've been unfaithful to me?" she asked him in a voice that seemed to come from somewhere far off, although it was her mouth that moved, her tongue that formed the words.

She thought he flinched slightly, a small tremor passing over the wooden mask of his face. "I'm sorry," he said again.

"When?" It wasn't what she'd meant to say, but it was as good a question as any. "I mean, was it a one-night stand? I suppose anyone can make a mistake, and I know it's been difficult lately—" Although she hadn't thought things were that bad.

He cut across her desperate rationalising. "No, Celine. It wasn't like that. It's no casual encounter."

"How long has it been going on, then?"

"Does it matter?" He frowned, and when she didn't answer, said curtly, "Several weeks."

"What does that mean? Three? Six?"

"More like six," he muttered, "if you mean how long have we been sleeping together. It hasn't...been all that often, actually."

"Oh? Why? Did your conscience bother you?" She heard the waspish note in her voice with surprise. She hadn't even realised that she was angry. She felt too numbed for that.

Max said, "As a matter of fact, yes." He shut his teeth on the last word.

Celine had sometimes wondered what she would do in a situation like this. Not that she'd seriously thought Max would ever betray her. "I didn't think that you would—" She found she was unable to finish the sentence.

Rather hoarsely, Max said, "Neither did I. But it has happened, and—well, you had to know."

For a moment she wished passionately that he hadn't told her. Maybe if she had never known, if he'd kept his lapse secret, she'd have gone on forever in blissful ignorance. "While I was away," she said, jumping to a conclusion. She'd been away a lot, lately.

"The first time it...happened, yes. You were away."

"You couldn't do without sex for a few days?"

"You know damn well I can." A frisson of resentment laced his voice, although he kept it level.

Celine moistened dry lips and lifted her chin, looking him in the eye. "Is it over?" she asked baldly.

"No," he said. "It isn't over."

Celine felt the ground spiralling away from beneath her feet. She clenched her hands on the fabric of the pretty peignoir, suddenly conscious of its incongruity in the circumstances. She had dressed for seduction, to lure her husband to bed with her. And he'd just told her he was having an affair with another woman. For all the impression her satin and chiffon was making on him, she might just as well be wearing sackcloth. The only expression she could see in his face was a stony resolve to get something unpleasant over and done with, and his eyes seemed to hold—of all things— compassion.

Minutes ago she'd been sitting on his lap, kissing him, wooing him, pressing his hand to her breast. Humiliation burned through her entire body. He didn't want her. His physical reaction had been nothing more than a reflex, just a fleeting, automatic lust.

"What do you expect me to do?" she asked him, trying to keep any shrillness out of her voice. "Wait until it *is* over?"

He shook his head. "You don't understand, Celine."

"How could I?" She had to suppress hysteria. "I'm only your wife, after all. Of course I don't *understand!*"

"I've told you I'm sorry," he said. "It doesn't do any good repeating it." His chest heaved. "Celine—if you can't understand at least try to accept it. It will never be over." His eyes were almost desperate in their dark demand. "I'm in love with her."

# Chapter 5

"In love." Celine stared blankly. "You said you'd never fall in love again."

"I know."

Her voice rising despite her best intentions, she said, "You spelled it out for me before we got engaged. You warned me! All you could promise me was loving friendship in a stable marriage. You'd never be tempted to stray because your heart—the part that could fall in love, anyway—was buried with Juliet!"

"*I know what I said!* I was wrong." He looked almost haggard. "I was wrong," he repeated. "I was wrong to think it, wrong to say it, wrong to build my marriage to you on a mistaken belief. I can only hope that in time you'll forgive me."

"Forgive you? When you've just told me you intend to go on seeing—who is she? Anyone I know?" Mentally she started running through a list of their friends. None of the women seemed a likely candidate.

"You've met her." He bent his head, one hand massaging the back of his neck.

Celine momentarily recalled how she'd caressed him there, five minutes ago—aeons ago. "Well—" she said. "—Who?"

"I'd appreciate it if you didn't make this public," he said.

Why? she wondered wildly. Was he ashamed? Or protecting the woman? "Hasn't she told her husband? A bit less honest than you, is she?"

"She isn't married," he said. "It's Katie...Kate Payne."

At first sheer astonishment held her silent. Immediately on its heels came a feeling, rather than a coherent thought—*of course.*

*"Bo Peep?"* she said at last, and began to laugh, peal after peal, her head going back.

"Don't, Celine!"

But she went on laughing, a hand at her midriff, the laughter welling out of her until he grabbed at her shoulders and gave her a sharp little shake. *"Stop it!"*

His face was white and furious. Celine choked to a stop and stared at him, her eyes wide and clear. "You fool, Max," she said distinctly. She knew her face had gone tight, hard. "You think you're in love with that little blond bombshell? You and how many of your balding, pot-bellied, fatuous, middle-aged colleagues? I'll bet half the office is in love with the girl. You'll all get over it!" Impatiently she knocked aside his arms, so that his hands left her. "You're better-looking than the other senior partners," she said, her voice cool and expressionless. "I can understand why she's plumped for you, but for heaven's sake, you're ten—*eleven* years older than she is. And married."

"Celine, I'm serious about this—about her."

She stared, and finally shook her head faintly in wonder. "Oh, I can see you are. And I suppose you think she is, too."

He opened his mouth, and she knew he'd been going to say that Kate was just as serious as he was. But he changed his mind. "I needn't discuss her feelings with you," he said instead. "That's between Kate and me. I hope that we—you and I—can remain the friends we've always been. It may not be easy at first, but I'm sure we can work it out."

They'd always been able to work out any problems. But this . . . this was different. She looked at him, her husband of twelve years, her friend since so far back that she couldn't remember when he hadn't been a part of her life. And she saw a stranger.

"Max," she said, almost gently, as something inside her seemed to crack in all directions, "you surely don't expect me to accept this, go on as if—as if things are the same as they always were?"

He looked shocked. "No," he said. "I don't expect that. I'll—I'll have to leave, of course." He looked around his study as though mentally assessing what he'd have to take with him. "If you can give me a couple of days," he said, "to get organised . . . or do you want me to go now?"

In films people left their spouses dramatically at all hours, packing bags in haste and departing into the night, apparently with no problem of where they would go. Englishmen would say "I'll be staying at my club." Max didn't have a club to go to. She pictured him entering a motel or hotel in the early hours, or trying to explain to his parents that he needed a bed.

Stupid. He had Kate, didn't he? He'd go to her. "Are you going to move in with . . . your mistress?" she asked stiffly.

"Kate isn't my mistress."

"You're sleeping with her, you said."

"We're lovers," he said stubbornly.

"That's different?" Without waiting for an answer, she asked, "How often *have* you made love—behind my back?" He'd said, *Not that often.* So exactly what did that mean?

A faint line of colour darkened his cheekbones. "I really don't think that's—"

"*Don't* tell me it's not my business," Celine said, in the grip of a fiercely controlled anger. "*I want to know!* So—how many times?"

"What does it matter?" Restlessly he spun away from her to walk towards the window and swung round to face her again, as though he'd needed distance between them.

That made her angrier still. She held it in, repressed a primitive urge to shriek abuse at him. "It matters to me!" she said tensely. "I'm your wife, *damn you!* I have a *right* to some answers!"

His mouth was a clamped line, his jaw clenched. She knew he was rigidly containing his own temper. "Not to that question." He paused there, and she thought he wanted to turn away, his body making a slight movement, but he checked it, staying where he was. "The first time," he said, "I thought it would never happen again. I hadn't intended it to happen at all—and neither had Kate."

Celine suppressed a snort of disbelief. She believed that Max had intended to keep to his wedding vows—as for Kate Payne's intentions, she had serious doubts.

Doggedly, Max went on. "I might not have told you—if it had stayed at that. I tried to put it down as an indiscretion, one I had to live with, rather than ease my guilt by burdening you with a confession—"

Of course he'd felt guilty. Max was an honourable man. He'd always been honest with her. They'd been honest with each other.

He said, "But the second time I could no longer pretend that it wouldn't happen again, and again, when the opportunity arose."

"You make 'it' sound like an act of God," she said scornfully. Max had always been in control of his life, his emotions. "A thunderstorm or a lightning strike."

One shoulder lifted briefly. "It is a bit like that," he said with perfect seriousness. "The thing is, Celine—I never expected to feel this way again."

As he had felt for Juliet, he meant. Juliet, the girl he'd been going to marry, whose photo he still kept in a drawer of his desk. As he'd never felt for Celine.

Surprised at the depth of the pain she felt, Celine tightened her lips against a tendency to tremble, and drew in a breath. She had never been jealous of Juliet's place in his heart, never attempted to take his dead fiancée's place, and he hadn't wanted her to. But now he thought he'd found someone who could.

She had a sudden mental picture of Max naked in bed with Kate Payne, his dark head bent over her tumbled blond curls, his eyes gazing into hers. She closed her own eyes briefly, trying to shake the image. Opening them again, she looked straight into his. "You didn't bring her here, did you? You haven't—not in our bed?"

"Good God—*no!* Of course not."

Of course not. Max had more sensitivity, more style than that. She was almost ready to apologise when he added, "I wouldn't do that to Katie—or to you."

At the afterthought, Celine's teeth snapped shut on the apology. She had an urgent desire to throw something heavy at his well-groomed head. Instead she said nastily, "She doesn't mind *you* calling her Katie?"

Max flushed, and she wished she'd kept her mouth shut. Obviously the pet name was a private thing between *Kate* and him. Celine was glad that he didn't answer.

She felt hot herself. The atmosphere in the small room seemed stifling. She had to get out of here before she lost control, and either fainted or gave vent to a fit of uncontrollable temper. She wouldn't lower herself, wouldn't let him see how deeply wounded she was, how he'd shattered her belief in herself, in him, their whole life together. "I'm going to bed," she said. "I don't think you know what you're doing, Max. But I can't stop you. I don't suppose you intend to join me tonight."

"I'll sleep here," he said. There was a couch in the study where they sometimes put up overnight guests if the bedrooms were full. "Celine—"

About to go out the door, she reluctantly looked back at him.

"Thank you," he said, "for taking it so well."

Had she taken it well? she wondered as she went along the curved gallery to their—*her*—bedroom. It had never seemed such a long way before. The floor appeared to be receding in waves before her feet. He meant, she supposed, that she hadn't succumbed to tears or tantrums. Either would have made him very uncomfortable. Max had never been one for showing a lot of emotion, and he didn't particularly like it in others.

Although, she recalled as she climbed into the big double bed, when her mother had died, it was Max who had held her in his arms while she cried. She'd not wanted to cry in front of her father, who was devastated himself, pale and numbed with his own grief, not wanted to make things harder for him. And she'd tried to be strong for her younger brother, who hadn't been able to contain his sobs at the graveside. She and her older brother had taken the main responsibility for planning the service and the burial, and Nancy had stepped in to help with the gathering afterwards in their home.

Only when it was all over, the last of the mourners had gone home and the house had been returned to order with the invaluable help of Max's family, she'd found herself alone in the kitchen with him, and he'd put a sympathetic arm about her shoulders and said softly, "Poor old Lina— they all lean on you, don't they?" And the tears had come.

He'd held her and let her cry. Once she thought someone came to the doorway, and Max shook his head and whoever it was went away again. And when the wracking sobs finally died he'd found a handkerchief for her and then dampened a towel and sponged her flushed, tear-stained face and swollen eyelids, giving her a final hug when she muttered that they'd better go and see what the family was doing.

Tears stung again at the back of her eyes as she remembered that Max of long ago, and the one she'd just left in the study, who'd told her that their marriage, as far as he was concerned, was over, and that he hoped they'd remain friends.

Such a cliché, she thought, leaning over to switch off the bedside light. She supposed it was possible. They had friends who had been invited to their ex-spouses' weddings to new partners, and who had actually wished the couple well with seeming sincerity. She knew divorced parents who managed to bring up their children in apparent accord and to enjoy family outings, despite their separation and sometimes the founding of a new family, perhaps of two.

Yes, it was possible. Just at the moment, though, it seemed that she could never accept such a relationship with Max.

In the blessed darkness she let one tear fall before blinking the rest away, savagely sinking her teeth into her lower lip. She would *not* cry. Not tonight when Max might hear, or worse, when he might come into the room and see.

But he wouldn't. He was sleeping alone in his study tonight. That was the arrangement.

There'd be other arrangements to make in the coming weeks, months. Would he want to move out all his things—his clothes, books, furniture? Should she ask him to? What did people do in this situation?

Worked things out, she supposed. In a sensible and civilised fashion.

She wished she felt sensible and civilised. Instead she felt as though she was burning up inside, with rage and pain and a sort of bewildered disbelief. If—heaven forbid—Kate Payne had walked into the room at that moment, Celine truly believed she might kill the girl.

She didn't expect to sleep, but at some point in the night she must have dropped off. She woke with a slight headache and a feeling of dread, not knowing immediately what caused it. Before she opened her eyes, the memory of the scene last night in Max's study returned. She sat up, hoping it had been a dream, but the heap of chiffon on the floor where she'd discarded her glamorous peignoir brought it back in hideous detail.

It was no dream. Max really was leaving. He didn't want to be her husband any longer.

She heard her father go down the stairs. It must have been the sounds of his morning ritual that woke her. She ought to go and make him breakfast. Max, of course, had always made his own. But she'd usually joined him before he left for work, and kissed him goodbye.

That was in the old days. Lately, she realised, he'd avoided even that cursory peck on the doorstep. She'd put it down to reticence in front of her father, or just forgetfulness, now that their normal routine had been disrupted by Ted's presence at the breakfast table, lingering over his third cup of tea.

She would have to tell her father that they were separating, that Max wasn't going to live here anymore.

She went down and served Ted's breakfast, finding her movements oddly dreamlike, slow. But he didn't appear to notice anything unusual.

When Max entered the kitchen later she saw that he was a little pale, the bones of his face seeming more prominent. Perhaps he hadn't slept well, either. *Good,* she thought involuntarily, immediately shocked at her own vindictiveness.

She turned away before her eyes caught his, and slotted some bread into the toaster. She didn't want toast but she needed something to do.

The men exchanged their usual morning greeting, and Max came over, holding two slices of bread. "Oh, sorry," he said, realising the toaster was in use.

"You can have these," Celine said, hastily backing away. "I'll eat later."

"No, you go ahead. I haven't had my cereal yet."

He always put the toast in before he ate his cereal so that it was ready for him.

"It's all right," she said, "really." They were like two strangers, awkwardly trying to be polite and considerate. "I put them in for you," she lied, "because I thought you were running late."

"Thank you." He looked at the clock. If anything, he was a little earlier than usual. Probably, Celine thought, he couldn't wait to get out of the house. She moved away and spooned instant coffee into a cup, then went to the fridge and opened the door, staring at the contents for several seconds before remembering that the milk was already on the table.

Max ate his breakfast quickly, while she alternately sipped at her coffee and pretended to be busy clearing Ted's breakfast things.

When he finally stood up, he brought his dishes over to the sink, like a guest being helpful. She muttered, "Thank you," and as he turned to go, added, "Are you going to be here tonight?" Her hands closed hard on the cup she held.

He hesitated. Dropping his voice as he glanced at his father-in-law, he said, "I'll pick up some of my things, if that's all right."

"Of course." But he wouldn't be staying, sharing their bed with her. He would never share it again. "I'll expect you in time for dinner," she said brightly, glancing over at Ted.

Max looked uncomfortable. Under his breath he said, "I didn't mean—you don't need to—"

Her voice brittle, she said, "No problem. I'm cooking, anyway."

"Thank you," he said, his brows low over his eyes as they searched hers, apparently looking for something, before she flicked her glance away.

Max lingered as though uncertain whether he ought to kiss her. She couldn't have borne it if he did. She picked up his cup and concentrated on rinsing it. He turned away at last, and she heard him say goodbye to her father before the door shut behind him.

All day she thought she ought to break the news to Ted, but didn't. Perhaps some small part of her wanted to believe that Max's decision was not irrevocable. She told herself that it was better to wait until he'd gone, anyway. It was bad enough the two of them being awkward with each other. Involving a third party could only make things worse.

She went upstairs after doing the breakfast dishes and walked into the bedroom. And stopped, her heart pounding, at the sight of an open suitcase, half packed with Max's clothes, sitting on the floor by his wardrobe. Thoughtfully, he'd placed it in the corner of the wall and the wardrobe so that it didn't get in the way.

The delicate peignoir she'd worn last night lay across her dressing table stool. She'd made the bed this morning but hadn't tidied the room. Turning her back on the suitcase, she walked over to the dressing table and picked up the flimsy garment—Max's gift to her, that she'd worn last night when she'd hoped to lure him into bed. She thought about all the lovely garments he'd bought for her over the years, and shivered with revulsion. His studied selection of glamorous, expensive presents was no longer an intimate, loving gesture. Instead she saw that he'd been trying to turn her into the kind of woman who attracted him, because she wasn't interesting enough as she was. Perhaps he'd needed fancy packaging to make himself desire her at all.

She found her hands had closed hard on the filmy material. Suddenly hating it, hating all those beautiful, sexy things he'd bought for her, that she'd paraded in for his benefit, she lifted the seductive garment in her hands and pulled hard until her hands hurt and first the stitching, then the material gave way. Deliberately, viciously, she tore it in two, then four, dropping the pieces on the floor. Panting, she stared down at the ruined garment, then scooped up the ragged remnants and went into the bathroom, where she stuffed them into the rubbish bin near the basin.

Straightening up, she caught sight of herself in the mirror. Her eyes were brilliant and her cheeks flushed. She put a hand to her hair, the familiar sleek bob. As yet there was no grey in it, but the dark brown colour was unexciting. There were tiny lines fanning from the corners of her eyes, a faint crease on her brow, and a smile line by her mouth. She thought of Kate Payne's smooth, unlined skin, her abundant blond curls and lush young breasts. The flush died from her cheeks, and she turned away.

When he'd come home from that conference Max had asked her why she didn't wear her hair long anymore. And later he'd mentioned "Katie something" so casually. And denied that he wanted to see her jumping out of a cake.

No, he wouldn't want that, she thought, going back to the bedroom. Max preferred a bit of sophistication in his entertainment, and he wouldn't enjoy watching any woman cheapening herself, especially a woman he cared for.

The day dragged by. Alice came in to clean the house, and Celine, recalling the half-filled suitcase in the bedroom, said she'd do the upstairs today.

Not that Alice would have commented—she was far too discreet, and anyway, Max did go away occasionally for conferences or to attend to legal business elsewhere. Still, it gave Celine something physical to do, cleaning bathrooms and vacuuming carpets.

When she went downstairs again Ted was chatting to Alice, who was cleaning the stove. He had the paper open in front of him at the real estate pages.

"Shall we go and see some flats?" Celine asked him, desperate to keep herself busy, stop herself thinking.

He was lukewarm about the idea, but she persuaded him to fill in a few hours looking at flats that he thought too small for comfort, too close to a noisy road, too big for one person, too isolated from the shops and public transport, too damp, too hot—

Celine in the end lost count of their various faults. She reminded herself that this would probably be Ted's last home and he was entitled to be happy with it. "There's plenty of time," she assured him, "to find the right place."

They were late getting back, and she found herself disorganised for once in the kitchen. Max arrived as she and Ted were sitting down for dinner.

"I'm sorry," he said awkwardly, hesitating in the dining room doorway, his eyes taking in the empty place at the head of the table. "I expected you'd have finished eating by now. I tried to phone to say I wouldn't be here for dinner after all, but the machine wasn't on."

The answering machine was in his study, and she hadn't wanted to enter that room today.

"You haven't eaten, have you?" Celine asked.

"No, but—"

Celine got up. "I've kept it warm."

He followed her to the kitchen. "I thought you'd prefer, really, that I didn't come in for dinner. I can get something later—"

"There's no need. It would only get wasted, you may as well have it."

In the end he excused himself for a few minutes and then joined them at the table.

Celine sat opposite him as usual, trying to act normally. Their eyes kept sliding off each other. Ted concentrated on his food, and Celine, desperate to fill the silence, told Max that she and her father had been flat-hunting.

He looked at her then as though he was surprised, but his voice was neutral. "Any luck?"

"Not yet. We'll know when we find the right one, won't we, Dad?"

Ted looked up and said something noncommittal before returning his attention to his plate.

"What exactly do you want?" Max asked, persevering.

Ted deliberately chewed and swallowed a mouthful of food, then said, "I'm not fussy."

Max turned a quizzical look from him to Celine. She'd exchanged a discreetly smiling glance with him before she remembered, and the smile in her eyes died.

She saw pain in Max's eyes, too, and she dropped her gaze to the tablecloth, clenching her hands on her knife and fork. The plate in front of her went fuzzy, and she took a hasty forkful of vegetables, chewing fiercely to keep the tears at bay.

After that she gave up the effort to make normal conversation. Max could try if he liked, she thought resentfully. And he did, asking Ted more questions and eliciting some kinds of reply. She wondered if he was listening to them.

She took their plates to the kitchen and carried in the apple pie and cream. When they'd been alone she and Max hardly ever had a sweet course, often preferring to finish with fruit and cheese or just coffee. But Ted was accustomed to a pudding. He'd have missed it.

She didn't want any herself tonight, but was unfairly irritated when Max said he'd skip it, thanks. She cut herself a small piece of pie to keep her father company, and ate it in tiny spoonfuls.

Max said, "If you'll both excuse me, I have things to do."

Like packing his bags. "Don't you want coffee?" she heard herself say, as though that might delay him.

"Not now, thanks," he said.

He'd probably found this meal just as excruciating as she did. She ought to be glad that he was ending it. But as she heard him cross the hallway and start up the stairs, she wanted to run after him and beg him to reconsider.

Perhaps he had? Perhaps if she did go after him he would tell her that he'd changed his mind, hadn't meant it after all. Her muscles tensed, ready to rise from the table, but she quelled the impulse. Pride wouldn't allow her to plead with him.

She forced down the rest of the pie, almost screaming with frustration as her father finished his generous portion with what seemed infinite slowness. The moment he'd spooned down the last mouthful she grabbed his plate and said, "I'll make the tea." Ted seldom drank coffee, and she'd taken to sharing a pot of tea with him.

When she finally was able to go upstairs, she entered the bedroom to find Max had closed the suitcase and was taking things from his dressing table drawers and placing them into an overnight bag.

He glanced up and she closed the door quietly, leaning back against it because her legs suddenly seemed wobbly. Then he went on methodically removing folded underclothes and a pair of pyjamas and placing them in the bag.

"You'll give me an address, won't you?" she asked in a detached voice. "For mail and . . . so on."

"Yes, of course." He closed a drawer, then picked up the bag and went into the bathroom.

She followed, putting a hand on the doorjamb, watching him take his toothpaste—they favoured different brands—and toothbrush, then his electric shaver and his shampoo and after-shave from the shelves of the mirrored cupboard, leaving his side of it empty. His hands, she noticed, were perfectly steady. As he shut the mirrored door she briefly glimpsed her own face, surprised to find it looking quite composed, although there was a tightness round her mouth. Deliberately, she relaxed the muscles. "You're going tonight, then," she said.

He looked calm, too, as he turned to face her. "I thought it would be easier for you if I didn't hang about."

"Thank you." Would it be easier? She didn't know.

"I'll have to come back for my other things. If you like, I can make it sometime when you're not here."

"That won't be necessary." She was really doing quite well, she thought. No one would know that inside she felt like a fragile piece of old china, riddled with tiny cracks but somehow still holding together. She stepped back as he came to the doorway. "Any time."

"I'll phone first. You can tell me if it's not convenient." He placed the overnight bag on the bed and glanced about the room before zipping it up, checking for anything he might have forgotten. The set of silver-backed brushes, her wedding gift to him, was still on top of the dressing table. She saw his eyes skip over them. Perhaps he didn't want to be reminded...

Turning to her, he said, "You haven't told your father?"

Celine shook her head. "Not yet."

"I suppose it will be easier when I've gone."

She nodded, not trusting her voice. *When I've gone.* It sounded so final.

Max placed the overnight bag with the suitcase and said, "I need a few things from my study."

When he came back holding his bulging briefcase, she was standing by her dressing table, fiddling with a crystal perfume spray, his latest Christmas present. She put it down with a small thud and turned to face him.

"Here," he said, offering a square of paper to her. "This is where I'll be, for a while, anyway."

She took it, resisting the urge to tear it up. "Is it her address?"

She thought he flushed slightly. "No. I thought you'd find it more...acceptable if I stayed on my own for a while. You can tell our friends that we've made a mutual decision to part. Or tell them it was your choice, if you like. Later..." He shrugged.

She ought to be grateful. He was giving her a chance to salvage some pride before he moved in with Kate, announcing his new love to the world. She looked down at the paper in her hand. It was an apartment in downtown Auckland. The city centre, once deserted between five, when the shops closed, and seven, when the entertainment centres and restaurants drew people back to its heart, was becoming a fashionable place to live, especially for business people without families. He would be only a few streets away from his office.

She stood staring down at the piece of paper. "You're renting it?"

"Yes. It's partly furnished."

So he could move straight in, she surmised. Convenient.

Max said, "You'll be able to have your father with you, after all."

As if that could make up for losing her husband. She didn't answer, afraid that if she opened her mouth it would be in an undignified howl of anger and hurt.

"Do you want me to say goodbye to him?" Max asked.

"No. I'll explain later."

"Right." He hesitated a moment longer, then turned to pick up his bags. "I'm sorry, Celine."

"I know," she said. He was, and she knew that this wasn't easy for him, either. But it was his choice, and her happiness was the price he was willing to pay for his own...and Kate Payne's.

"I couldn't have gone on pretending," he said. "I thought for a while that I could. I tried."

Yes, she supposed that he had.

"Sooner or later," he said, "this was inevitable...once I'd met Kate." He was telling her that her happiness couldn't have lasted, that she'd been living in a fool's paradise. Not for the first time, he'd picked up on her thoughts.

"You don't have to explain," she told him distantly.

He wanted her to understand. She didn't. They'd had something good, something worthwhile, solid, *loving*. It might not have been all moonlight and roses, but they'd had those, too, from time to time. And he was throwing it all away for the sake of some kind of emotional high. Because he'd fallen in love.

Perhaps she should tell him she'd wait for it to blow over, that there was no need for him to leave. But even if her own emotions hadn't balked at the prospect of turning a blind eye while he conducted a raging affair, she knew that Max would never have accepted that. His sense of integrity wouldn't allow it.

"Let me know if you need anything," he said. "I'll always care for you, Celine. That won't alter. Only, this is...different."

Tightly, she said, "I don't want to hear this, Max. It would be better if you'd just...*go!*"

He bowed his head slightly. "If that's what you want. I'll be in touch."

If he kisses me, I *will* scream, Celine thought, clenching her hands at her sides.

His eyes searched hers, and she looked back at him stony-faced. He nodded again, jerkily, and turned to the door.

Burdened as he was, he'd have to put down the bags to open it. Celine stepped in front of him and did it for him.

"Thanks," he said, not looking at her as he passed through. Watching him walk along the gallery and disappear down the stairs, she hoped her father wouldn't choose this moment to come out of the lounge where he was watching TV.

She heard Max's footfall on the marble floor. He must have left his car in front of the house, because he went out the front door. It snapped to behind him, and a few minutes later the car started and went off down the drive. She listened until the engine note died away, standing very still as though that would hold her together, her mind oddly blank, her emotions temporarily in a blessed limbo.

"Max gone out?" Her father glanced up from the paper as she entered the lounge.

"Yes." She ought to tell him now, of course. But instead she sat down and pretended to be watching the television while he rattled through the paper, glancing up now and then to comment on what was on the screen.

She'd tell him tomorrow. She didn't think that tonight she could cope with questions, comments and helpful suggestions.

Once she might have looked to her father for comfort, but now their roles had reversed. She looked at him and saw how his cheeks had sunk inward below his cheekbones, and his eyes were dulled behind his spectacles. She saw the prominence of his wrist bones as he turned the pages of the newspaper, and watched him squinting to read the print, even though he wore his reading glasses. Maybe it was time for a new prescription. She remembered how he'd been when he was younger, when she'd thought him a big, strong man, although now he was scarcely taller than herself. Then, she'd known with utter conviction that her father would always look after her.

Everything changes, she thought sadly. Max had said there was no reason now why Ted shouldn't stay. She ought to be glad. Instead she felt an unutterable depression.

# Chapter 6

Ted took the news, when she broke it to him after breakfast, surprisingly calmly. He was shocked, of course, but then he picked up her hand and held it, saying, "Poor Lina. I've been so wrapped up in my own troubles, I didn't realise things weren't going right for you."

Grateful for the sympathy, she blinked away tears. She hadn't mentioned Kate Payne. That could come later. At least Max had given her time.

She hadn't asked Max if or when he would tell his family. Nancy or Michelle would have been her first confidante in any other crisis. But how could she talk to Max's mother or sister about his defection? With sudden dread, she wondered how they would react to her being Max's ex-wife. Surely they wouldn't exclude her? Their friendship was too long-standing for that.

But Max would want to introduce his new love to his family. She imagined the awkwardness that would result if she spent as much time with the Archers as she'd been used to, sharing their birthdays and celebrations, being invited to impromptu gatherings, sometimes popping in unexpectedly for coffee or bringing a treat for lunch. Sooner or later she would find herself confronted with Kate hanging on Max's arm.

No, she would have to distance herself from his family. They'd probably be grateful.

Nancy phoned that evening. "Celine, dear, are you all right?"

"I'm fine," she answered steadily.

"Max has just been here."

"He's told you, then."

"I can't believe it!" Her mother-in-law sounded shell-shocked. "You two are so right for each other. We thought you had a perfect marriage!"

*I thought we did, too.* But she'd been blind, fooling herself. She wondered if Max had confided the real reason to his family.

Nancy's next words dispelled that thought. "You're probably going through a bad patch," she said. "Everyone has them, you know. I tried to tell Max, but he said he doubted you'd have him back. Would you like to talk about it? I could come round, if you like."

So Max had put the blame on her? Made his mother believe it was Celine's idea? Anger clamped her fingers more strongly on the phone. "No," she said. "I can't talk about it yet. Maybe... maybe later."

"Well... any time. You know I'll always be here for you both."

Will you? Celine thought bleakly. What if Max divorces me to marry Kate? She didn't want Nancy to be torn between her loyalty to her son and to the daughter of her old friend. "Thank you," she said noncommittally. "I'm all right, really." She paused, then asked, "Did Max seem... okay?"

"A bit strained," Nancy said. "I suppose you both are. A separation, he said. Well, that's not final, is it?"

*Ask Max,* Celine was tempted to say. But instead she said, "It will give us both some time to think."

"Yes." Relief entered Nancy's tone. "He made it seem so... definite. When I see him again, can I tell him you're thinking about things?"

*"No!"* Celine bit her lip, trying to control her voice. "Let us work it out in our own way, please, Nancy. I'm sure Max will... will keep you posted."

"I hope so. I don't want to interfere, but Celine, I think of you as a daughter, you know."

"Yes, and I'm grateful."

How would Nancy feel about being asked to think of Kate as a daughter? she wondered as she hung up. As Max's wife?

She'd welcome the girl with open arms, Celine guessed, for her son's sake.

Michelle phoned the following day. Obviously the news had gone around the family. Michelle, probably primed by her mother, tried to express her dismay and bewilderment without prying or apportioning blame, but she finally said, "I can't believe that you and Max—I mean, you've known each other *forever*—you seem so... well, perfect together! You're both so calm and sensible and—and strong."

So everyone thought, Celine supposed. What a boring, predictable couple they must have appeared, even to their own families. "Maybe that was the problem," she said aloud. "Max wanted something different."

"Max?" There was a blank silence. "I thought that *you—*"

"No." Why should I take the blame? Celine decided rebelliously. His family, at least, could know the truth. Or a part of it. "It was Max's idea," she said, "to separate. I... went along with it."

"Oh. Oh, Celine, I'm so sorry!"

Celine winced. Pity was the last thing she needed. Maybe she should have let well enough alone.

Michelle rushed on. "What's the matter with him?"

"I think he's... bored. He wants a bit of freedom, I suppose."

"Freedom? Bored? *Max?*"

"Lots of men do it."

"Yes, but *Max?* And to do it to you! How could he, the pig! Next time I see my brother, I'll put a flea in his ear!"

"Michelle—"

"How *dare* he!"

"Michelle—"

"Doesn't he know how lucky he is? Men! I could *kill* him."

"Michelle, *please!*" Half laughing, but fighting tears, Celine broke into the diatribe. "Don't!" she begged. "I don't need you to fight my battles for me. Truly. We...we're working it out. The last thing I want is a rift between Max and his family."

Michelle sighed. "I suppose the two of you just sat down and had a calm discussion and decided to part? You wouldn't even have a row about that, would you?"

Celine admitted, "I guess it was something like that." She recalled Max formally thanking her for taking it so well. At least she'd kept some dignity.

Michelle said darkly, "I'd box Tony's ears if he did it to me."

Celine couldn't help a little laugh. "I know you would. But I'm not you, and Max isn't Tony. I'm sure that Tony wouldn't—" He adored Michelle, a fact that was obvious to everyone. They quarrelled sometimes, often noisily on Michelle's part, but the sparks soon died.

"He'd better not," Michelle said grimly. "I don't know what's come over my brother! Celine—"

Dreading the question, Celine took a deep breath.

"—it's not another woman, is it?"

Celine closed her eyes, letting the breath out. "Ask Max," she said.

"You don't know?" Michelle guessed sceptically. "I don't suppose he'd tell me if there was," she added.

She'll find out in due time, Celine thought. But that was up to Max.

He called her two days later. "If it wouldn't inconvenience you," he said, "I'd like to collect some books and a

few other things this evening." He was talking like a lawyer.

Celine said graciously that it wouldn't inconvenience her.
"In case we're not here," she said, "you still have your keys,
don't you?"

Of course he did. "When I've removed the rest of my
stuff," he promised, "I'll hand the keys over to you."

"The house is still half yours."

"Yes, but—well, we can sort that out when the time
comes," he said. "I can make over my half into your
name."

What would Kate think of that? she speculated. But Kate,
of course, had a well-paid job of her own. Celine suspected
that Max imagined her interior design business was a source
of no more than pin money. He'd never enquired how much
she earned from it. If she took it on full-time, she supposed
she'd be able to support herself adequately.

She asked her father if he'd care to go to a film. Ted
shook his head, then seemed to think better of it. "Do you
want to go out?" he asked, suddenly alert. "Shall we find
out what's on, then?"

He made a show of studying the entertainment pages of
the paper in his hands, and asking her what she wanted to
see. Touched, she chose a film at random. At least she didn't
have to tell him that Max was coming round and she simply
wanted to avoid meeting him.

The film wasn't what she'd have chosen if she'd been
thinking about it. It was a thriller concerning a jealous
woman who stalked and killed her husband's lover. Celine
found herself in some sympathy with the villainess.

The film was over earlier than she'd expected. When they
came home Max's car was parked in the drive. She edged
hers past it and into the garage, which seemed enormous
with only one car in it. Ted said, "That's Max, isn't it? Do
you think he's—er—"

"He's just collecting some of his things," Celine said. "I
thought he'd be gone by now."

"Oh—ah—I see." Her father shot her a sympathetic glance. Once they were inside, he hovered uncertainly in the hall. "Well," he said, "um—I'll go up to bed, unless you—"

Unless she needed his moral support, she supposed. She smiled at him. "I'll just make myself a hot drink first. You go on up." He didn't like to drink anything this late because it meant he'd need to get up in the night.

She made coffee, taking her time and doing it properly in the percolator. The study was almost directly over the kitchen, and she heard one or two subdued thumps on the ceiling as she waited.

She poured herself a cup of the brew, realising that she'd unthinkingly made too much for one. After a moment she took another cup from the cupboard and filled it, spooning in sugar, and carried them both upstairs.

The door of the study was ajar, a wedge of light shining onto the gallery carpet. Celine pushed it open with her shoulder and stepped inside.

Max had been emptying his bookshelves into several large cartons on the floor. Stooped over a box, he straightened to look at her as she paused in the doorway.

"Coffee?" she offered, surprised at the shock of pleasure it gave her to see him. The sleeves of his white shirt were rolled up and his collar was open. A jacket and tie lay over the back of the swivel chair.

He smiled, and she felt her heart make a quiet revolution in her chest. It was the same smile he'd always given her, warming his eyes and softening the slightly austere lines of his face. "Thanks," he said. He reached out to take the cup she gave him, and glanced at the watch on his other wrist. "I'm sorry, I didn't expect to take so much time over this." He surveyed the nearly emptied shelves.

Celine just stopped herself from offering to help. It was a natural reflex, which she stifled with a shrug. "It doesn't matter." Leaning back against a bookcase, she took a sip of her coffee.

Max propped himself on the edge of the desk, his long, dark-trousered legs stretched in front of him, one ankle propped on the other. He drank some coffee and looked across at her. "How have you been?"

It was only a couple of days since they'd seen each other, but he asked as if he cared. Conscience, Celine told herself sharply. She shrugged again. Meeting his eyes, she said, "I will survive."

"Yes," he said, "I know you will. It isn't as though—"

When he stopped there, she asked curiously, "As though what?"

"Well—" he absently swirled the coffee in his cup "—as though you really need me. I mean, you've always been very self-sufficient."

"Does Kate need you?" Celine asked baldly.

The gentle movement of his hand halted. He looked up from his study of the coffee. His eyes seemed distant and expressionless, perhaps purposely so. "I don't think I can answer that."

Because he didn't know? Or because he wouldn't discuss Kate with her? She looked at him, searching for clues. She had never thought that Max was the type to be attracted to a needy woman. "Do you want her to?" she pressed.

He lifted the cup to his lips and half emptied it before straightening away from the desk and turning so that he almost had his back to her. He'd cleared the desktop except for a glass paperweight that Celine had given him a long time ago. Putting out a hand, he shifted it a few inches to one side. "I think I need *her*," he said, so quietly that she almost missed the words.

Celine felt a painful tightening of her throat. Hastily she drank some more coffee. When she could trust her voice again, she said thinly, "Well, I hope it works out for you."

He shot her a quick look. "Thank you. That's very generous."

Bitterly, Celine reflected that she was making this all too easy. The trouble was, she'd had no practice at being the wronged wife. In most social situations she was able to behave in the appropriate manner—it was one of the things, she knew, that Max liked about her. She'd never embarrassed him in public. But now she wasn't even sure how she should feel, let alone how to act.

The woman in the film she'd seen tonight had never had any doubts or hesitations. She'd simply solved her problem in the most direct and crude way possible by removing her opposition, using a horrifying level of violence. But it hadn't given her husband back to her. He was revolted by what she'd done. The ironic ending left them in a deadly relationship, with both of them knowing that vengeance and murder lay between them for the rest of their lives.

Celine knew she wasn't capable of murder, and she didn't want vengeance. She wanted Max, she wanted her marriage back, she wanted—she supposed what she wanted was for everything to stay as it had been. And that was never going to be possible. No matter what happened now, their lives were irrevocably altered. Nothing would ever be quite the same again.

"How's Ted?" Max asked.

"Much the same," Celine answered automatically. Then she amended it. "Actually, a bit better, I think." One thing this had done was to go some way to pulling her father from the lethargic aftermath of his loss. He'd been making an effort to take an interest in her problems, offer her a level of comfort. "We went to a film tonight."

"Oh? What did you see?"

She told him, and he said, "Isn't that the one about—"

"Yes," she said. Their eyes met and she saw the quizzical gleam in his. "Kate's safe," she told him dryly, and saw his mouth curve with humour, his body infinitesimally relax.

"I'll tell her."

Oddly, she thought she'd always treasure this moment, the shared laughter. "I don't think so," she said huskily.

"No." The smile died from his eyes. "I won't. She wouldn't—"

Wouldn't think it was funny, Celine finished mentally for him. Not that one could blame her. It was the kind of joke that long-married couples shared. Or freshly separated ones, perhaps.

Perhaps shared laughter would make him realise that he was indulging in a ludicrous fantasy, that their marriage was more real and precious than any temporary infatuation. But beneath her determinedly composed facade she was too perilously close to hysteria to allow herself the luxury of laughter.

Her mouth took on a wry curve. She lifted her cup and finished the coffee in it. "There's some mail for you," she said. "I left it on the hall table. I was going to readdress it, but as you're here..."

"Thanks. I'll pick it up on my way out. I shouldn't be long in here." He finished his drink, too, tipping back his head. She watched the movements of his throat, and the way his hair fell over his forehead when he lowered his head again. Assailed by an unexpected wave of desire, she clenched her teeth to stop it showing on her face.

He stood, looking slightly awkward until she stretched out a hand, offering to take his cup.

"Thanks," he said tersely. "Don't let me keep you up."

Dismissed, she took the cups and trailed downstairs with them. Leaving them in the dishwasher, she climbed the stairs again, lingering outside her bedroom, the room where last night she'd slept alone. Where from now on she would always sleep alone.

The study door was firmly closed. Max had shut her out, just as he wanted to shut her out of his life.

When she made herself open the door of the study the next day the shelves were bare, the top of the desk swept clear. Even the glass paperweight had gone. She wondered what Max had done with it. Several boxes, neatly sealed with wide sticky tape, were piled in a corner. The desk drawers, when she opened them, were empty. Would Kate mind that he still kept a picture of his first love? Or perhaps for Kate he had got rid of it. Celine had never been able to erase his memory of Juliet, but had Kate taken her place in his heart?

He phoned at lunchtime, saying, "I didn't want to disturb you and Ted by carrying everything out last night. I'll pick up the boxes later today, probably this evening. And . . . the rest of my clothes."

"Yes," she said. "That's fine." Tonight she'd be playing bridge. "Do you need your desk, or anything?"

"No. Do what you like with it. Perhaps I'll have the chair if I can fit it into the car. You wouldn't mind?"

"Take whatever you want."

"Thanks. I do appreciate . . . your attitude."

Sure, she thought. He'd have hated her to make scenes, throw tantrums, act like a jealous woman. He probably thought she was being pragmatic, sensible, even sporting about the whole thing.

No, not that. Max wasn't crass enough not to imagine that his actions hadn't deeply affected her, at the very least dealt a crippling blow to her self-esteem; his face-saving gesture in not publicly going straight to Kate's arms and her bed were evidence of that. But he'd left Celine, anyway. And that was the clearest, unequivocal indication of how desperately important Kate was to him.

After she had returned from her evening of bridge, grateful for the fierce concentration needed so that for minutes at a time she almost forgot what was going on in her life, she forced herself to open Max's wardrobe. There had been no sign of his presence in the house, although when she asked, her father said yes, Max had been in, briefly.

The shelves and hangers stared back at her, patently empty. She closed the wardrobe doors. He'd left nothing of himself behind, except the silver brushes that still lay on his dressing table. Perhaps he hadn't known what to do with her wedding gift to him.

She went over and swept them into an empty drawer, firmly closing it.

She'd seen the exercise machine still in the corner of the garage when she got out of the car. Max wouldn't have forgotten it, so he didn't want to take it. He'd hinted that he wasn't interested in belongings that couldn't be easily taken in the car. The Red Cross Society was having a garage sale next week. She'd phone someone and ask them to collect it. And the desk that he didn't want. They could have the shelves, too, from his study. And anything else she couldn't bear to look at.

Next morning she noticed the two keys lying on the small table in the hall. Max must have taken them from his key ring and left them there last night. She picked them up, feeling as though a huge leaden weight had descended on her chest. There was something very final about them lying there, signifying the end of Max's right to use them. They made a small sound, a metallic chink, in her hand as she closed her fingers on them, so tightly that the serrated edges left marks on her palm for hours afterwards.

Celine went on somehow with her life. It was lucky she had a full calendar, she told herself. Only it was difficult somehow to enjoy her various activities with the same zest. In time perhaps it would return. No one could live in this fog of bleak bewilderment and resolutely buried anger forever.

One day she had lunch in a city restaurant with Nancy, feeling slightly guilty about leaving her father on his own, but after placing a ham salad in the fridge for his midday meal, she'd left him happily poking about among the plants with a gardening fork.

Nancy tactfully let Celine steer the conversation away from the subject of her marriage, for which she was grateful. After they parted with a warm hug she was walking to her car when a dress in a shop window caught her eye.

She passed the shop, then hesitated and turned back to look again. It was a striking dress, with a vaguely thirties look, slim and flowing, low at the neck, elegantly longish in the skirt, and bias-cut to cling. The kind of dress that might make a woman with a voluptuous figure look overblown, but on her, with her modest bust, narrow waist, almost flat stomach and gently curved hips, it would be supremely sophisticated.

The most eye-catching thing about it was its colour—deep violet at the neckline, gradually shading to palest mauve at the floating hem.

"Yes," she said to herself, and walked into the shop. The price tag was considerable, but she had just received a substantial cheque from the Chatswoods for the redecoration of their home. She could afford it. And it fitted her like a dream.

She walked out of the shop feeling better than she had in weeks. Heaven knew when she would ever get to wear the dress. Most of the evening functions she'd attended had been something to do with Max's work or Max's friends. And it wasn't a daytime dress, unless for a very special occasion. But, she reminded herself, she did have friends of her own. Anyway, just seeing herself in the dress had given her spirits a much needed boost.

Hanging it in her wardrobe, she wondered if she was a very shallow person, that the purchase of a pretty dress could even slightly soothe the wound of a broken marriage.

But of course it hadn't healed it.

Sharon Chatswood phoned. "Stephen and I are holding a small party to show off our new decorating. You and Max will come, I hope?"

Celine presumed that Max had let his colleagues know discreetly what the situation was, but obviously the news had yet to filter through to ex-colleagues. "That's very kind, Sharon," she said warmly, "but perhaps you haven't heard that Max and I are not together anymore."

"Not—? Oh! Celine, I'm terribly sorry. I had no idea—"

"How could you?" Celine answered reasonably. God, she hated this! "It's quite recent—just a few weeks ago we decided to part." She might as well get the speech off pat. "I'd be delighted to come, if you still want me on my own. But if you want Max, I'll give you his new telephone number and you can invite him separately.''

"Well, you must come, dear, naturally. It's your skill we're showing off, after all.'' Hesitantly, Sharon added, "You're still good friends, then? You won't mind if we invite Max, too?''

Hoping he'd have the discretion to decline, Celine said pleasantly, "I'm sure that neither of us wants to force our friends to take sides. And we're still talking to each other. Please invite him if you want to. I have the number right here. Or you could phone him at work, of course.''

Ted was still half-heartedly house-hunting, and although she had several times almost told him that there was no need to move if he'd prefer to stay with her, something stopped her. Despising herself, she supposed it was a subconscious hope that Max might change his mind and come back. And he had made it very plain that he didn't intend permanently sharing a house with her father.

Somehow Celine had found neither the time nor the inclination to get her hair cut lately, and it was much longer than she was used to. She'd taken to holding it back with a clasp to keep it away from her face. Before the Chatswoods' party she decided to get something done about it.

When she phoned for an appointment she was told that her regular hairdresser had gone on leave to have a baby. Celine hadn't even known the woman was pregnant. For the first time in years, she felt a once-familiar pang of envy. Whatever lingering hope she might have retained of one day having Max's baby, it had gone now.

"There's a new girl, Sophie,'' the receptionist said helpfully. "She's come to us from another salon, very experienced.''

"Yes, all right.'' Celine wrenched her mind back to the business at hand.

Sophie seemed young to have so much experience, but then, Celine reflected, police officers and ministers tended to look young these days, too.

Perhaps because she was new to the salon, Sophie appeared to have plenty of time. She suggested a colour rinse. "Just to liven it up a bit, give it some amber lights." And when Celine described her usual style, explaining that a cut was way overdue, Sophie demurred. "It's just at the awkward stage, I know, but if you let it grow a bit more, we could really do things with your hair. Give you a body wave and restyle it—look, I'll show you a picture."

In the end Celine put herself in Sophie's hands. The hairdresser snipped a little here and there, shaped the dark brown mass and blow-waved it into a graceful, swinging shape with a chestnut shine. "There," she said, "that'll keep it nice for a while. A few more weeks and you'll be able to put it up if you like. I can show you lots of ways of doing it that would suit your face."

Celine left the salon feeling if not a new woman, at least a renovated one. When she put on the new dress that evening, she was careful not to disturb the hairstyle.

It was the first party she'd been to without Max. She felt odd walking into the house alone, but Sharon welcomed her and introduced her to everyone as "our clever decorator," and no one seemed to find it in the least unusual that she was without a partner.

She wasn't the only one, anyway. One man was so interested in her ideas about the decor that Sharon urged her to take him on a guided tour of the whole house and show him what she'd done with it.

He was tall, with greying hair and a pleasant, intelligent face, and she saw him glance surreptitiously at her wedding ring, but he made no comment on it. He walked at her side without touching her, and asked sensible questions. In answer to her eventual query, he said, "I've just acquired an old house. It needs some work, and I'm looking for ideas."

They were coming out of the master bedroom as Sharon passed them to answer a peal of the doorbell. "Did Celine show you how she did the curtains?" she queried in passing, reaching for the door handle.

"Yes, very nice." He put a light hand on Celine's waist, allowing her to precede him into the passageway.

Just as she did so Sharon swung open the front door to reveal Max standing on the step.

Involuntarily, Celine came to a dead stop, and the man behind her almost stood on her heel. She felt his body brush hers, and his hand slid about her waist as he instinctively tried to steady himself without actually cannoning into her.

"Sorry," they both murmured, and exchanged the embarrassed, forgiving smiles that the small incident demanded.

Sharon said rather loudly, *"Max.* Lovely of you to come," and cast an anxious look at Celine as she ushered him in.

Celine couldn't retreat now, it would look too pointed. Instead she gave him a stiff smile as she edged away from the other man and said, "Hello, Max."

"This is Roland Jackson," Sharon said hastily, waving towards her companion. "Max Archer."

Roland held out a hand, and after a tiny pause Max took it in his, nodding curtly.

Sharon tucked a hand into Max's arm to lead him towards the lounge. "Celine's been showing Roland what she's done with the house," she said brightly as Max's gaze flickered sideways to the bedroom doorway.

"Archer?" Roland queried, his eyes going from Max to Celine and back again.

Max said, "Celine is my wife."

Startled, Celine looked at him, finding his eyes as glacial as his courtroom opponents might have. Technically it was true, of course. She still wore his ring. Perhaps Max, like her, shrank from making explanations to a stranger.

"I see." Roland obviously didn't quite, but he also obviously knew this wasn't the time to question any further. They were entering the lounge now, and Sharon went into hostess mode, making sure everyone knew Max.

"Can I get you a drink?" Roland enquired while Max was busy greeting the other guests.

"Thank you." Celine smiled gratefully at him. "Gin and lime, please." She could do with one. She was profoundly thankful that Max had not brought Kate with him.

She crossed the room, getting as far away from Max as she could, and was deep in conversation with one of the women when Roland handed her a glass. "Thanks." She smiled at him again, and he stayed and joined in the discussion.

Max didn't come near her all night, although she was acutely aware of his every move. She knew when he went to the bar and got himself a drink—three times—and when he sat down or stood with a group near the fireplace, and who he was talking to. The whole evening was an exquisite form of torture.

At some stage Roland had drifted off, but later he came back to her and said, "Would you be interested in looking over my house sometime? I'd welcome some professional advice. And I'm impressed with what you've done here."

"I'd be happy to have a look." She could do with some work if she was not to be dependent on Max. And dependent she didn't want to be, if they were no longer husband and wife.

"Good." Smiling, Roland took a card from his pocket. "Could you phone me when you're not too busy, and we'll arrange a time." He looked younger when he smiled.

Pleased at the prospect of another job, she gave him a friendly smile back. "Yes, I'll do that, thank you." She ought to have some cards made for herself, she reflected. It would have been more professional if she could have given him one.

Apparently he was leaving. "I . . . couldn't give you a lift, could I?" he asked.

For the first time she considered that he might be attracted to her. Had he checked with their hostess and been told that she and Max were separated? "No, thanks," she said pleasantly. "I brought my own car. But it was nice of you to offer."

"I'll see you again, then," he said casually, and tossed a general "Good night" to all those nearby before going in search of his hosts.

Half an hour later Celine decided that she could leave without anyone concluding that she'd run off early. She said goodbye quietly to Sharon and Stephen and went out to her car. Only to find that it wouldn't start.

She tried it again and again, then rested it, counting off five minutes before turning the key once more. All it produced was a sickly whine.

As she tried yet again, the door opened and two people came out, while Sharon stood in the doorway to see them off.

"Having trouble?" The man stopped as they passed, and peered into the side window. "Can we help?"

Sharon came over. "Celine? Are you still here?"

Curbing an urge to snap, Celine said, "I'm afraid so. I think it's the starter. I had a new battery put in just a couple of weeks back."

"Didn't leave the lights on, did you?" the man asked helpfully.

"No," she said with calm courtesy. "I haven't left anything on."

"I'll get Stephen," Sharon offered.

"No, please! I'll come inside and call a taxi."

But no one was going to settle for that. The man was itching to get his hands on the motor, while his wife stood by looking resigned, and Sharon insisted that Stephen would either fix the problem or run Celine home, it was no trouble, really.

Someone else came to the open door of the house, and inside of three minutes Celine and the car were surrounded by helpful males offering contradictory advice and suggestions.

Then Max strolled into the small but growing knot of people and said, "I'll take Celine home, of course. We'll arrange for someone to pick up the car in the morning, Sharon. It's not blocking anyone's way there." And he simply took Celine's arm and put her into the passenger seat of his car and drove off.

"I could have got a taxi," she said after a few minutes. "I don't want to put you to this trouble."

"Don't be silly, Celine. It's no trouble."

"It's out of your way."

"A few minutes," he said indifferently. "Don't fuss."

"I'm not fussing!"

He glanced at her, perhaps surprised by the unusual note of asperity in her voice.

"I could easily have got a lift with someone else," she muttered.

"Stephen still has other guests."

"Roland Jackson offered to take me home earlier."

"Know him well, do you?"

"I only met the man tonight."

"Then you wouldn't be stupid enough to accept his offer, I hope."

"He's a friend of the Chatswoods! I'm sure he's quite trustworthy."

"And I'm sure he thinks you're fair game."

"I beg your pardon?" Celine said frostily.

This time his swift look at her was definitely irritated. "He could hardly keep his hands off you—not that you seemed to be minding much. If you were trying to make me jealous it was a cheap trick."

For a moment she couldn't speak at all. Then she said between her teeth, "I was not trying to make you jealous! I didn't even expect you to be there tonight. And don't you *dare* accuse me of using cheap tricks." It was on the tip of her tongue to ask him if he preferred them coming from Kate, but that *would* make her sound like a jealous shrew.

He looked sceptical. "You must have expected me. Sharon said you'd given her my phone number."

"I knew she was inviting you. Only I thought you'd have the consideration to stay away."

"And *I* thought you'd like me to pay you the compliment of coming to see what you'd done with the Chatswoods' house. I'm sorry if my presence upset you."

"It didn't upset me!" she denied hastily. "Sharon was embarrassed."

"Rubbish," Max said brusquely. "If she was embarrassed it was because you were practically in Roland Jackson's arms when I walked in."

Celine opened her mouth to deny it, to explain, and then thought better of it. She didn't owe Max explanations, not anymore. "If I was," she said, "it's no concern of yours."

"Of course it concerns me. I told you, I haven't stopped caring about you."

Oh, he cared, did he? Some lukewarm emotion that was more insulting than if he'd said he hated her. "I'm a free agent, Max," she said. "Thanks to you. At least *I* wasn't casting about before we separated!"

He drew to a halt for a red light, drumming his fingers on the wheel until the signal had changed, while Celine sat in seething silence. As the car glided off again, he said, "Then who is the new dress for? And the hairstyle?"

"What?" The change of subject threw her for a moment. Who was it *for*? "It's for myself," she said. "To make me feel—good."

"Advertising, are you?" The car picked up speed as his foot pressed down on the accelerator.

"What are you talking about?"

He looked at her again, this time casting a comprehensive eye over her entire body. "You're not an innocent, Celine. You must know damn well that dress makes you look—available."

Celine was so astonished that she laughed. "You're being ridiculous! In any case, you have no right to comment on what I wear, or question my actions. And you're way over the speed limit!" she added.

He eased his foot off the accelerator, and a moment later she saw his lips curl at the corner. "Pots and kettles?" he said softly, slanting a brief look at her. "It's okay for *you* to comment on my driving, is it?"

"It's my life, too," she told him acidly. But she couldn't help smiling a little.

"You're right. I guess I overreacted," he said. "Maybe I've a possessive streak that I didn't know I had." He moved one hand from the wheel and found hers, holding it in a casual, companionable clasp. Celine stayed perfectly unmoving, almost not breathing, remembering the hundreds of times they'd sat hand in hand like this, feeling the warmth of his skin against hers, the hidden strength in the fingers about hers.

After a while he put his hand back on the wheel to go round a corner, and then drove the rest of the way in silence.

"You needn't get out," she said when he drew up at the door, but he did, anyway, coming round to help her from the car.

It was odd to come home with him and know that they weren't going into the house and up the stairs together. She said, "Would you like a cup of coffee?" And thought it sounded as though they were young again and had been on a date.

Max seemed to hesitate. Perhaps he felt awkward, too. "No," he said finally, "but thanks for asking." He bent and kissed her lightly on the mouth. It was totally nonsexual, just a friendly gesture, she warned herself, perhaps a sign of truce. Or even the result of long habit. "Good night, Celine."

"Good night." He stayed by the car until she'd found her key and opened the door. When she'd stepped inside and turned, he was getting back into the driver's seat. As he started the engine she closed the door. She didn't think she could bear to watch him drive away.

# Chapter 7

Upstairs, Celine switched on the bedroom light and crossed to the wardrobe, opening the door to examine herself in the full-length mirror fixed inside it.

*Available?* She studied the dress. Certainly she seldom wore such daring necklines, but with her meagre endowment it was hardly indecent. And although the flowing cut and soft material made the most of her figure, it wasn't skin-tight. The dress was in no way a blatant come-on. She didn't think anyone could have accused her of being obvious.

Except Max.

*Had* he been jealous? The thought was enough to stir a faint excitement—a glimmer of hope.

He'd been annoyed, angry. And had come close to accusing her of deliberately flaunting herself. In fact he had been less his urbane, strictly controlled self than she'd seen him since their marriage. Except perhaps for the night he'd come home from the firm's Christmas party and almost dragged her into bed.

In the mirror her eyes looked dark and mystic, her face delicately flushed. The light shone on her hair, picking up, as Sophie had promised, gold and amber glints.

She tried to see herself as Max had. Was it possible that he'd found her more attractive than he remembered? That somehow the sight of her had unsettled him, even made him doubt his feelings for Kate?

Celine shook her head. *Don't assume too much,* she warned herself. She might have surprised him by looking more glamorous and more desirable than he'd come to expect, but Max was far from shallow. A new hairdo and a low-cut dress weren't enough to change his feelings or bring him to her feet.

He was madly in love with Kate. She mustn't lose sight of that. But . . . his reactions did give her food for thought.

A couple of days later Celine phoned Roland Jackson and arranged to meet him at his house just after five. He was waiting for her when she arrived.

"I like the place because the rooms are a decent size," he explained, "but it's about fifty years old. The outside has been quite well maintained, though it needs a coat of paint. I can do that, all right, but I've no idea what to do inside. My wife used to take care of all that— I'm divorced."

"I see." As he pushed open the front door for them, she looked down a wide but dim passageway.

"I think this is the original wallpaper," he told her, waving a hand. The paper was speckled with brown, and peeling.

The other rooms were equally neglected. "But it's sound," Roland told her, stamping gently on the bare boards of one of the bedroom floors. "I used to do a bit of building, so I know what to look for."

After touring the whole house, Celine said, "I'd love to take it in hand, it could be a beautiful home, but the kitchen and bathroom should be totally remodelled, and the other rooms at least repapered. I'd like to keep some of the cupboards, but they'll have to be stripped—I should think there are at least three or four layers of paint on that wood. If you can afford it—"

"I want the job done properly. I expected it to be expensive."

"We must talk about what you like and don't like, and what use you want to make of the rooms. And any ideas you have."

Celine went home feeling almost cheerful. Roland seemed able to afford pretty much what he wanted, and it promised to be a lucrative commission, besides being a challenge to her skills.

The mail that morning had contained several bills that she'd readdressed to Max. For several years she'd been using her own earnings for most of her clothes and personal needs, but lately she'd begun to feel uncomfortable about him paying for her electricity and phone calls when he no longer lived in the house.

She voiced that thought to him when he rang her to enquire about an account that seemed to be overdue, but he brushed off her tentative offer to take over the payments. "We can sort out those things later," he said. "I'm quite happy with the arrangement meantime."

"Is Kate?" she asked.

After a moment's cool silence, he said, "I'm not married to Kate yet." Then he added, "Anyway, I don't think you can afford to pay all the household expenses on your own."

"Dad helps out, and I make money from the decorating."

"Still, it's only intermittent, isn't it? You can't be sure of a steady income."

"I'm working on it. I have another commission."

"Good. We'll still leave things as they are for now, though."

Shopping for a sixtieth birthday present for Max's mother, Celine found herself standing shoulder to shoulder at a cosmetics counter with Honoria Harding.

"Celine!" Honoria cried, a pair of outrageously large, bright cerise earrings swinging violently as she swivelled her head. "I haven't seen you in ages. You look wonderful! Are you growing your hair? I remember when we first met in Rarotonga you had lovely long hair. I always thought it was a shame you cut it." She broke off to take a parcel and her credit card from the shop assistant. "Thanks. What are you looking for, Celine? They have this stunning new makeup range—" She turned back to the girl behind the counter. "Show my friend the Spellbound special, would you? They're having a cut-price promotion," she explained to Celine, "to introduce it."

Between the saleswoman, who swung into her pitch instantly with the skill of practice, and Honoria, whose idea of a good time Max had once said was to spend the greatest amount of money in the shortest possible time, Celine had no chance. By the time she was settled at a table in a nearby café with Honoria, she was holding a silver-printed bag containing not only a complete set of scented bath salts, toilet soap and talcum powder with a large fluffy towel and matching hand towel for Nancy's birthday, but also a number of assorted containers bearing the Spellbound logo.

"And how's darling Max?" Honoria asked, choosing a filled pastry case from the assortment before her.

She ought to be getting used to this, Celine told herself as she unclenched her teeth. "You haven't heard," she said. "We've split up."

"No!" Honoria dropped the tart back onto the plate. "Oh, Celine, I had no idea. Last time I saw you the two of you seemed just the same as when we first met you on your honeymoon! What went wrong?"

She had told no one about Kate Payne. Max had promised her a period of grace, and she'd been grateful for it. But now, with Honoria's shocked and sympathetic gaze on her, she said baldly, "He's found another woman."

"*Max?* Oh, well..." Honoria's tone held a mixture of disgust and resignation. "He is a man, I suppose. How old is he now?"

"Thirty-seven—nearly thirty-eight."

Honoria nodded wisely. "That's the age for it, all right. How old is the floozy?"

Despite herself, Celine couldn't help smiling. "Twenty-five. But she's not really a floozy. She's a high-powered lawyer who works with him."

"Twenty-five, huh?" Honoria nodded again, unsurprised.

"He . . . he wants to marry her."

Honoria snorted. "Give it time. He'll grow out of it—Tom did."

"Tom left you?"

"Not exactly. He was having an affair with his secretary and I threw him out. That brought him to his senses, I can tell you."

"Max has already walked out. I didn't even have to ask him to go."

"Hmm. Is he living with her?"

"Not yet. Not openly, anyway."

"So what are you going to do about it?"

"What *can* I do?"

Honoria gave her a pitying look. She leaned across the table. "If you want him back, hon, you've got to get out there and fight her for him."

Experimenting with the new makeup that evening at her dressing table, Celine remembered Honoria's advice. "If you want him back—"

Did she want Max back, at any price, on any terms?

She'd been so busy hurting, and bottling up her anger, hanging on grimly to some semblance of dignity and self-respect, that she'd never sat down and thought about what exactly she did want. Except the impossible, to have everything remain as it had been.

Max had told his mother that he didn't think Celine would have him back. He thought he knew her well enough to predict that.

He'd deliberately burnt his boats, then, by walking away from her. She knew his decision to leave had been no impetuous action. Max had always known exactly what he wanted, and gone after it single-mindedly. Now he wanted Kate, and he was prepared to discard his marriage to get her.

He'd said he hoped that Celine and he would remain friends. Did he find it as difficult to imagine a life without her as she did without him? But friendship wasn't what she wanted.

And why, she thought with a hot surge of resentment, should Max assume he could have it both ways? She was his *wife*, and if she wasn't going to be his wife for much longer, she wouldn't damn well be his friend, either!

Telling him so wouldn't make a scrap of difference, she supposed. She'd have to adopt a more effective strategy.

She put down the makeup brush she'd been wielding and looked at herself in the mirror. She'd used rather more eye makeup than she usually did, and outlined her lips with a lip pencil before colouring them, so that her mouth was more clearly defined. The dusky rose lipstick the saleswoman had pressed on her suited her, and the eyeshadow, a soft shade between violet and brown, lent her eyes a slumbrous look. She picked up a small container of dusky rose blusher and applied some of the colour to the skin over her cheekbones. The shape of her face looked instantly different, as if it had acquired interesting new contours.

She didn't think for a moment that a change of makeup would bring Max crawling back to her, she wasn't that stupid. What it would do was help her to face him with some confidence next time they met.

Which, she realised, would probably be at Nancy's birthday dinner. Michelle had insisted that Nancy would want her to attend, and to bring her father along. "He's known Mum and Dad forever, after all. You won't mind Max being there, will you?" she'd asked. "You two aren't going to start throwing the plates at each other?"

"No," Celine assured her. Neither of them could imagine Max throwing plates at anyone. And obviously Michelle thought Celine equally incapable of it. "But," she added cautiously, "perhaps Max will want to bring someone—"

"It's a family occasion, for family only. Mum specifically asked for it to be that way."

"Then I'm not sure—"

"You're family," Michelle told her firmly. "You're Mum's goddaughter and Maxine's godmother, besides being still legally married to Max. So you're coming, aren't you?"

Ted declined the invitation, surprising Celine.

"Why don't you want to go?" she pressed him. "I'm sure Nancy will be pleased to have you there. You must be one of her oldest friends."

"Your mother was her friend, and I don't want to be reminded of your mother just now. Somehow, losing Dora has brought it all back too clearly. And you know I'm not one for going out to restaurants and such. I'd rather spend a quiet evening alone. Just give Nancy my best wishes. She'll understand."

Max had arranged for Celine's car to be fixed and delivered to her after the Chatswoods' party, so she was surprised when he phoned and asked her if she'd like a lift to his parents' house. About to tell him she'd drive herself, she recalled Honoria Harding's advice and said, "Thank you. What time shall I expect you?"

She heard the door chime as she was fixing her hair. Max was a few minutes early, and she was having some trouble getting her hair into the style Sophie had shown her last time she'd visited the salon.

Inclined to hurry, she made herself slow down, although her fingers were trembling. Her father would let Max in. She was going to look her very best tonight, and if it meant keeping Max waiting, so be it. She wondered how he felt, having to ring the doorbell of his own house and wait to be invited inside.

Carefully she inserted the last pins, and picked up a hand mirror to see the back of her hair. She checked her makeup without haste, slipped a pair of garnet earrings into her lobes and stood up to inspect herself.

Extravagantly, she'd bought another new dress, a dramatic tomato-red silk, a colour she seldom wore, but it suited her.

The wide, stiffened collar framed her shoulders and neck, and dipped in front to the shallow hollow between her breasts. Large buttons fastened all the way down the front. There was no belt because it was cut on slim lines, and she had to leave the bottom two buttons undone to allow her to walk with freedom because the skirt fitted snugly over her hips and thighs.

Sheer nylon encased her legs, and she had dark red high-heeled pumps on her feet. A whisper of the new eyeshadow on each lid, finished with navy eyeliner and mascara, enhanced her eyes.

She felt like a teenager on her first date—nervous, excited, anticipatory. Her cheeks didn't really need the blusher that she'd touched them with.

Downstairs, Max was talking to her father in the lounge. As she entered the room she had the satisfaction of seeing a look almost of shock cross his face when he rose from his chair.

She didn't apologise for keeping him waiting.

He took her elbow to guide her out to the car, and as he opened the door for her he cast her a searching glance. When he slid in beside her, he looked at her again, fumbling for the ignition key. "You look very nice," he said quietly.

"Nice?" She swivelled her head to look at him, brows raised.

His fingers had found the key, but he didn't turn it immediately. "Beautiful," he said, making her blood suddenly run faster.

"You approve, then?" This dress was defiantly sexier than the one he'd been so censorious about before.

He smiled as though acknowledging a hit, but didn't answer as he started the engine and moved off.

The car stopped in the gateway while he checked for traffic. As they turned onto the road, she asked casually, "How's Kate?"

"Very well," he replied formally.

"She doesn't object to you taking me to this party?"

"I didn't ask her permission."

Did that mean she didn't know? Celine wondered. "Does your family know about her now?"

"Yes. My mother...doesn't want to meet her yet. She needs a little time to adjust to what's happened."

She wasn't the only one, Celine told him silently. *And perhaps some of us don't want to adjust.* Supposing she just decided not to? "What about Michelle?"

His lips twisted wryly. "Michelle is very loyal...to you. I'm not sure if she'll be speaking to me tonight."

"I'll talk to her if you like." It distressed her to think of Michelle and Max being at odds. Theirs was a close-knit family.

"Magnanimous of you," Max said, "but don't worry about it. She'll come round when she meets Kate."

Celine bit her tongue and counted to ten. She wondered if he'd met Kate's family. What would they think about their daughter having an affair with a man who had to wait two years to obtain a divorce before he could marry her? He might have his work cut out to bring them round to the idea.

"How's the decorating business?" Max asked her. "You said you have another commission."

"Yes, Roland Jackson asked me to do a house he bought recently." Looking at him covertly, she saw the involuntary frown that he quickly dispelled.

"Oh, yes?" he said politely. "Are you enjoying that?"

"Very much. He's given me pretty much a free hand."

"Does he have a family?"

"Two children. They live with his ex-wife, but he has them for holidays and some weekends."

"What does he do?"

"He's a property developer, specialising in commercial buildings. If he likes what I do with the house, I'm hoping he might give me a chance to work on some of them."

"A new departure for you."

"A challenge. I've had a lot of new experiences lately."

The frown reappeared between his brows, and he cast her a sharp glance. Celine kept her eyes serenely fixed on the view through the windscreen.

He said, "I never stopped you doing anything you wanted to."

"I'm not accusing you, Max. But I suppose," she said thoughtfully, "you never really cared enough for it to be an issue."

"That's a hell of a thing to say!" His frown deepened.

Celine shrugged. "It's the truth, isn't it?"

"It wasn't like that at all."

Tempted to ask what it was like, for him, Celine firmly closed her mouth. It wouldn't do to start a quarrel. They couldn't walk into Nancy's party scowling at each other. She looked down at the gift-wrapped parcel in her lap, fiddling with the ribbon bow.

When they drew up outside the house he helped her out of the car, but dropped his hand from her arm to remove a large package from the back seat.

The door was unlatched, and as they entered Maxine and Susan ran to greet them, small faces alight with excitement.

"Can I give Nana the parcel?" Maxine asked, taking the wrapped box from Max's hands.

Susan, always less forward than her sister, looked wistful, and Celine offered her own present. "Would you like to give her this?"

"You brought *two* presents?" Maxine commented. "Look, Nana, Uncle Max and Auntie Celine brought you a present each!"

Celine felt a small pang. Always before, their gifts had been joint ones, usually bought by her. Obviously the girls didn't see the significance of the separate gifts, and Nancy, surrounded by discarded wrappings, smilingly presented her cheek first to Max and then to Celine, but Michelle, catching Celine's eye, looked sympathetic.

Celine gave her a determined smile. Nothing must spoil Nancy's evening. Max's father, standing by his wife's chair, looked rather piercingly at his son as he gave him a nod of greeting, and his clasp on Celine's hand was firmer than usual when he kissed her cheek.

They had booked a restaurant table, but first they had a round of drinks together, toasting Nancy, once the presents had been received and admired. Max's gift was a particularly elegant coffee-maker.

The children begged to be allowed to travel to the restaurant in Max's car, and although Michelle and Tony demurred, Max acceded to the request with alacrity. Celine, too, was rather relieved to have their company.

"Who's allowed to drink tonight?" Tony asked when the wine came. "I'm limited to two glasses—it's Michelle's turn to get tiddly."

"I won't get tiddly," Michelle asserted loftily.

"Oh, no?" Her husband grinned at her and asked Celine, "What about you?"

"Go ahead," Max said as she turned to him. Usually they would have had a discussion as to who was going to limit their drinks and drive home. "I'm driving," he told Tony.

There were times during the evening when Celine almost forgot that she and Max were estranged. He sat next to her, and as they lingered over coffee draped an arm over her chair behind her shoulders. It seemed much like many other family occasions they'd shared over the years.

Michelle, at first stiff with her brother, unwound gradually as she saw that he and Celine appeared to be at ease. Celine was glad to see her, later in the evening, laughing with him over some remembered childhood escapade. As different in personality as it was possible for siblings to be, they were nevertheless too fond of each other to be at odds for very long.

Outside the restaurant everyone said good night, and the girls climbed into the back of their parents' car.

"I think my mother enjoyed her evening," Max commented as he drove out of the carpark.

"It seems to have been extremely successful," Celine agreed. Was this how conversation was going to be from now on between them, limited to platitudes in order to keep them away from the dangerous shoals of accusation and recrimination? "She was very taken with the coffee-maker."

"I bought one for my flat," he said. "And she'd mentioned that their percolator broke down recently. I found mine very good, so it seemed the ideal present."

His flat. "What's it like?" she asked. "The flat." She didn't really want to know, but she had to make conversation somehow.

"Basic. Two bedrooms, a large lounge. The decor is bland, I'm afraid," he admitted. "It could do with some pizzazz. I know you'd—"

She would have dressed it up, made it interesting and comfortable.

"Well," Max said, leaving that thought unfinished, "it's a place to eat and sleep."

And a place to make love to Kate, she supposed. She wondered if the girl lived with her family, or flatmates. "Does Kate have a place of her own?" She hadn't meant to ask, torment herself like this. Clasping her hands tightly in her lap, she turned to look out the side window.

"Yes," Max said, without offering any further information. Patently he didn't intend to talk about that. "I should tell you," he said carefully, "the fact that Kate and I are seeing each other is common knowledge now at the office."

"Well, you couldn't keep it a secret forever." She moved her head, staring unseeingly at the windscreen.

"They think it's recent," he said. "We haven't told them anything."

"You mean they don't know that you left me for her."

"Celine—"

"I suppose you haven't told your family that, either. Did you deliberately give them the impression that I'd thrown you out?"

"I told them what I've told everyone else, that we'd made a mutual decision to separate."

"Michelle thought it was my idea."

"Michelle is all too prone to jumping to conclusions, you know that. I certainly didn't intend to lay any blame on you. But I thought you might not relish—" He hesitated, his hands moving on the steering wheel as he took a bend in the road.

"—Being known as your discarded wife?" she finished for him. She actually saw him wince as they passed a bright orange streetlight, and felt a shameful spurt of pleasure in his discomfort. "The one you traded in for a younger model?"

"For heaven's sake, Celine! Age has nothing to do with it."

She couldn't help a short, scornful laugh. "Be real, Max. I'm thirty-six years old. Kate is twenty-five. You've seen it happen to other people often enough. I think what I most resent is that the situation is such a commonplace one. I feel as though I'm living in a soap opera! If you weren't so damned honourable you'd probably have had an affair with the girl and hoped that I'd never find out."

His head turned sharply for a moment. "Would you have preferred it that way? Anyway, I told you it isn't like that."

Celine didn't know what she would have preferred. She shook her head and turned again to the window. The atmosphere in the car remained prickly, the very air bristling with unvoiced thoughts.

She was relieved when they reached the house and he parked the car in front of the door. The porch light was on, but otherwise the place was dark. The pool of light didn't quite reach the car.

"Got your key?" Max asked as he helped her out.

"Yes, of course." She opened the small purse she carried and found the leather tag, tugging impatiently as the key caught on something inside the bag. She meant to hold it up for him to see, but the stitching in the leather must have given way, for she was left with the tag in her hand while the key spun into the air, glittered briefly and then disappeared into the night without a sound.

"Famous last words," Max said. "It can't have landed on the drive or we'd have heard it. It's on the lawn or in the garden."

There were roses and alyssum planted in a narrow bed between the drive and the lawn. "I'll get a torch from the car," Max said, going back for it. "Pity I didn't hang on to my keys after all." The torch beam flicked among the rose bushes. Celine squatted, thinking she spied a gleam in the alyssum, but it turned out to be elusive. Max caught her arm. "Careful, you don't want to get your dress dirty."

Celine stood up and he dropped his hand.

"I could back up the car and use the headlights," he offered.

That didn't work, either. The headlights only cast deeper shadows.

"Don't worry," Celine said. "I'll ring the bell and wake Dad to let me in."

"If you like." But she pushed the bell several times and nothing happened.

"Fast asleep?" he murmured.

"I guess so. He has seemed a bit hard of hearing lately. And you know that bell isn't very audible upstairs."

"Mmm. What about the kitchen window?"

Once before they'd accidentally locked themselves out, each thinking the other had a key. Max had forced the window with a chisel from the toolshed and got inside that way.

"I've had all the windows fitted with burglar-proof locks," she told him. It had seemed a wise precaution for a woman whose husband had left her. "Dad will have checked them before he went to bed. He always does."

Max went off to inspect the windows, anyway, and Celine returned to the garden and, regardless of her dress, began hunting through the alyssum again.

When Max returned, he said, "All locked up tightly. No chance of getting in without smashing some glass, I'm afraid."

Celine stood uncertainly, her teeth worrying her lower lip. Finally Max said, "You'll have to come back to the flat with me."

"I can't!" She'd rather he drove her to a hotel. But she knew without asking that he'd turn down the idea of abandoning her to one in the middle of the night. He'd think she was being stupidly coy about spending the night in his flat.

"Why not?" Max asked. "It's the only sensible thing to do. You can phone your father in the morning and let him know what happened before he starts to worry. I certainly can't leave you stranded."

His parents would be in bed by now, and she discarded the idea of rousing any of the neighbours and begging for shelter at this hour. There were two bedrooms at the flat, he'd said.

"Come on." Max touched her arm. "You're getting cold out here."

It was true that the night was turning cool, and once or twice she had shivered. She looked with a certain amount of exasperation at the dark window of the spare room where her father slept. Calling to him or throwing something at the window would disturb the neighbours and probably have them phoning the police, and Ted wouldn't hear, anyway. Reluctantly, she said, "I suppose you're right. Thank you."

He'd been right about the apartment, she thought when he unlocked the door and ushered her in, switching on a light. The decor was unobtrusive to the point of dullness. A small entryway led to a pleasantly spacious lounge, furnished with a wide sofa and a couple of unmatched chairs grouped about a round coffee table. Max opened another door and led her into a room containing a double bed covered by a cheap, Indian cotton spread, and a dressing table. A kitchen chair by the bed apparently served as a bedside table. Two books lay on it, and a tie hung over its back.

"You can sleep in here," Max said.

"It's your room."

"I'm using the spare bedroom as a study. I'll be quite comfortable on the sofa."

"I can use the sofa." She began to back out of the room.

"It's okay," he said. "Do you want something to wear?"

"I suppose so." She couldn't sleep in the red silk dress, and all she had underneath was a strapless bra and a pair of satin panties over the lacy suspender belt holding up her stockings.

Max rummaged in the built-in wardrobe and handed her a paisley-patterned pyjama shirt.

"Thank you."

"I'll show you the bathroom. I don't think I've got a spare toothbrush, but you can use mine if you like."

He left her to it, and she washed out her panties in the basin before hanging them over the shower rail. Using the toothbrush he'd handed her, she thought what an intimate gesture that was, and wondered if Kate kept a toothbrush here. She hadn't seen another when Max had opened the mirrored door of the cupboard over the basin.

She rolled up the sleeves of the pyjama top, and removed as much makeup as she could with soap and a facecloth, resisting the urge to look in the cupboard for a jar of cleansing cream.

Even if Kate had left some here, she couldn't have brought herself to use it. In any case, inspecting the contents of Max's bathroom cupboard would be close to conducting a search for incriminating evidence. Which she didn't need, because he'd frankly admitted his adultery.

Picking up her clothing, she returned to the lounge, to find Max putting a couple of sheets, a pillow and a blanket on the couch. "I've left you two pillows," he told her, "and a duvet. I hope you'll be comfortable." He bent to adjust the blanket.

"I'd prefer the couch, really."

"There's no need. Take the bed."

"Max! I don't want to sleep in a bed where you and—" Celine choked to a halt, her cheeks hot.

Max straightened and looked at her. "I see," he said quietly. "In that case, it makes no difference. Take your choice, the couch or the bed."

Celine swallowed hard, afraid she was going to be sick. Of course he and Kate hadn't confined their lovemaking to the bed. The couch was long enough to accommodate Max's length, and wide enough to be comfortable for two, if they were sufficiently close.

With an effort she banished the image of them from her mind. "I'd still prefer the couch," she said.

Max looked surprised, but shrugged and suggested, "Perhaps you'd rather have the duvet, then?"

She couldn't bear this. In a minute she'd be screaming at him. "Just leave me alone please, Max, and go to bed."

"Okay. Sleep well," he said, and went towards the bathroom.

Celine draped her dress and underclothing over the back of the couch, and when she was sure Max had finished in the bathroom and gone to bed, she pulled the blanket and pillow from the couch onto the thin, nothing-coloured carpet. Wrapping the blanket about her, she tried to sleep.

# Chapter 8

The floor was hard, and the night air rapidly cooled. Stubbornly, Celine closed her eyes and willed herself to sleep. Outside she could hear cars passing, and somewhere in the distance a burglar alarm pulsed. It seemed no one was taking any notice, because it went on for at least half an hour.

She was almost dozing off at last when a motorbike roared past the building, startling her awake again. Then an ambulance came by, its siren wailing loudly. She wondered if it had woken Max.

When she heard voices in the street, and then a scream, she got up and pulled the window curtain aside. Across the street several young people were milling about, and she heard laughter and raised voices. She watched for a few minutes as they walked along, jostling and whooping, and guessed that the sound she'd heard was a scream of laughter rather than a signal of distress. With relief, she dropped the curtain into place and turned to go back to the makeshift bed.

In the dark she groped for the sofa, trying to avoid the coffee table, but her foot caught in the rumpled blanket and she tripped, barking her shin on the edge of the table. Unable to stifle a cry of pain, she sat down on the sofa, her hands tightly clasping the injured leg.

"Celine?" Max appeared as a shadow in the doorway and the light went on. "Are you all right? What have you done?" He came swiftly towards her, kneeling in front of her to prise her hands away. As usual, he wore only the bottom half of his pyjamas.

"I bumped into the table. It's nothing. Sorry I woke you."

"You didn't—those idiots out in the street did that. I thought someone needed help."

"Me, too. That's why I was blundering about in the dark."

"This is bleeding a bit." He stood up. "I'll get a plaster."

As he left the room she peered down at the small graze, and stopped a trickle of blood with her finger, to save the carpet.

Gazing absently about the room, she mentally refurnished it. A picture that used to be in Max's study hung on the opposite wall, a Rita Angus that he was particularly fond of. That and one of the chairs, simple and functional, were about the only things she'd keep.

He came back and knelt again, pressing a plaster over the graze.

"Thank you," she said.

He got up and looked at the bedding on the floor, then at her.

"I couldn't," she said.

A look of enlightenment came into his face, followed by a fleeting expression that might have been embarrassment. "You misunderstood, I think," he said shortly. "Kate has never been here."

"But you said—oh." He'd said it didn't make any difference if she chose the sofa or his bed. About to ask him why

Kate hadn't seen his flat, she hastily swallowed the question. Probably he didn't think the place was good enough for her, with its minimal furniture and air of functional impersonality. Briefly she speculated on what Kate's home would be like, picturing a wide double bed with a pink valance and a bouffant broderie anglais duvet. Hardly Max's style...

He said, "Have you had any sleep?"

"A bit." She lifted her hand to cover a yawn.

"This is stupid." Before she could protest, he'd bent and picked her up in his arms and was striding towards his bedroom, pausing to switch off the light with his elbow.

"We've shared a bed for twelve years," he said as he deposited her on the big mattress and twitched a sheet and duvet over her. "One more night isn't going to make any difference." Then he settled beside her. "Go to sleep, Celine." Pulling the other half of the bedclothes over his shoulders, he turned his back.

Perhaps lulled by the familiarity of the sound of his breathing and the dark hump of his body next to hers, or simply tired after the sleepless hours she'd spent on the living room floor, she dropped off almost immediately.

When she woke it was daylight and Max's side of the bed was empty. She heard his voice in the distance, followed by the ting of the telephone receiver being put down.

A minute later he appeared in the doorway. "You're awake," he commented. "I just phoned your father to let him know you're safe. You looked as though you might sleep for hours."

"You should have woken me. I must be holding you up." She pushed back the sheet and duvet, sliding her feet to the floor. The bed was higher than at home, and her legs looked long, her narrow, tapered feet pale and fine-boned. Once, a long time ago, Max had called them aristocratic feet, as he held one of them in his warm hands, caressing the soles and tracing the high arch of her instep with a leisurely finger. She'd laughed and said they were darned difficult to find shoes for.

"No hurry," he was saying. "It's Saturday, remember. I'll make breakfast while you're in the bathroom."

He turned away and she padded to the bathroom for a shower. She retrieved her panties and stepped into them, then wrapped a towel about her, and slipped out to the lounge for her other clothes.

She folded the stockings and suspender belt into her little bag, making it bulge, and buttoned the red silk dress over her bra and panties, then went barefoot to the kitchen, absently removing pins from her hair. "Could I borrow a comb?" she asked.

Max looked up from dropping a rasher of bacon into a smoking pan. "Bathroom cupboard," he said, "though I rather like your hair the way it is. Don't be too long," he cautioned her. "This'll be ready in a few minutes."

The bathroom cupboard contained a small range of masculine toiletries and first-aid supplies. She found the comb and fought the tangles out of her hair. Some of the pins she'd had yesterday seemed to have disappeared, and it was difficult to achieve the style again.

"Celine!" Max called. "Will you be long?"

Ages if she was going to do this, she thought, grimacing at the unsuccessful result in the mirror. She hadn't been able to get all her eye makeup off using plain soap and water, and her eyes looked smudged in a pale face. Sighing, she removed the pins and combed her hair back from her ears. Why fool herself? She couldn't compete with a girl more than ten years younger and twice as good-looking.

She went back to the kitchen and sat down in the chair he indicated. The sky outside was grey, despite the warmth of the air, and rain pattered against the window. A glass of orange juice and a bowl of cornflakes and milk was set before her, and Max sat opposite, tucking into his own.

The bacon and eggs that followed were perfect—it was Max's one culinary skill. He'd sometimes made breakfast at the weekends as a special treat—for her birthday, their anniversary, or occasionally for no particular reason except that he felt like it.

"You haven't lost your touch," she told him as she finished.

He took the plates to the sink and poured coffee from the machine that was a twin to the one he'd given Nancy.

The surroundings were different, but everything else was much like scores of Saturday mornings they'd shared over the years. He even had the newspaper folded by his plate. On Saturday he enjoyed the luxury of reading it in the morning instead of skimming the headlines over breakfast before leaving for the office.

But this morning he didn't open it, eyeing her reflectively as he drank his coffee. Putting down the cup, he said, "I haven't seen that dress—have I?—before last night."

Celine shook her head. "It's new."

"It suits you, that colour. You don't wear red very often."

She'd always thought red a bit too flamboyant for her. Perhaps subconsciously she'd been breaking out when she bought it. She finished her coffee and held the empty cup in both her hands, and glanced down at the red silk. "It's not really breakfast wear."

Max gave her a lazy smile. "Oh, I don't know. It's rather like having an exotic rose on the table—unnecessary but nice."

"Yes, well—that just about sums me up as far as you're concerned, doesn't it?" Celine pushed back her chair and went to place her cup with the dirty dishes.

She heard his chair scrape on the vinyl-covered floor, and when she turned he was standing before her, his face grim. "You know I didn't mean it that way," he said. "It was a compliment."

"I don't think you have the right to give me compliments anymore, Max," she said coldly. "You should save them for Kate."

A spasm of irritation crossed his face. "That's crazy. Why should loving Kate stop me from saying something nice, and sincerely meant, I might add, to—to any woman friend?"

Quietly, Celine was simmering with that dangerous fury that kept threatening to overwhelm her. "I'm not 'any woman friend,'" she reminded him. "I'm your—your *ex*-wife. And if I no longer have your love, and your loyalty, I don't want your shallow compliments!"

A frown line appeared between his dark brows. "I didn't mean to offend you, Celine." He paused. "And I haven't stopped loving you. It's just...different from—"

"Oh, spare me! I know! You're *fond* of me, the way you'd be fond of a dog or a cat that had been around for years. You have some lukewarm affection for me, a pale shadow of your feelings for Kate!"

Stubbornly, he said, "I wouldn't call it lukewarm. I value it—a lot. I always have."

"But not enough to stand by your marriage vows," she said flatly, glad to see him recoil slightly.

"Is that what you really want? To be locked into marriage with a man you know has given his heart to another woman?"

If she had flicked him on the raw, it was nothing compared to what she felt now—he had flayed her. Unable to speak, knowing from the cold dampness at her temples and a sudden disoriented sensation that her face had paled, she brushed past him and walked into the lounge, with some vague idea of collecting the rest of her things and getting out of here.

Of course he followed. Before she could reach the couch and her bag and shoes, he caught at her arm, turning her to face him. "I don't mean to cause you pain, Celine," he said in a low voice. "But you have to face up to what's happened."

"I have!" She lifted her head to look at him. "But have you?"

"What do you mean?" he asked blankly.

"You can't have it both ways!" Spelling it out, she said, "You can't have Kate's love and my...friendship. I'm not asking you to choose—you've already chosen Kate. Well, I wish you every happiness," she managed, bitterly. "But don't invite me to your wedding. I would really rather never see you again."

"You don't mean that—"

"I do mean it!"

"I understand that you're upset—hurt," he added quickly as her brows rose derisively. "I accept that I'm to blame, and believe me, I'm not proud of it. I wish there was some other way. But cutting yourself off completely from me means cutting out my entire family—my mother, Michelle. Next to your own parents, we—they are the people you're closest to in all the world. You know you can't do that to them—to yourself."

"If you can do it to me," she said starkly, "I can do it to your family. And you can add that to your guilty conscience."

He frowned. "Revenge? That's not like you, Celine."

Not revenge, self-preservation. But obviously he couldn't see that. Wonderingly, she said, "I don't believe you've ever known me at all."

"Only all your life," he argued dryly.

Celine shook her head. "Perhaps that's why—" Gropingly, she added, "Maybe we took each other too much for granted. I thought I knew you, too. But I never imagined that you'd bring us to this."

Releasing her, Max made a helpless gesture with his hands. "I didn't plan to. One day you may fall in love—really in love— yourself. Then you'll understand."

Her throat ached, and she felt her shoulders droop, her interior rage swamped by hopelessness.

He was standing just feet away, and she could almost feel the barrier between them, like a sheet of invisible but armour-tough plate glass. She didn't know how to get through to him. Did he honestly think that her feelings for him were so mild and feeble that she could face with equanimity the prospect of casually bumping into him—him and Kate— when she visited Nancy, of having to pretend she didn't care when Michelle mentioned his name?

She turned from him again and groped for her shoes, slipping them on, then picked up her bag. "Are you taking me home or shall I call a taxi?" Her voice sounded cool, remote and steady. She had herself firmly in hand again.

"I'll take you, of course," Max said curtly. "Go out the front way and pull the door to. I'll bring the car around." The garage was at the rear of the block of flats, and outside it was still drizzling. "Do you want to borrow a coat?" he asked her.

The silk would spot, even during a short dash from the front door to the road. "Yes," she said, "thank you."

He found his raincoat and handed it to her. Taking it, she asked, "What about you?" She had an umbrella at home, but Max disliked them and didn't own one.

"A little dampness won't hurt me." Despite the rain, the temperature was warm and humid, and he wore no jacket with his cotton shirt and casual trousers.

She heard him lock the back door, and went to the window of the lounge to watch for the car. The phone rang, and she hesitated, then went to answer it. It might be important. Picking up the receiver, she said neutrally, "Hello?"

Silence on the other end, then an uncertain female voice said, "Do I have a wrong number? Is Max Archer there?"

"You have the right number," she confirmed. "He's just about to go out. Can I take a message?"

"I...um...who am I speaking to, please?"

"His wife."

"Oh," the voice on the other end said blankly. "No...no message, thank you."

There was a click in Celine's ear, and she slowly replaced the receiver.

She was still staring at it when a discreet toot outside took her to the door, wrapping Max's coat about her. She pulled the door to and raced along the short path as he opened the passenger door from inside. As soon as she took her seat, he reached across and shut her in.

Celine shook back her hair and brushed tiny droplets of moisture from her forehead. The motor was running, and

Max swung the car out onto the road while she was still getting her breath back and fastening her safety belt.

"You had a call," she said. "I answered it, but maybe I shouldn't have."

"Why not?" He glanced at her.

"She didn't give a name or leave a message, but I think it was Kate."

"Thanks," he said. "I'll call her back later."

"Perhaps it had better be sooner rather than later. I think I upset her."

He frowned. "What did you say to her?"

"She asked who I was. I told her." It had been automatic, she'd taken hundreds of messages for Max before. And what else could she have said? *I'm his soon-to-be-discarded wife—his deserted wife—?*

Max let out a breath. "I see."

Had it been so automatic? Celine challenged herself. It had been a short conversation, she'd barely had time to think about what she was saying. But hadn't she known, really, from the first syllable uttered in that young female voice, that it had to be Kate? And taken a certain pleasure in telling her, *I'm his wife.* Even if it was no longer strictly true.

She didn't much like the picture of herself she was seeing. Spite, vengefulness, was out of character for her. She said, "If you like, I can explain to her what happened."

"Thanks, but it won't be necessary. I'll explain to Kate myself."

"And tell her I slept in your bed?"

"I'll tell her anything she needs to know."

Which might or might not, in his opinion, include that information, Celine deduced. She shrugged. "Well, if you need corroboration—"

"I'm sure Kate trusts me."

Celine couldn't suppress a small, cynical laugh. At Max's sharp glance, she said, "So did I."

She found herself taking a mean satisfaction in the flush that darkened his cheeks. A muscle twitched under the taut skin as his jaw tensed.

What a nasty person she was turning into, Celine thought bleakly. It was the first time in her life she'd been tempted to deliberately hurt someone she loved. She really felt that if she opened her mouth again it would be to say something horrible, as wounding as she could make it. She swallowed and clenched her teeth tightly together. For the rest of the journey neither of them said a word.

When he pulled into the driveway it was still raining. She said, "Do you want to come in, and take your coat back? You might need it."

She saw him hesitate, then he said, "Yes, I might. Okay."

Just as they got out and he closed her door behind her, the rain suddenly intensified, coming down in sheets, and Celine gasped as it hit her face.

Max's hand on her back urged her to the shallow steps and onto the partial shelter of the porch, but even there the rain drove in, and Max impatiently jabbed a thumb at the electric button a second time before Ted finally opened the door.

"Sorry," he said, standing back as they tumbled in, Max shoving the door closed behind them. "I was watching the cricket on TV, and wasn't sure I heard the bell."

"Never mind," Celine told him automatically. Her hair was dripping, and rain ran off the coat huddled about her, puddling on the floor. Max's hair was sleeked to his head, and his soaked shirt clung to his torso, his trousers moulded to his long legs.

She made to swing the coat away from her shoulders, but he said, "You'll have to dry your hair before you take that off if you don't want to spoil your dress."

He was right. "Yes, I will. You'd better come up and dry off, too." Hastily she added, "Dad won't mind you using the other bathroom."

"Help yourself," her father said. "It's pelting down out there, isn't it?"

"You can use the phone if you like," Celine offered. "Do you want to put your shirt in the dryer for a few minutes?"

Perhaps he recognised it as an olive branch. After the briefest pause, he said, "Thanks. I'll do that."

As he began unbuttoning it, the muted sound of the commentary emanating from the lounge was drowned by a cheer. Ted said, "Sounds like another wicket gone," and hurried back to the game.

Max stripped off his shirt as he made for the utility room.

Upstairs Celine wrapped a towel about her head and wiped the raindrops from her face before removing the raincoat and hanging it over the bath. After shedding her dress, she took off her bra, thankful to be rid of the restrictive, underwired garment, and slipped her green robe on.

If she went along to the spare bathroom now she could leave Max's raincoat in there. He'd no doubt take some time to soothe Kate's wounded feelings and allay her suspicions.

The coat wasn't actively dripping anymore, and she took it down and made for the door.

She'd already taken a step out of the room when she saw Max walking from the top of the stairs along the gallery towards her. He had taken off his trousers as well as his shirt, and was wearing only a pair of blue briefs.

Startled, Celine stopped dead, holding the damp raincoat in front of her.

Max stopped, too. "Shocked?" he asked sardonically.

"Of course not—surprised, that's all. I didn't expect you to be up here so soon."

"It was a short call."

Did that mean that Kate had cut him off in pique? Or she'd accepted his explanation instantly? "Is everything all right?"

"I've arranged to see her later." He looked down at his scanty clothing and said, "My pants were soaked, too. You don't mind my drying them off, as well?"

"Of course not. Your coat," she said, thrusting it at him.

"Thanks. I suppose I could put it on in the interests of modesty. I think I'd feel a bit like a flasher, though."

Remembering a roomy towelling robe she'd been given by Nancy, luxurious but so heavy she seldom wore it, she said, "Just a minute."

Walking back into the room while he waited, she dragged the garment out of her wardrobe. "You could borrow this." It might be a bit short but at least it would cover him better than the skimpy underpants.

"Thanks." He took it from her, a hint of ironic humour lurking in his eyes. His hair was still wet, and his skin gleamed damp. "Ted says there isn't a clean towel in his bathroom. You won't mind if I take one from the linen cupboard?"

Celine was unsure if he was baiting her in some way or simply trying tactfully to find his way through the complicated nuances of their situation. He could hardly be classed as a guest, but he was no longer a member of the household, either. It seemed plain silly for him to be asking her permission to open the linen cupboard, and yet he had forfeited the right to treat this house as home.

"Help yourself," she said.

He nodded, his mouth quirking a little quizzically, his gaze for an instant looking beyond her shoulder. She realised she was standing in the doorway as though barring him entry to the bedroom they'd shared for twelve years. Max thought she was being ridiculously petty and prim—and she supposed she was.

They'd shared a bed last night. What was a bathroom between friends? she asked herself cynically, fighting a childish desire to slam the door in his face. Stepping back, she said, "Come in, for heaven's sake! I've finished with the bathroom here. There's a clean towel on your rail." She still kept one there because when the rail was bare its emptiness was a reminder of his absence.

"Thanks." He crossed the carpet without haste and disappeared into the bathroom.

Celine stood biting her lip, surprised at the sensations coursing through her body. She felt hot and breathless, and her breasts tingled. Just watching Max casually walk across the room, as he had done hundreds if not thousands of times during their marriage, had brought her to a pitch of desire that shocked her with its intensity.

She was sitting on the bed vigorously towelling her hair when he came out of the bathroom, a towel slung around his shoulders and the robe carelessly belted, showing a wide vee of chest. "Maybe you can return the favour and lend me a comb," he said.

Celine lowered the towel and flung back her half-dried hair. "There's one in your drawer." She dragged her eyes away from him, afraid he'd notice the longing in them, the desire to go to him and touch him, lean her face against that tantalising wedge of bare chest.

She must stop feeling this way. Max was not in the slightest aroused. That reaction was reserved for Kate these days.

Woodenly, she got up and went over to her dressing table, the towel draped about her shoulders. She heard Max open a drawer, and bent her head to find her own comb, starting with shaking fingers to pull it through the rough-dried tresses.

The comb hit a knot and she heard the small snap of the plastic tooth. *"Damn!"* she said forcefully, venting some of her frustration in the expletive.

"What's the matter?" Max came into view in the mirror, strolling towards her. His hair was combed back, making his face look more starkly masculine than ever.

"I broke my comb." She flung it down on the dressing table. "I'm not used to having my hair so long. It's all tangled."

"It doesn't look broken." He leaned over from behind her and picked it up, running his fingers along the row of teeth. Two of them came away, and he said, "Mmm. I see. Do you want to use mine?"

He had it in his hand. As he proffered it, Celine shook her head. "I have a hard-bristled brush," she said, rummaging in the drawer. "I suppose I ought to have used that first."

She found it and began dragging it viciously through her hair. He was still standing there, looming behind her. She remembered the feel of his skin against her hands, the swell of his arm muscles under the warm flesh, the wiry hairs on his chest that tickled her palm.

The hard nylon brush caught, and she tugged at it impatiently, but it only turned in her hand and became more entangled. "Damn!" she swore again, trying to free it. "Damn, damn, *damn!*"

"Here." Max's fingers moved hers aside. "Let me try."

She sat still while he worked at it, slowly and carefully. When he lifted the brush away, instead of handing it to her, he began stroking it over her hair. "I'll do it," he said. "Just relax."

She couldn't relax. While the bristles massaged her scalp, she watched his face, his eyes down as they focused on what he was doing, a faint frown of concentration between his brows, and his chest rising and falling with his steady breathing. Her throat felt locked, and something inside her seemed to be melting, warmed by his closeness. His fingers touched her nape when he lifted a hank of damp hair and gently untangled the knotted strands, putting down the brush for a minute to separate them with his fingers. As he bent to pick it up again, she felt his breath on her temple. Momentarily, Celine closed her eyes, willing her own breathing to stay as even and unhurried as his.

He was brushing smoothly and rhythmically, only pausing now and then to struggle with another knot. "Why have you grown it?" he asked.

"I wanted a change," she said, matching his casual tone. If this was some kind of sweet torture for her, he obviously didn't share her feelings. On that thought, she added, "*You* know—you got bored with your marriage, I got bored with my hairstyle."

The brushing stopped for an instant, then went on in the same rhythm. "You know it wasn't like that," he said.

"Are you so sure?" she asked huskily. "Honoria said—"

"Honoria?" His eyes flicked up briefly to meet hers in the mirror. "What made you choose *her* for a confidante?"

"She isn't a confidante. I just mentioned to her that we were separated, that's all. And that there was another woman involved."

"So," he asked after a second, "what did Honoria have to say?"

"Nothing much."

"That I find hard to believe."

"She said this kind of thing is common at your age. Ouch!"

"Sorry. There's a stubborn knot here." On a very dry note, he asked, "Did the phrase 'male menopause' come into this conversation, by any chance?"

"No, actually." She couldn't help a small twitch of her lips. Honoria did have a penchant for pat, if not clichéd, analyses of personal and social dilemmas.

"You surprise me." Max placed the hairbrush carefully on the dressing table. He picked up his comb that he'd left there and drew it several times through the damp tresses, then replaced it on the polished wood. "There, all done."

"Thank you." As he moved back, Celine stood up. Honoria had also said, *If you want him back, you've got to get out there and fight her for him.*

Right now she wanted him desperately, with a fierce sexual need that bewildered her. Sometimes during their marriage she had taken the initiative, but never had she felt this overwhelming desire before they'd even touched.

Deprivation, she told herself. It was ages since she'd made love, and her body was telling her what she'd been missing. It probably would have reacted the same way to any personable, half-naked male. Men weren't the only ones who had purely physical urges. Hastily, she walked away and opened the door of her wardrobe.

She wondered if she had the bravado to strip off her green wrap and change into a dress. But Max would either turn away to spare her modesty or he'd recognise the action for a blatant invitation, and she didn't want to be humiliated again as she had been the last time she made the first move.

He was lounging against her dressing table, his arms folded. The robe wasn't long enough—it stopped at about mid-thigh—and the gap in the front had grown wider, the belt sagging at about hip level. To her own chagrin, Celine heard herself say sharply, "I wish you'd do that thing up properly!"

Straightening, Max looked down at the robe in patent astonishment. "What's the problem?"

Was he being deliberately obtuse? Or did he simply not think of her anymore as a sexual being? "If I didn't know better," he said, taking his time about retying the belt round his waist, "I might have thought the sight of my naked chest was giving you an unexpected thrill."

From Max, the gibe was startlingly crude, rousing confused emotions. She sensed a surprised query behind the apparent insensitivity.

"I'm used to your naked chest," she retorted, self-preservation winning out over her other mingled feelings. "It's no novelty to me."

His eyes scanned her face, detecting the faint flush in her cheeks. Then his gaze slid down, and she was suddenly acutely conscious that the thin green fabric wasn't hiding much. She ought to have kept her bra on. Trying to distract him, she added, "Try flaunting yourself at Kate. She might appreciate it."

As his eyes moved back to her face, he made a tiny negative movement with his head, as though throwing off an unlikely thought. "She does," he said, almost absently. "I'm well aware that you've always been distinctly underwhelmed by the sight of my body."

Celine gaped. "What on earth do you mean by that?"

Max seemed to mentally shake himself. Shrugging, he strolled away from her towards the door. "That was probably in bad taste," he said. "I'll wait downstairs."

"You've forgotten your coat," she said, and marched into the bathroom, scooping it up from where he'd left it.

He was halfway across the room to meet her when she thrust it into his hand. He gave her a curt nod of thanks and turned to leave. She watched him, biting her tongue until his hand touched the door.

"What did you mean about my being 'underwhelmed' by your body?" she repeated finally, glaring at his back as he walked to the door. "There's nothing wrong with it."

He dropped his hand from the doorknob and turned to face her, his expression rather caustic. "Except that it doesn't turn you on. Not your fault."

"Of course it does—*did!* What makes you think I don't—didn't find you attractive?" As his brows rose in scepticism, she said, "We've made love so many times, you must know I enjoyed it with you!"

"Oh, yes," he said coolly. He thrust his hands into the capacious pockets of the robe, standing with his feet apart. "In the dark, in bed, under the blankets."

"Not always," she protested. Admittedly she preferred the comfort of a double bed to less orthodox settings, and she didn't often have the impulse or the time to make love in daylight. But there had been occasions—

"Mostly," Max claimed, cutting across her thoughts. "And then there's the exercise machine. I did get the message, from the impressive photos of pleased users flexing their muscles, but I'm afraid building pecs isn't actually a top priority in my life."

Astounded, Celine said, "That wasn't what I wanted at all! The pictures just happened to come with the machine. It was to help you keep fit when you didn't have time for any other form of exercise. It's good for your health, when you have an essentially sedentary job. I don't *like* huge, muscle-bound men. Most women don't. As a matter of fact, I've always admired your looks—both your face and your body."

He said slowly, "That's the first time you've said anything of the kind. You used to barely look at me when I was less than fully dressed—unless you were already thoroughly aroused."

She supposed that was true. Having a high degree of modesty herself, inculcated by her mother and perhaps reinforced by being a teenage girl living in a household of males, she had tended to look away from Max's unashamed nudity, out of some instinctive desire to accord him the privacy she required for herself. Even though he didn't give a damn. But sometimes she hadn't been able to resist—

The heat in her cheeks intensified, and she muttered, "I peeked."

"What?" Max took a step forward and inclined his head, obviously unsure if he'd heard right.

"I peeked," she confessed. "Sometimes. And—it never occurred to me that *you* needed to be told that—that I liked looking at you, enjoyed touching you. But I do—I did." Emboldened by his dumbfounded expression, she added, her voice scarcely above a murmur, "I love the way your hair feels in my fingers—like cool silk—and the way your shoulders are so smooth and yet firm, and your 'pecs,'" she said with a glimmer of a smile, "sort of ripple when I run my hands over them, so I can feel the muscles, how hard they are. I like the way the hair on your chest grows mostly down the middle, but curves up over your nipples, and how it's not too thick, so when I run my hands over it I can still feel the texture of your skin."

Max's gaze seemed riveted, his body turned to stone. She discovered that her heart was pounding. "Didn't I ever say," she asked huskily, "that I was proud of the way you look in swimming togs, when so many men are pot-bellied and flabby or covered in thick hair, or have skinny little legs? That I like to watch you walk, with that long, confident stride. That your smile gives me a thrill. And your hands— you have such nice, masculine hands. I like the way the fingers are long but almost square at the ends, not tapered and feminine, and the palms are so broad. Your hands made me feel cared-for when you took my arm while we were walking, or put one on my waist to cross a road. I used to watch them when you drove the car, because they looked so competent, so in control. And they were so strong and so gentle when we made love.'' She caught a quick breath. "Haven't I ever told you how much pleasure your body gave me, in bed and out of it?"

"No." His voice was hoarse, and she could see his jaw was rigid. His cheeks had a dusky flush, and his eyes met hers with a look that held a sombre, sullen fire.

Celine moistened her lips with the tip of her tongue. "Perhaps," she said hesitantly, "I should have. I'm sorry."

Max shook his head, whether in negation or an attempt to clear it, she wasn't sure. "It's too late, now."

But she had moved him in some way, she could see. "I wish I had," she said softly, and walked slowly towards him. Willing her fingers not to tremble, she took one of his hands in hers and laid her cheek against the back of it. "I wish it wasn't too late."

She saw the shock in his face, felt his fingers convulse around hers. *"Celine!"*

She turned her head and put her lips to his hand. Tears stung her eyes, and one escaped down her cheek and landed on the hand she held.

"Don't!" Max said, sounding shaken. As she raised her head, he lifted his other hand and clumsily wiped the skin below her eyes. His pupils were enlarged, very dark. He looked as though he was suffering. "I didn't mean to do this to you. I'm not worth it, you know."

If anyone had told her that about another man in these circumstances, she'd have agreed. "Our marriage is worth a few tears, Max," she said, trying to smile as another hot droplet slid down her cheek. "You'll have to allow me that, even if you can't shed any yourself."

His mouth twisted in some kind of anguish, and he said, "I have. It's probably not going to help you much, but a lot of the time I feel as though I'm being stretched on the rack. This decision wasn't made lightly, Celine, or in a hurry."

Celine felt her heart plunge. Max would have considered every angle, including the fact that she would be dreadfully hurt, that his own family might support her, perhaps even condemn him, that he was giving up a whole way of life. But his desire for Kate had outweighed everything else. "Oh, Max—we had so much!" she cried. "Everyone thought we had the perfect marriage! It was a *nice* life—and if you found it unexciting, we could have worked on that the way we worked on all our problems. You didn't need to throw away twelve years of happiness. You *were* happy! *We were!*"

"We were contented," Max said, freeing his hand. "Even complacent. Do you call that happiness?"

"It was good enough for you for twelve years," she said, her voice hardening as the tears dried. "I put a lot of work into this marriage, Max," she said fiercely. "Too much to just tamely surrender it to your romantic whim." She looked defiantly at him.

"I'm afraid you don't have a choice, Celine," he said quite gently. "I know I'm being selfish and unfair, because you've done nothing to justify my leaving you. You always kept your side of the contract, and I respect you for it, more than you can know, but I don't love you in the way that you deserve to be loved, and I...can't pretend, year in and year out. I'd need to be superhuman."

"Have you been pretending all these years?" she asked him, pushing down the pain of his blunt repudiation. "I thought our love-life was pretty satisfactory—you never complained. And there was certainly no sign that you didn't enjoy it. What about when you came home after the firm's Christmas party and couldn't wait to make love to me?" she asked. Seeing him flinch, she followed up her advantage. "That wasn't so long ago, Max. Are you going to tell me that you didn't love me then? You certainly felt *something* pretty potent. And you assured me you hadn't had much to drink. Or were you lying?"

"No," Max said in a strange voice. "Not about that. It was the lovemaking that was a lie."

# Chapter 9

Celine stared at him, puzzled, and then an inkling of his meaning penetrated her mind, setting off violent waves of heat and light inside her. Her head jerked up a little, her eyes hot and questioning. "What are you *talking* about?" *No!* she thought. *It's too monstrous.*

"It isn't important," Max said uneasily. "I was thinking aloud."

"What happened at the party?" she demanded. "She was there, of course—Kate. Did you sneak off to a back room together? Was that the first time you made love to her?"

"*No.* Celine, there's no point in this."

She felt sick. His wooden expression only goaded her further. "But you came home with all systems on go," she said. "What happened? Did someone interrupt at the crucial moment?" That was vulgar, she thought, even as a flicker of expression in his eyes gave her a paltry thrill of triumph. "Or hadn't you persuaded her to come through at that stage?"

"*Stop it,* Celine." He had gone white. She knew that her own face was hectically flushed.

"I'll stop when you tell me what happened!"

His eyes were furious, too. He was hating this. "*Nothing* happened. Nothing that couldn't have taken place in public, at any Christmas party!"

Couldn't have, he said. So whatever it was hadn't been in front of all the others. The two of them *had* sneaked off to be on their own.

Wearily, he said, "Leave it, Celine. There was nothing to upset you."

"You're *lying!*" She felt cheapened and defiled, possessed by a scorching anger. She lifted her hands, curled into fists, and thumped them hard but harmlessly against his solid chest. Max took a step backwards, and she followed. "Tell me!" she said, doing it again.

"All right!" He warded her off with his arm, so that she hurt herself on the hard bone. "We kissed, that's all. It was nothing—an innocent, friendly kiss under the mistletoe. Everyone was doing it."

Max had always avoided that sort of meaningless, playful behaviour; he was too reserved by nature to enjoy it.

But he'd kissed Kate. Kissed her and wanted her, and then he'd come home to tell Celine she was beautiful, with that deliberate, assessing—*comparing*—stare. And practically forced her into bed with him. Because he'd wanted Kate and couldn't have her. So he'd made do with his wife instead. And probably fantasised that it was Kate in his arms, Kate laughing softly, surprised but pleased at his importunate passion, Kate discovering a buried passion in herself that she'd not known she possessed, Kate, not Celine, responding eagerly and adventurously and making Max's excitement even more intense, fuelling hers in turn, so that her body turned to a white-hot flame that flared in his arms, that consumed them both in a great primal explosion of pleasure that engulfed them again, and again, and again. Kate, Kate, Kate.

All of it had been for Kate, not for her. Not for the wife he'd held hundreds of times, who had learned how to please him and taught him to please her, so that their lovemaking was always successful, always satisfying—*and always the same?*

"You *bastard!*" It was a cry raw with rage and pain. Celine wasn't even aware that she'd swung her hand back until it flew forward and connected stingingly with Max's cheek, so fast and hard that his head was jerked aside. She was conscious of being, for once, out of control, and in a strange, heady fashion of being freed by it. Her fury was incandescent, so that she felt it like a leaping, all-consuming fire, her veins liquid and burning, her head singing.

She tried to hit him again, and when he caught her wrist she bent her head without a second's thought and sank her teeth into his hand. He wrenched away but without releasing her, and she raised her free hand, fingers clawed, reaching for his face, but he was holding her well away, and she only connected with his arm and shoulder as she hit out again and again.

She shifted her feet—they were bare so she couldn't kick him—and he staggered momentarily but he soon regained his balance, swinging her with him in a half circle. She pulled away, straining to twist out of his grip, but he said grimly, his face ashen and obstinate, "No, you don't—not until you calm down."

That made her more frenzied than ever, and she fought him with a desperation and ferocity that lent her strength, so that he had to follow when she moved, and for a time she thought they were almost even.

Her hair tumbled about her shoulders, fell across her eyes as she tried to bite him, scratch, hurt him in any way she could. She didn't realise that Max had edged her back towards the bed until she felt it behind her knees, lost her balance and fell backwards.

He had captured both her wrists, and was breathing almost as hard as she, his face showing nothing but a gritty determination to win. He leaned over her, holding her wrists down against the bed cover, and said, "All right, Celine, *that's enough!*"

He must have seen in her face what she meant to do, perhaps felt it in the tension of her arms, and as she brought her knee viciously up, he twisted, avoiding it. So she tried to kick him instead and encountered only the bruising bone of his shin.

*"No more!"* he said forcefully, and in one movement he had hitched her further back onto the bed and flung himself over her. "No more," he repeated as his hands, his body, his legs imprisoned her struggling limbs and pressed her down on the mattress.

He freed her wrists, but as she pushed and thumped at his chest and shoulders he trapped her hands between their bodies, his arms behind her back, holding her tightly. "Shh," he was saying. "Settle down, Lina. Hush."

It was the pet name from their childhood days that made her abruptly stop struggling, all her energy concentrated on stemming an unexpected tide of piercing, overwhelming grief. She was *not* going to cry again.

Feeling her sudden surrender, Max changed his hold, cradling her against him, his arms a haven, not a prison, his cheek touching hers, his voice murmuring broken words of comfort in her ear.

Gradually their breathing slowed. She felt with blank shock a tiny dampness against her cheek, and stirred, moving her head so she could see his face. He lifted his head, his eyes glittery with tears, and she saw the effort he was making at control, the set of his mouth, the taut sinews of his throat. "I'm *sorry*," he said hoarsely. "I know I've done you an enormous wrong, Celine. I wish there was another way..."

His eyes were tortured, and she knew he'd been speaking the truth when he said he was on the rack. The last remnant of her anger faded, leaving her oddly calm, almost detached. She freed her hands of his slackened hold on her, and touched his face, the moistness of a tear meeting her fingers. "Oh, Max," she whispered, compassion swamping the last of her bitterness. She slid her hand behind his head, into the silky strands of his hair, and kissed his cheek in a gesture that was tender and passionless.

He smiled at her, bent closer and returned the kiss, first on her cheek, then her forehead. As he drew back slightly, Celine's lips parted. They were hot and throbbing. She looked into his eyes and mutely begged for more, her eyelids drifting down, and heard him say in an unsteady voice, "Celine?"

She didn't dare open her eyes.

After a pause of several heartbeats, she felt the tentative brush of his mouth against hers, and sighed contentedly, allowing her breath to mingle with his.

She was conscious of his instant stillness and, terrified that he'd leave her, tightened her arms and held him. Opening her mouth, inviting him to more intimacy, she angled her body subtly, hardly more than a flexing of her leg muscles, so that her bared thigh lay snugly between his.

He lifted his head an inch or so, a frown between his brows. "Celine, I don't think—"

"Don't!" she whispered. She brought her imprisoned thigh up a fraction, and saw the flare in his eyes, felt the stirring of his response. "Don't think!" she urged him, pulling his head down until their lips met again, slipping her tongue into his mouth, gliding it over his, moving it back and forth in a way that had always excited him. She raised her knee, and heard him give a moaning grunt, felt his resistance ebbing. His mouth enclosed her tongue, gently sucking, encouraging, before he reversed their roles and silently asked her to receive his.

As he kissed her more and more deeply and his breathing quickened, she let her hands drop from his neck to explore his shoulders, sliding her fingers under the thick towelling, then peeling it away so that she had access to his back and his chest, running knowing hands over him, identifying again the pattern of his crisp chest hair, the flat coins of his nipples with their tiny centres, the rise of his ribs, the taut, hollowed plane of flesh between the lower ones, and the almost invisible scar on his hip, legacy of a childhood encounter with a broken branch when he'd fallen from a tree.

He had one hand curved under her nape, his thumb caressing her earlobe as he kissed her, and the other made a leisurely journey from her armpit to her thigh, lingered there and then without haste made its way to her breast, stroking it firmly through the silk the way she liked, until she parted the front of the gown herself, signalling him that she wanted his hand on her skin.

He obliged, pushing the edges of the gown further back so that with lazy-lidded eyes he could watch the effect of his caresses, and later his kisses. She touched his hair again, and combed her fingers through it over and over, pretending not to notice or concern herself with what he was doing, until her breasts were tense and full, the furled centres so sensitive that the mere brush of his breath across them made her gasp with pleasure.

Her hands were plucking at the belt of his robe even as he shifted aside to remove hers. Not bothering to shed them fully, they smiled at each other and came together again, flesh to heated flesh.

He settled himself against her, his hands cupping her shoulders, his forearms taking his weight, and she aligned her body with his so that when he came in, it was with one slow, sure thrust. His hips were cradled between her thighs, and she rocked slightly, gently, while he matched the rhythm, his hands moving to her head, his fingers in her hair as he kissed her.

They had learned, over the years, how to prolong the plateau with small movements and snatched kisses and feather-light touches that brought murmurs of enjoyment as they exchanged taut, expectant smiles. She knew that he liked the light play of her fingers over his shoulder-blades and back, and that the moist tip of her tongue in the hollow of his throat would make him shiver and close his eyes, inciting her to do it again. And he was aware of the erotic torture he inflicted when he caught her earlobe in his teeth and teased it with his tongue.

When Max felt her breathing begin to alter, he lifted his mouth from where he'd been idly nuzzling the curve of her neck and shoulder, and showed his white teeth in a tight feral smile.

She didn't need to tell him what she wanted him to do—he did it instinctively, knowing when to make the provocative rhythm faster, when her body was feverishly begging him to go even deeper, when she had attained the pitch of unbearable excitement that preceded the ultimate cresting of pleasure, so that he could let go the iron rein of his restraint and join her, hurtling into the void.

As their breathing steadied, Celine's hand strayed from his hair down the back of his neck to his shoulder. She raised her head to kiss him there, his skin slightly salty and dewy against her lips. She felt his hand tighten for an instant on her hair, tugging it, and then he was dragging himself away from her to lie on his back with one arm flung across his eyes.

The harshness of his breath gradually diminished. The sheet was tangled about his waist, leaving little for Celine. She reached for tissues from the bedside table, then pulled her gown across her breasts, her eyes on Max.

At last he heaved a huge sigh, and took away the concealing arm from his face. Celine propped herself on her elbow, still watching him. It seemed to be an effort for him to look at her.

"Are you all right?" he queried.

"I'm fine." She wanted to smile at him, snuggle down against him as she usually did after lovemaking. But the bleakness in his expression warned her before he said, "This should never have happened. I—I have no right to—"

No right to make love to his wife? Disappointed hope was a knife turning just below her heart. "It takes two," she said remotely, determined not to let him see how let-down she felt, as though someone had just dropped her from the clouds onto the hard, cold ground.

He sat up, hauling the towelling robe closed as he stumbled to his feet. Almost violently he retied the belt, pulling the knot tight.

"It's all right," Celine said, acrid amusement colouring her voice. It was so unlike Max to be bothered by his own nakedness. "I'm not planning another assault on your virtue."

He flicked her an amazed glance. "It's no laughing matter."

"It's not the end of the world, either," she said tartly. "It isn't even immoral. We're still married."

"On paper," he allowed. "That doesn't mean a thing."

That caught her on the raw. "It may surprise you," she said, "but it does mean something to me. Once, I thought it did to you."

"You know what I meant," he said.

"No." Celine sat up, her back straight, her eyes hostile. "Explain it to me."

Stiffly, he said, "Our marriage is over. You know that."

"Well, it certainly didn't feel *over* five minutes ago! And I'm damned sure it didn't feel like it to you! Unless, of course, it takes the fillip of *not* being married to your partner to turn you on these days?"

"That's a hell of a thing to say!" Maybe she'd come close to pricking him, she thought, watching his sudden anger with interest. But he quickly controlled it, his voice turning frigid as he added, "Sarcasm doesn't suit you."

"Oh, don't be so stuffy!" Celine hurled back the remainder of the sheet and stood up, too, facing him across the width of the bed, tying her own robe with vicious efficiency. "Why *did* you make love to me, then? *Habit?*"

This time her sarcasm backfired badly. "I guess that's about it," he said heavily. "You seemed to need...comfort. And it got out of hand."

Celine momentarily closed her eyes. She'd asked for that. Out of sheer blind stupidity. Looking at him again, she said, "Will you tell Kate?"

Max shrugged. He had his hands in the pockets of the robe again. His jaw was clenched. "I don't know."

"Supposing *I* do?" she asked him, her chin held high.

"Is that a threat?" His eyes had narrowed. Hostility sharpened his features. "You wouldn't be so vindictive."

He knew her too well. The thought had no sooner entered her mind than she'd dismissed it. Even if it took Kate out of his life, it wouldn't bring Max back to her. He'd never forgive her.

"If you want my advice," she said, "you won't mention it to her."

A complicated expression crossed his face. But all he said was, "Thanks."

Celine shrugged. A little hysterically, she wondered what she was doing, playing agony aunt to her husband, giving him advice on his relationship with another woman. *I'm not doing very well, here, Honoria. I don't suppose this is the way to get him back.*

"I'm going to have a shower," she said, on her way to the bathroom. "You can leave the robe downstairs." His clothes ought to be dry by now.

As she reached the door, his voice stopped her.

"Celine?"

She turned her head. "Yes?"

"Why did you—just now . . . Was it habit for you, too?"

Why was he asking her? Did it matter? Was he hoping she'd say yes? The one thing she wasn't going to admit was that since he'd left her she'd realised how much she loved him, how much she wanted him, emotionally, physically, in every way. Confessing to it would only embarrass him, like an unwanted gift. And she still had her pride—it was about all that he had left her. "Lust," she said calmly, watching the ripple of shock on his face. "You're still the best lover I've ever had, Max."

She saw the flush that mounted to his cheeks, and made to turn away, pausing when he said harshly, "Better than your building tycoon?"

For a moment she didn't even know who he meant. She hadn't seen much of Roland lately; he'd been involved on another of his commercial projects, and once they'd worked out what was wanted for the house he'd only called in briefly a few times to see how the work was going. "Roland?" she said at last. "I'm not sleeping with him. Or anyone. Except you," she added with a bleak little smile.

The glimmer of relief that crossed his face then should have amused, or perhaps angered her. Instead she was only dully, distantly surprised. "I'm inclined to be cautious," she said. "Things have changed since you and I got married. Sex wasn't a life-threatening activity, then. You didn't use any protection just now, did you? I hope you've thought of it with Kate."

Startled, he said, "You don't really think I'm a danger to your health?"

"One can't be too careful, they say."

"You've no cause for concern," he said shortly.

"You can hardly be certain of that," she pointed out, "unless Kate was a virgin."

She was quite unprepared for his sudden, dark flush. Her heart made a sickening, unexpected plunge. "*Oh, God, Max!*" she said. "Did you know?"

He shook his head, his mouth extremely grim. "In any case," he said, "I don't want to get her pregnant—"

*Yet.* The unspoken word hovered in the air between them. Once they were married they would, naturally, like a family. Kate was young and fit and presumably fertile, and Max had been told there wasn't anything wrong with him. It was just bad luck that for some reason the chemistry between him and Celine wasn't ideal for conception. But with Kate...

"I hope she's not relying entirely on you to prevent it," Celine said dryly.

"I'm not selfish enough to forget."

"I don't suppose you are. But everyone seems to have conveniently forgotten that when we were teenagers we were forever being warned about the high failure rate of that particular form of contraception, though now it's somehow supposed to stop people from contracting a deadly illness."

"Thanks for the warning." Max's tone was ultrapolite. "I'll bear it in mind."

She supposed it was ludicrous for her to be lecturing him on the subject, but this had started, after all, as a query concerning her own safety. "You're welcome," she said, trying to keep any hint of sarcasm out of her voice, and this time she stepped into the bathroom and closed the door.

Was it true that Kate was inexperienced? she wondered as she stood under the shower, the jets on at full blast. She thought about the younger woman's air of girlish, innocent coquettishness, and decided that it probably was. A circumspection that had been distinctly unusual when Celine was that age must be much more common among intelligent young women now. And despite appearances to the contrary, Kate was intelligent, all right.

Intelligent enough to deliberately engage on her first sexual experiment with a man who'd been faithfully married for years?

Max seemed sure that Kate was as much in love as he was, that she wanted to share his life, be his new wife. Had he discussed all that with Kate, Celine wondered, or was he just taking it for granted?

Clutching at straws, she told herself. She had no reason on earth to believe that Kate wasn't as committed as Max. In fact, this new revelation strengthened that likelihood. A woman who looked like Kate and yet hadn't succumbed to temptation earlier wasn't likely to have lightly given herself to anyone. No, she was serious about Max.

"But he's *my* husband," Celine muttered, reaching to turn off the faucet. "Damn her, she hasn't any *right!*"

The ends of her hair were damp again, and she dried them roughly, then the rest of her body.

*It takes two,* she'd told Max earlier. It was no use casting Kate in the role of vamp, exonerating Max from blame. Any outsider would conclude that it was he who had seduced a younger, innocent girl. Perhaps it was true?

She wandered into the other room, for once not bothering to cover herself. Max would be gone by now. There was no one to see her.

The bed showed the effects of the half hour they'd spent on it. She stood looking at it, remembering, her body warming as she relived the feel of his hands on her skin, the silk-sheathed iron of his body under her fingers. She had a wild urge to lie down on the bed, among the tumbled sheets that would still hold the scent of him, of their lovemaking, to lie with her eyes closed and relive those thirty precious minutes.

Instead she walked briskly to the wardrobe and dragged out a blouse and a pair of jeans, hauled undies from a drawer and shut it with a bang, dressed hastily and pulled her hair carelessly back with a clasp. Then she stripped the bed with quick, efficient movements, got clean sheets from the linen cupboard to remake it, and left the room without a backward glance, to go downstairs and hurl the linen into the washing machine.

"Max has gone," her father said, looking up briefly from the TV set when she walked into the lounge.

She hadn't realised that she'd hoped he'd still be here. But of course he'd gone, raced off to keep an appointment with Kate and explain to her why Celine had been breakfasting with him this morning. And now he had something else to explain . . . if he could.

"What do you fancy for lunch?" she asked. "There's some leftover chicken, and tomatoes, but no lettuce, I'm afraid. Or I could do some egg-and-cheese sandwiches." Ted was particularly fond of those.

"Whatever's easier for you," he said, not taking his eyes from the screen. "I'll come and help you soon."

Celine laughed. "Don't bother, you watch your game. I'll bring your lunch in here on a tray."

"You spoil me," he said when she placed the tray on his knees. "What about you?"

"I had a sandwich in the kitchen," she lied. She didn't feel like even looking at food.

Ted settled the tray more comfortably and picked up a sandwich. "I reckon it's about time I got myself out from under your feet."

"You're not under my feet," Celine protested.

He cast her a rather bothered look. "I can't help wondering," he said slowly, "if Max's leaving had anything to do with the fact that I'm here."

"It didn't," she said. Sitting down, she leaned towards him. "Honestly. It wasn't that."

"Oh, I don't mean that I caused the break-up, exactly, but maybe you two would have worked it out if you'd not had a third person in the house."

Celine shook her head. "Dad, Max is in love with some-one else. That isn't something we can work out easily."

Ted frowned. "Another woman?" The noise from the TV increased as the crowd cheered, but Ted's eyes didn't waver from her face. "I'm sorry to hear that, my dear. But it isn't necessarily the end of your marriage."

"Max thinks it is," she told him quietly.

"It was his idea to move out?"

"Yes."

"So you were ready to forgive and forget?"

"I never got the chance, Dad."

"Would you," he asked, "if you got the chance?"

Would she? Could she swallow her pride if the miracle happened and he wanted to come back to her? "I don't know," she confessed. "Sometimes I think I'd give any-thing to have him back, on any terms. And other times I'm so angry, and hurt, and humiliated, I just want him to feel the same. If he wanted a reconciliation, I wouldn't make it easy for him. I don't even know if I could bear to have him back."

An interior voice jeered, *Then what was all that about upstairs? He touched you and you melted! You weren't standing on your pride then!*

"That's natural," Ted said. "But you know, if you love him, you'll find a way."

"I'm not likely to be given the opportunity," she said. "He wants to marry her."

"Is she younger?"

"Yes," she said. "Aren't they always?"

"Not always. Sometimes—look, switch that thing off, will you, please?"

Astonished, she said, "But the cricket—?"

"Pah! I can tell who's going to win, anyway. The Pakistanis are walking all over us." He waited until she'd turned the TV off. "There's something I was never going to tell you, but maybe you need to know now."

At his solemn tone, a tremor of apprehension ran through her. Carefully she reseated herself on the edge of the chair, her hands clasped before her. "What is it?"

"I loved your mother very much," he said. "When she died I thought I couldn't even go on living without her. Except that she expected me to look after you and the boys for her. If it hadn't been for that—" he shook his head "—I don't know what I might have done. I was very fond of Dora, and we had some good times together. I never regretted marrying again. But your mother—she was the love of my youth. And the mother of my children. If you and Max had—but that can't be helped." He paused, staring down at the plate of food on his lap but obviously not seeing it.

"The thing is," he continued, "when you were all young, and I was trying to get ahead at work, and your mother was busy caring for the family and trying to budget on not a lot of money, she was always tired, and afraid of getting pregnant again. The pill wasn't available then, and she didn't quite trust the things that were. It was a time when we sort of lost sight of each other."

He paused again, and Celine, guessing yet disbelieving what was to come, held her breath.

Ted cleared his throat. "I never wanted to hurt her, but it seemed to me she didn't really care. She was tied up with the house and the kids and her sewing—you remember, she used to get a little money by sewing for other people, besides making clothes for herself and you kids—and she never had time for me. And there was another woman—one we both knew. We saw a lot of her, and somehow I fancied I was in love with her.''

Celine caught her breath. A fantastic thought entered her head. She bit her lip, silencing her mind.

''For a while,'' Ted said, ''she thought maybe she felt the same. Later she said she realised that mostly she'd just felt flattered, and excited. She was in much the same boat as your mother, really, surrounded by children and house-work, and pretty bored with it. She'd stopped thinking of herself as a woman, she told me. She was a mother first, a wife second, and it was nice that some man—a nice man, she said—desired her. Oh, it was all very innocent, really— just looks and whispers and secret telephone conversa-tions. It would have been almost impossible for us to—well, to go any further, the way we were situated. Too difficult to arrange.''

Celine said, ''How long did this go on?''

''About a year. She came to her senses sooner than me, and tried to cool things off. Only I wouldn't listen. Until the day I realised that your mother knew—'' his voice trem-bled ''—and I saw how hurt she was.''

''What . . . did she say?'' Celine whispered.

''She told me she loved me. That's all. She said nothing at all about—about the other lady, or my disloyalty. But I could tell she knew. All she did was let me know that she loved me. And I knew then that if it came to a choice, I'd have chosen her.'' He picked up the sandwich again with an absent air, and lifted his gaze to Celine's face. ''I don't know just how things are with you and Max, except that they're bad. And maybe my advice won't be any use at all. But for what it's worth, here it is. Just ask yourself two questions. Do you love Max? And does he know it?'' He waved the sandwich in a slightly random fashion, and dropped his eyes. ''This looks very good,'' he said in an almost embar-rassed way.

Celine smiled faintly. "Do you want me to switch on the game again?"

"Oh, may as well," he said, trying to hide his interest. "Not that much has changed, probably."

Later after dinner as he was having his hot drink, he said, "I want you to be honest with me, Celine. Do you want me to stay here, or would you sooner be on your own?"

"I like having your company," she said. "You must know that."

"For good? I've asked you to be honest."

Celine's gaze wavered. "If Max isn't going to be here," she said, "it really doesn't matter, Dad. What do *you* honestly want to do?"

"You've been very good to me," he said, "but if I stay here I'm going to be an old man whose daughter looks after him. I don't think I'm ready for that. And maybe you're not, either. When I really need looking after, if I can't fend for myself, I don't want you to be doing it. I had a letter from the estate agent in Rotorua yesterday."

"Yes, I know." She'd seen the return address on the envelope, but Ted hadn't said anything and she'd assumed it was just a routine progress report.

"He's got an agreement on the house. When it's final I'll be looking in earnest for somewhere not too far away from you—and not too close. That last village arrangement that we looked at—I met an old friend of mine there, remember?"

She did. The two men had taken a while to recognise each other, but they'd been delighted at the reunion.

"Well, Charlie seemed to think the place was okay. What's good enough for him is probably good enough for me. I've got my name down for one of those self-contained flats. If the time comes when I can't manage for myself, I can move into a room in the rest home next door."

"When did you do that?" Celine asked, astonished.

"The day after we were there. It doesn't hurt to be on the waiting list, and I'm not committed to taking the first vacancy. But I can't do anything definite until the money from the house comes through, and I wasn't sure how the wind was blowing between you and Max. I don't want to leave you in the lurch when you might need me."

"Thanks, Dad." She went over to him and kissed his cheek. "But I'm a big girl, now. Whatever happens, I can look after myself."

# Chapter 10

Celine had finished the decorating of Roland's house, and the furniture had been moved in under her supervision. He came to inspect the result and said she'd done a wonderful job. "Let me take you out to dinner as a gesture of appreciation," he suggested.

"There's no need," she told him. "You're paying me very well to do this."

"I'd still like to take you to dinner," he insisted. "No strings, I promise. I have another proposal lined up for you that I'd like to discuss."

Roland was a nice man. She knew he was attracted to her, but his tentative overtures had met with no encouragement, and he seemed content to settle for a friendly business relationship. Celine appreciated his tact, which had allowed her to concentrate on the job in hand without having to fend off unwelcome advances at the same time. "All right," she said. "Thank you."

She wore the red silk dress, taking care to look her best. If this wasn't exactly a date, it was the first time she'd been out alone with a man other than Max for many years, and she couldn't help a small flutter of nervous anticipation.

Roland called for her in a taxi. It wasn't until they were in the restaurant, seated at the table with its starched white cloth and the small floral centrepiece, that he looked at her properly and said, "You look wonderful. Even lovelier than the first time I saw you."

"Thank you." Naturally she was pleased at the compliment, and its obvious sincerity, but the look in his eyes warned her that perhaps this evening wasn't going to be all business.

The waiter presented the wine list, and Roland turned his attention to it, asking Celine if she had any preference and conferring with the waiter before ordering a white wine.

"When will you be moving into your house?" Celine asked after they had chosen their meal.

"Next weekend, I thought. It's only a matter of clothes, some books and records, and a few bits and pieces. You've made it virtually ready to walk into." Roland was twirling the wine glass in his fingers. "I'll have the boys, then. They're keen to sleep in their new rooms."

Celine smiled. She'd met the two boys to discuss with them what kind of decor they wanted for their bedrooms. "They're nice kids," she said. "I liked them."

"You don't have children, do you?" he asked.

Celine shook her head. "Perhaps it's just as well."

"Because of your marriage break-up?" When she nodded, he said, "I understand, but I wouldn't be without my two for anything in the world. At least something good came of my marriage, even though the relationship didn't survive."

Celine wondered if having Max's child would have helped her to cope with his defection. Or if they'd had a family, would he have left at all? Shaking away the thought, she picked up her wine and said lightly, "To your new home."

Roland smiled, lifting his glass, too, but his eyes were shrewd and kind. Too kind, perhaps. Returning her glass to the table, Celine said, "What was it you wanted to talk about?"

He gave her a slight, wry smile and said, "I mentioned to you that I was buying an office block, didn't I? The whole place needs refurbishing, and I hope you'll be interested in designing the interior."

"I'd love to try," Celine said. "How big is it, and what did you have in mind?"

The subject occupied them throughout the leisurely meal. By the time they'd finished she had a fair idea of the magnitude of the task he'd asked her to undertake. "But I'll have to see the place before I can come up with specific suggestions."

"Of course. The sooner the better. I've only been waiting for you to finish my house. Will Monday do?"

"I'll look forward to it."

He ordered coffee, and as he spooned sugar into his, he said, "The boys took a liking to you, and I think they'd want to thank you personally for doing up their rooms to their taste. Would you happen to be free for lunch next Sunday? *En famille,*" he added. "I make a great salad, and my grilled T-bones are the best in town, the kids tell me."

Celine hesitated as he replaced the sugar spoon and looked at her expectantly. "I don't know," she said. "It's kind of you, but it's a family occasion, moving in."

"And you're not sure what you might be getting into."

Celine shrugged a little, casting him an apologetic look.

"I know you're still working through your separation," he told her, "and you're wary of starting any new relationship too soon. You're wise," he added bluntly. "When my wife and I split up I was so darned hurt and angry and insecure I plunged straight into an affair with a woman who was in the same boat, only it didn't last. Both of us had a lot of baggage to unload before we could establish a successful new relationship. But I'm over that stage now. I'm lonely and I'd like to share my life again with someone, but not just anyone. The minute I saw you at the Chatswoods' party, I knew you weren't just anyone."

Celine stiffened, and he said, "I'm not going to try to push things or hurry them up, because I know you're not ready to look at anyone else yet. But when you are I'd like to be around where you can see me."

Cautiously, she asked, "Is that why you've hired me to refurbish your office block?"

He looked surprised, then laughed. "Celine, I'm a businessman. I can't afford to make gestures like that, believe me! No, I need a good job done on this project, and I believe you're the one to do it. The other—that's a personal matter, and whatever happens I'm not about to start pressuring you with promises of work, or threats of withdrawing it. Have I ever given you the impression that I might?"

Relieved, she said, "No, I'm sorry. I didn't mean to imply that you would."

"Okay, I can't blame you for checking, when I've made my personal interest crystal-clear—I hope?"

Celine nodded. "Roland," she said carefully, "I'm really— grateful. But I can't imagine—"

"That's okay. I know you can't right now. Maybe some day, and maybe not. I just want you to know. And now, how about lunch on Sunday?" He smiled at her, the skin about his eyes and mouth crinkling in a disarming way.

"Well—yes, I'm free," she said. "Thanks. I'll look forward to seeing the boys again. Can I bring a salad, or a sweet?"

"If you bring a sweet the boys will be your slaves forever. I should warn you—be prepared for some very unsubtle matchmaking."

Celine laughed. "I guess I can stand it."

She didn't have to, though. The boys, perhaps warned by their father, behaved impeccably, and Celine had a very pleasant afternoon. She hadn't realised how circumscribed her life had become since their friends had learned that she and Max were no longer a couple. The book group discussions and committee meetings, badminton and bridge—her solo activities—continued as before, but invitations to parties and other social occasions had dwindled since she'd become that social spare wheel, a lone woman.

Max's car was on the drive when she got home and parked hers in the big garage. For a few moments she didn't get out. It was more than two weeks since the fiery confrontation in their bedroom had led to that unforeseen, passionate conclusion. Her cheeks burned at the memory. One letter had arrived for him and she'd readdressed it to his flat. Otherwise they'd had no contact at all. For a day or two she had nursed a wild hope. But as the week slipped by, and then another, she had to concede that the episode had made no difference to Max. He wasn't going to turn from Kate to her.

He was in the lounge talking to Ted. Celine stopped in the doorway and Ted looked up, saying, "Ah, you're back! Had a nice time?"

"Lovely, thank you. Hello, Max."

He stood up. With one swift glance he took in her blue cotton shirt and slim-fitting jeans, returning to her face, almost bare of makeup, and the casually tied scarf that held her hair back. "Ted asked me to do the conveyancing on the sale of his house," he said. "We've just been talking about his plans."

"I see." Since Ted had asked Max to do the legal work when he and Dora had bought their property, it was only sensible that he'd handle this deal, too. And it was like Max to offer to come round and talk about it, rather than ask Ted to trek into his office in the city. "Dad made you some tea?" The tray holding a plate of biscuits, a jug of milk and a bowl of sugar, and the empty cups and saucers on the floor told her he had. Advancing into the room, she said, "I'll take those away."

Max forestalled her, stacking the crockery on the tray.

Celine expected him to hand it to her, but instead he picked it up and headed for the kitchen. She followed him, and as he placed the tray on the table by a half-emptied cellophane pack of biscuits, she said, "I could have carried it myself."

"They're not your dishes," he said. "I'll do them if you like."

"A couple of cups!" She scooped them up and opened the dishwasher, inserting them in the rack. When she turned, he was putting the milk away in the fridge. It was so long since she'd seen him in this room that it was like having a stranger here, and yet he knew his way around it almost as well as she did. Finding an airtight tin, she began carefully transferring the biscuits into it.

"Ted said you'd made meringues yesterday," Max told her, retrieving the last biscuit before she removed it from the plate, "but he couldn't find the evidence. We had to make do with these." He bit into the biscuit.

"You seem to be enjoying them, anyway. Dad had some of the meringues last night. I took the rest with me as a contribution towards lunch."

"Enjoy yourself?" He popped the remainder of the biscuit into his mouth.

"Very much." She hadn't exactly told Ted who she was lunching with, just that she'd be out.

"You looked very relaxed when you came in."

"Did I?"

"Now you're tensing up. Is it me?"

"I suppose," she said, "it's the situation. I wasn't expecting you to be here."

"Do you want me to leave?"

"No, of course not. Finish your talk with Dad—"

"We've finished. My mother says she's worried about you."

Nancy? "She hasn't even seen me lately."

"That's what she's worried about."

"I've been busy. I've just completed a commission."

"That's good. Will you have time for your friends now?"

"I have time for my friends. It's your family that I . . ."

Into the pause he said, "That you don't want in your life?"

"I told you—"

"I couldn't believe you really meant that. Surely you're cutting off your nose to spite your face? And hurting your oldest friends in the process."

"You started this, Max. So don't complain—and don't blame me—when the fall-out affects people you love."

His mouth went grim, and he shoved a hand into one of his pockets, staring fiercely at the empty plate on the table. "All right," he said at last. "I guess I deserved that."

She picked up the plate and went to tuck it in the dishwasher with the cups and saucers.

"That must have been some lunch," Max drawled. "Was it a picnic?"

"No." She closed the machine and turned a puzzled gaze to him. "Why?"

The smile on his face didn't look real. "I just wondered what sort of lunch it was that left you with a grass stain on the seat of your pants, and—" he stepped over to her and she felt his fingers in her hair "—hay in your hair."

"It isn't hay," she said as he showed her the withered bit of vegetation in his fingers. "Grass clippings, I suppose."

"Grass clippings?"

"I must have got it playing rounders with the boys."

"The boys?" Max's brows shot up.

"Roland's two boys." After lunch the four of them had taken a bat and ball to a nearby park and played for about an hour. "I slipped making home base."

"Roland Jackson? I didn't know you two were that close."

About to deny it, she changed her mind. Instead she said, "He's given me another commission—a big one, designing the decor for an office block."

After a short silence Max said, "Congratulations."

"It should be worth a good deal of money. I don't need you to pay the bills anymore, Max."

"Your father tells me he's moving out. You won't have his contribution then."

"Nor his expenses," Celine pointed out. "For that matter," she added, "I won't need this big house. Perhaps I should look for something smaller."

"There's no hurry," Max said curtly. "Give yourself some time. I thought you were fond of this place. You put a lot of effort into it."

"I put the effort into it for us. It was all done with your taste in mind."

"Mine? Ours, surely?"

"Exactly. There isn't any 'us' or 'ours' anymore. You've seen to that. I could fix up a new place just to please myself."

"If that's what you want," he said. "Still, don't rush into anything. And let me have a look at the legal angles."

"Thanks."

"I told Ted to contact me when he's moving, and I'll help with the heavy stuff."

"I'm sure we could manage. There's not a lot of furniture to move."

"Your father won't want you trying to shift it, and he's not strong enough anymore. He could hurt himself."

She supposed he was right. If her brothers had been here . . . but they weren't. "I'm sure he's grateful for the offer," she said.

"You'll be alone. Will it bother you?"

"It's not your worry." Some demon urging her on, she added, "I may not be alone for long."

His head gave a little jerk. "What?"

"Just thinking aloud. If I am, it'll be from choice. I certainly don't need to be."

She seemed to have disconcerted him. "No, I suppose not. You told me you weren't sleeping with Jackson."

Celine hoped her smile was enigmatic. "It was true."

"Was?" She saw his jaw clench. He swung around and marched to the door as if he could no longer bear to be in the same room as her. But when he reached it, he turned. "I hope you know what you're doing," he said. "It's not just your way of getting back at me, is it?"

"I like Roland, very much. He's a super person and a good father. And he understands how I feel."

"You *like* him? Is that enough for you to go to bed with him?"

"It was enough for me to go to bed with *you*," she reminded him.

"I wanted to marry you."

"So does Roland." He'd practically told her it was in his mind, even if the words remained unspoken.

That brought him up short. "It's gone that far?"

Celine shrugged. "Maybe what happened last time you and I ... met ... made me realise what I was missing."

"Sex." His tone was contemptuous. "You and I had a lot more than that, Celine."

*Oh, we did!* she thought. But it was Max who had carelessly thrown it all away. "Whatever we had wasn't enough for you," she reminded him.

She could see him fighting the urge to say something more. He quelled it, his mouth tight, his jaw rigid. "I'll go and say goodbye to your father," he said at last.

She had been childish, Celine supposed. There had been no reason to let Max think that she was sleeping with another man except to salve her pride. Tit for tat. There was some satisfaction in his obvious displeasure, but that was only a dog-in-the-manger reaction. It didn't mean that he wanted her himself.

For the next several weeks she spent a lot of time on the office design project. Perhaps more than she needed to, but it was challenging enough to stop her thinking about other things for large stretches of time, although the constant aching regret she'd learned to live with never went away.

The sale of Ted's house went through and he was ready to move his things out of storage and into the small flat in the retirement complex.

"Max said he'll meet us there," he told Celine. Then, hesitantly, "You don't mind that he's going to help?" He must have been aware that she and Max had not had any contact for some time.

"Of course I don't mind." But Celine wondered if she would get over him better if she never saw him. It was what she'd told him she wanted, what common sense insisted she needed to get her own life together without him. Fate and perhaps Max himself seemed to conspire against it.

When she saw him climbing out of his car and coming towards them with a casual smile for Ted and a rather restrained one for her, she felt a deep sense of pleasure mixed with pain.

Max helped the driver of the removal truck with the heavy furniture, and after the truck had gone Celine took over the kitchen, filling the cupboards with crockery as Max opened boxes and cartons, and stocking the small pantry with tins and packets of food that they'd shopped for to start him off in his new home.

Later she helped Ted to arrange his books and a few ornaments onto shelves, and made up his bed. She'd brought some bread and salad vegetables with her, and at twelve-thirty made sandwiches. "Where's Max?" she asked her father, interrupting him as he was hammering a picture hook into the bedroom wall.

"Putting my tools in the shed for me. Hand me that picture, will you?"

She picked it up off the bed and stayed to help him get it straight. "Lunch is ready," she said. "I'll go and fetch Max."

The toolshed was small, but Max had Ted's gardening tools neatly stacked against the walls, and had erected some kit-set shelving. Boxes of nails, screws and carpentry tools were on the floor. "Do you know what he wants done with these?" he asked as Celine appeared in the doorway.

"I'd leave them for Dad," she advised. "He'll have his own ideas about where he wants them. I've made sandwiches."

"Heavens! Is that the time?" Max glanced at his watch.

"Is Kate expecting you?" she asked coolly.

He shot her an odd look. "No. She knows I'll be tied up all day."

Stepping out of the shed, he closed the door. "Ted may want a padlock on this," he said, sending the metal bolt home. "It's good that he's got some garden attached to the place. He enjoys it, doesn't he?"

"Mmm. I'll miss him at home."

"Why don't you get a gardener? Ted tells me you're working pretty well full-time on this latest project. I'll pay for someone to come once or twice a week if you like. They can at least mow the lawns."

"I could do it, but I've already arranged for that. There's a teenager down the road who's been looking after the neighbour's lawns. He's quite good—and cheap."

He stood back to let her go up the two steps to the door first. "Tell him to send me a monthly invoice—unless he insists on cash."

Impatiently, Celine swung round on the top step. "I wish you would stop trying to salve your conscience with—oh!" She broke off abruptly as Max's face and the view behind him tilted, and she felt herself sway off balance.

"Celine!" Max grabbed her arm, steadying her. "What's wrong? You've gone as white as a sheet."

She bowed her head and slowly lifted it again. Things were steadier now. Max still held her arm, and she was conscious of his familiar scent, and the faint line between his brows, the curve of his mouth as he bent close. "Celine?" He put an arm about her, and she fought the temptation to lean against him, to feel again the warmth of his body, the comforting strength.

Reluctantly, she drew away. "I'm all right. Just turned too quickly, I think, and I need my lunch." She gave him a pale smile.

But he kept his arm loosely about her waist until they entered the kitchen and he'd guided her to a chair. "You're sure you're all right?"

Ted, coming into the room, said, "What's up?"

"Celine's not well," Max told him. "Has she been okay until now?"

"I just got dizzy for a moment," Celine protested. "Once I've had something to eat and a cup of tea I'll be as right as rain."

"You were off your food yesterday morning," Ted said, frowning.

"Something I ate at the bridge club the night before," she said. "Maybe I'm not quite over it. Sit down, you two, and have your lunch."

She took a sandwich from the heap on the table, realised that she didn't really want it but determinedly bit into the fresh bread. If she didn't eat, the men would start fussing again.

They hardly allowed her to pick up anything heavier than a feather duster after lunch. At about two-thirty, stowing some linen in the narrow hall cupboard, she somehow dropped a small stack of pillowcases and bent to retrieve them. Straightening, she found herself waver, and hastily leaned against the wall, the pillowcases in her hand.

Max, helping Ted to store a few bottles of whisky and wine in a high cupboard, caught sight of her through the kitchen doorway and came striding over to her. "That's it," he said, removing the pillowcases from her loosened grasp. "Lie down."

He pushed her into the bedroom and onto her father's bed, while Ted hovered anxiously in the background.

"You should have said you were crook," Ted told her sternly. "I would have managed all right without you."

"I wasn't," she said weakly, hoping the room would soon keep still. "Honestly."

Max said, "You look awful."

"Flatterer!" she murmured, trying to focus on his face, seeing the faint answering grin before she closed her eyes because there seemed to be more than one of him.

"I'll get her a nip of whisky," Ted offered, and she felt Max's weight on the bed as he sat beside her and put a cool hand to her forehead.

"You're not feverish," he commented.

Daring to open her eyes again, she saw that there was only one of him again. "I'm okay."

"Your colour's coming back, but you're obviously not okay. What have you been doing lately? Overworking? Is that project of Jackson's too much for you?"

"No, I'm enjoying it." She sat up cautiously as her father returned with a small amount of whisky in a glass. Max adjusted the pillows behind her.

Ted said, "This'll brace you up a bit."

"Shouldn't it be brandy?" Max demurred.

"Never drink it," Ted told him.

The whisky did brace her, bringing some warmth into her cheeks. But there was no chance the men were going to allow her to do any more work. Even driving, apparently, was out of the question.

"I'm taking you home now," Max told her.

"Maybe I should come with you, stay the night," her father suggested.

But she firmly vetoed that. He was quite excited about his new home, and she didn't want to spoil his first night in it. Max said, "I won't leave her until I'm sure she's all right," and Ted subsided.

"It really isn't necessary," she argued, but admitted she probably shouldn't drive if she was likely to have an attack of dizziness at any time. "What about my car?"

"It'll be quite safe here overnight."

"Yes," Ted agreed. "You go on home and get into bed. Maybe," he added to Max, "you should take her to a doctor."

"No!" Celine protested. "It's probably just a tummy bug of some sort. I promise I'll rest, but there's no need to be bothering a doctor."

When they got to the house, Max followed her inside. "Can I get anything for you?" he asked.

"Oh, make me a cup of coffee if you like," she said. "I was going to offer you one, anyway."

"Right. You lie down and I'll get it."

She compromised by sitting on the sofa in the lounge with a cushion behind her and her feet up.

The coffee was welcome, but he'd found some of her favourite fruit biscuits and arranged half a dozen on a plate. The sight of them made her stomach turn over. She shook her head and hastily looked away. "Not just now, thanks. It isn't long since lunch." Remembering lunch, she swallowed an unexpected nausea. What on earth *was* wrong with her?

Max sat on one of the chairs, nursing a cup of his own. "You still don't look too good," he told her critically.

She didn't feel too good, either, she thought, making an effort at sipping the coffee.

Then, as quickly as it had come, the sick feeling passed off.

But Max seemed in no hurry to leave. He talked in a desultory fashion about Ted's new home, his family, the news headlines from the morning paper, watching her all the time.

Finally she swung her feet to the floor and stood up. "I'm sure you have things to do," she said firmly. "Thanks for bringing me home, but there's no need to stay any longer."

"I hope you don't have any plans to go out tonight," he said, standing up with apparent reluctance.

She didn't, but it was Saturday and she supposed that *he* did. "I'm not going anywhere," she told him.

"Good. I could stay and make you a meal."

"Not at all necessary." She discovered a temptation to pretend she was really unwell, simply to keep him by her for a bit longer. Annoyed with herself, she said, "Will you just *go!*"

He stiffened, his face changing from concern to a blank mask. "I suppose you're expecting company."

Company? What was he talking about? She blinked at him.

For a moment she thought he was going to say something else. Then he bit off whatever it was and headed for the door, quite fast.

Celine followed, but he flung over his shoulder, "You needn't see me out. I do know my way!"

She stopped in the middle of the entry hall as he threw open the door. "What about my car?" she asked.

His look was impatient. "I'll call you tomorrow. We'll sort it out then." From being inclined to linger, it seemed now he couldn't wait to get away.

Celine nodded and he stepped outside and closed the door behind him.


In the morning she was throwing up in the bathroom when the telephone by the bed rang. She didn't get to it before it abruptly stopped. Sinking down on the bed, she wondered if that had been Max. She waited a few minutes, then gingerly got off the bed and returned to the bathroom to clean her teeth and have a shower, fighting down nausea. It took her longer than usual to get dressed, and she roughly tidied her hair without bothering to tie it up, too drained to care.

After cautiously negotiating the stairs, she went to the kitchen for a cup of tea. She made toast and ate it dry, shuddering at the thought of butter.

Afterwards, feeling slightly better, she put the dishes into the sink. Now that she was on her own it didn't seem worthwhile to use the dishwasher. The doorbell burred, and she turned hastily, then gasped and grabbed the edge of the counter for a second.

The bell had rung again by the time she got there. She opened the door and found Max staring at her. "You didn't answer your phone," he said.

"I was in the bathroom."

He looked relieved. "How are you feeling?"

Celine shrugged. "Okay."

"Well enough to come with me and pick up your car?"

"Yes, sure," she said brightly. "I'll just run up and get my handbag."

She started up the stairs as he watched from the marble-floored entryway. Halfway up, she faltered and clung with both hands to the stair rail, her head hanging over it.

Everything was going black, and her head was swimming. She heard Max's sharp exclamation, and his footsteps heavy and quick on the stairs. He must be taking them two at a time. Then his voice was in her ear, and she was swung up into his arms.

Dimly she was aware of movement, and then of softness beneath her. As the blackness and dizziness receded, she was conscious of him at her side, holding her hand, talking to her.

She hadn't realised her eyes were closed. She opened them, and Max, his own face pale, said, "Thank God."

"It's just a faint," she said. She had fainted only once before in her life, when she'd been sickening for some childhood disease. "Nothing, really."

"There must be a reason. Well, this settles it—I'm calling Harry Parr."

Harry was their G.P. "It's Sunday," Celine protested. "He may not be on duty."

"Someone will be."

"Look, I'm not that ill. I felt fine last night after you'd gone."

Max's brows rose. "Is there a connection?"

"I didn't mean that. But I'm sure this is nothing serious. Maybe I'm a bit anaemic or something. If it doesn't pass off, I'll make an appointment on Monday."

He looked about to override her, but after a while, he said, reluctantly, "See that you do. Meantime, you shouldn't be alone."

"I can't ask Dad to come back now. He hasn't had time to settle in yet."

"I wasn't suggesting your dad should come back. I can stay."

"I wouldn't dream of expecting you to—"

"Don't be silly. You'll have to eat sometime. Did you have breakfast?"

"Yes, just before you came. I can get myself meals."

"Oh, yes? Suppose you got dizzy again going down the stairs to the kitchen? You could fall and break your neck."

They argued some more but it was obvious he was going to win—there was no way she could physically evict him. He stayed, and ordered her to remain where she was, and he got her meals and in between left her pretty much alone. Celine napped, and ate, and read a book, and in a half-guilty fashion enjoyed being waited on.

Once she heard the ping that meant the phone downstairs had been picked up, and she wondered if he was calling Kate, explaining perhaps why he couldn't see her today. Or cancelling an arrangement.

After he'd brought her dinner, an unambitious chicken soup from a packet and a pile of toast, with fresh fruit to follow, she asked him, "Are you and Kate... living together?"

"No." The bald monosyllable seemed designed to stifle any further questions.

Carefully casual, she said, "I thought you would be by now."

"We don't want to rush things."

For Kate's sake, Celine surmised. Perhaps Kate was less certain than Max of her feelings. Slowly tearing apart a piece of unwanted toast, she said, "I suppose there's no hurry. You can't marry her until you divorce me." She dropped the mangled pieces of toast back on the plate.

"No." He bit off the word. "Have you finished with that?"

"Yes, thank you." She let him take the tray. "I'd like to go downstairs."

He paused in the doorway. "Wait until I come back."

She didn't feel at all unwell now, but she waited, and he stayed at her side until she reached the lounge and sat on the sofa. Max made coffee and they watched the TV news and then a wildlife programme that they'd seldom missed, and a thriller serial. It was, Celine thought, like so many Sunday evenings they'd spent at home. Unexciting, she supposed, but comfortable.

But on those other evenings she hadn't found her attention straying from the screen to Max's face, her eyes studying the exact slope of his nose, the jut of his chin, the firm contours of his mouth, with longing.

*You didn't know what you had until you'd lost it,* she told herself as the credits rolled up the screen.

"Anything else you'd like to see?" Max enquired, waiting for her to shake her head before he switched off the set.

"Maybe the current affairs programme later," she said. "Do you want to stay for it?"

"I'm staying the night," he said.

"Oh, but—"

"I'm not leaving you alone," he told her. "Supposing you get sick or faint in the night? Don't worry," he added, "I'll sleep in the spare room—but leave your door ajar in case you need me."

Celine opened her mouth and shut it again. Why argue when she knew she'd lose? And why argue when she didn't really want to? At times she'd been bitterly hurt and angry, as she knew she had every right to be—even Max himself acknowledged that. But tonight she was very tired and in need of care and solace. It felt nice that Max was prepared to give it to her.

# Chapter 11

Celine opened her eyes on darkness. For some time she'd been experiencing discomfort, half waking and then dozing.

She'd gone to bed soon after nine-thirty, Max watchfully taking the stairs at her elbow although she'd assured him she felt perfectly fine. She hadn't slept for some time though, listening to the muted sounds of him preparing for bed in the guest room. He'd kept the light on for a while, the warm glow just visible through her obediently opened door. But long after he'd turned it off she had lain tense and rigid, fighting a desire to go to him, slip into bed beside him and ask him to make love to her.

The longing was almost a physical pain, and when she finally drifted into sleep she'd dreamed that Max was beside her, taking her in his arms, loving her...

She couldn't see her watch, but it must be well after midnight. The house was silent. Celine sighed. It was no use trying to go back to sleep now, she needed to use the bathroom. Reluctantly she pushed back the covers.

When she switched off the bathroom light and came back into the room it was very dark, and she didn't see Max standing there until she cannoned into him, with a little scream of fright.

"It's all right," he said. "It's only me."

He had his hands on her arms, and hers were flattened on his bare chest, her cheek resting on his shoulder. She inhaled his familiar male scent, and instinctively relaxed against him. "Max!"

Through the thin nightgown she wore the heat of his body warmed hers. His breath stirred her hair. "Sorry," he said, "I didn't mean to scare you. I heard the water running and thought you might have been sick."

"Not this time." She didn't want to move, and as his hands loosened she instinctively slid her arms about his waist, realising with a slight shock that he was wearing nothing but a skimpy pair of underpants. "Max," she breathed. Memories of her erotic dream floated into her mind. Maybe she was still dreaming...because she felt a stirring of his body, heard him catch his breath.

She let her hands wander down, smoothing the taut male flanks, and pressed her mouth to his skin.

"Celine!" His hands tightening cruelly on her shoulders, he pushed her away, putting a foot of space between them. He was breathing hard. *"Wake up, Celine,"* he said harshly. *"You don't want this."*

She wasn't asleep. She was burningly, tinglingly awake, and alive in a way she hadn't been for some time. "Yes, I do," she said. "And so do you."

He took a deep, shuddering breath and let her go, taking a step back. "Don't mistake a normal reflex for something it isn't," he said.

That hurt. Oh, it hurt. She bit her lip to stop herself from crying out. "Are you sure that isn't what you've been doing?" she asked.

"What do you mean?"

"Just that maybe you mistook a normal, passing attraction to a pretty girl for something more serious."

"I won't discuss my relationship with Kate, Celine." He sounded very remote.

"Are you afraid there might be some truth in what I'm saying?"

"I just don't think it's an appropriate subject for us to get into."

*"Oh, for heaven's sake!"* Furious and mortified at his rebuff, she was hot and shaking. "You've broken up our marriage because of her, discarded everything we had for the last twelve years, and we're not supposed to *discuss* it? This does happen to affect me, you know. It's *my* marriage that's being thrown on the dust heap! So don't you tell me it's *inappropriate* to discuss it with me!"

"You may have a point," Max conceded stolidly, "but this is hardly the time or place."

She supposed he felt at a disadvantage, standing almost naked in her—*their* bedroom.

"Anyway," he added, "you ought to get back into bed."

"You wouldn't care to join me?" she asked with a degree of sarcasm as she moved towards it.

His voice was strained as he said, "You don't really mean that."

"You know, I never realised," she said, getting under the sheet, "how omniscient you are, Max. You know what I really don't want, and what I really don't mean—next you'll be telling me what I really don't feel. Go on, why don't you?" she goaded him. "Tell me I don't feel hurt, or humiliated, belittled or betrayed. I don't feel that I've wasted twelve years of my life on something that was never what I thought it was. I don't feel anything that *you* don't want me to feel, anything that will make you uncomfortable."

"That's not fair, Celine!"

*"I don't feel fair!"* she almost shouted at him. "You wanted a marriage that was friendly and pleasant and didn't make too many demands on you. You got it. Now you want something else, and you expect me to make the divorce pleasant and friendly, too. Well, it doesn't necessarily work like that, Max. Divorce is messy and wounding and heart-

breaking. And I can't make it any other way for your convenience."

"*You* wanted that kind of marriage, too," he said accusingly. "Haven't you ever felt that you wanted something more?"

*Not until now,* Celine thought bleakly. Not until Max had found it—with someone else. "Why couldn't you have told me," she said, "if you were bored and restless? We've always talked about things. Couldn't you have talked about this?"

"I wasn't bored—or if I was, I didn't know it," he said, "until I met Kate. And I did try—I tried to bring some excitement, some variety, into our marriage. Remember the holiday we never had? Oh, I'm not blaming you, it was a collection of unfortunate circumstances, but the fact is we never did have that time away alone. Even that night that—the night of the party, I told myself how lucky I was having a woman like you, that many men would have envied me. That marriage didn't need to be a collection of habits, it needn't be predictable. That we had good, exciting sex together and a lot more besides."

"The night you substituted me for Kate, you mean," Celine said bitingly.

He said, "It wasn't like that—"

"You told me that making love to me was a lie."

"In a way. It's . . . complicated. I admit that when I came home my mind was full of Kate. Then I saw you and . . . I saw all that I was endangering, everything we'd built over the years of our marriage—even before. We've known each other so long. Our marriage—you—were important to me. I wanted to hold on to it. I thought if I made love to you I'd forget her."

"But you couldn't." Of course he couldn't, the girl was in the same workplace with him five days a week.

"For a little while I did. You were very passionate that night. More than you'd ever been."

Because that night his lovemaking had an edge, an extra dimension that she'd never known before.

"I thought we'd be all right," he said. "I wanted to take you away somewhere, make love and talk, perhaps find out new things about each other. But it didn't happen. You seemed uninterested. You liked your life as it was, and you'd filled it with a lot of things that didn't seem to leave any time for me. Oh, I know—" he added as she made a small sound of protest "— there was Dora, and your father. But even before that I didn't seem to be getting through to you. I suppose we'd lived on the surface for so long I could hardly expect you to head for deeper waters with me just because I was—discontented."

"You never said so," she said. "You might have told me."

"It wasn't easy to put into words. A feeling that something was missing from my life—from our marriage. Something that we'd never had. Something I was wanting, more and more."

"And that's what you've found with Kate?"

There was a long pause before he said quietly, "Yes."

That, Celine thought later, was the moment when she knew she had truly lost him. When she knew that despite Honoria's advice and her own feelings, she had to let Max go. Because with Kate he had found something he'd never found with her, that she would never, now, experience herself.

In discovering how much she loved him, she had sealed her own lonely fate. There was nothing she wanted more in the world at this moment than to embark with Max on that voyage of discovery, but now it was too late. He was committed to making the voyage with another woman. All he wanted from Celine was his freedom to make it. That was the only gift her love could give.

A great, hard lump in her throat almost choked her. Her eyes were burning and tearless. Into the silence, Max's voice said quietly, "Good night, Celine."

She couldn't answer him. The darkness shifted and she knew he was leaving the room, his bulk briefly silhouetted in the doorway, and then he silently returned to the other room. Faintly she thought she heard the bed creak as he lay down. And after that, nothing. She buried her face in the pillow and fiercely closed her eyes, willing sleep to come.

In the morning she kept herself aloof and composed. Max had brought her breakfast on a tray, remaining in the bedroom as a precaution while she showered, only taking the tray down when she was dressing.

"If you have time to drive me over to Dad's," she told him, "I'll bring my car back."

She must have looked better because he hardly demurred at all, only insisting on following her home again, "Just in case."

Once she'd garaged the car she went over to his, where he sat with the engine idling, and told him crisply, "Thanks for the help. I really don't need you now. You'd better go and make your peace with Kate."

"My peace?"

"You haven't seen much of her this weekend. She'll have missed you." Her voice, she noted proudly, was perfectly steady and casual.

Max gave her a rather penetrating look and said, "Look after yourself."

"I will." Celine mustered a smile and stepped back, lifting a hand. "'Bye."

When he'd left, she allowed the smile to fade and walked slowly up the steps and into the house, fighting a mood of black despair.

*It isn't the end of the world,* she told herself. But it felt like the end of hers.

It was Roland who finally took her to see a doctor. They had been walking around the office block, planning where partitions and cupboards and extra washrooms should go, and talking colour schemes, when she went suddenly pale and looked around for somewhere to sit down. The place was bare of furniture and she had to sink to the floor in the end, her back against a wall and her forehead resting on her raised knees while Roland knelt anxiously beside her.

When she was on her feet again, he refused to continue the tour, instead bundling her into his car and whisking her off to see his own G.P. whose surgery was close by.

Hovering in the waiting room, he took her arm when she came out and led her back to his car. "Anything serious?" he asked, his concerned brown eyes scanning her face.

Rather dazed, she was staring straight through the wind-screen. After a moment she turned and gave him an absent smile of reassurance. "No. I'm probably a bit anaemic. He wants me to have some tests done, but I said I'd see my own doctor."

"Will you?" Roland looked at her sternly.

"Yes. I will. It's nice of you to bother, Roland. Really, there's nothing to worry about."

Nancy came to see her, admitting when Celine asked her point-blank that Max had urged her to do so. "I told him I wasn't sure you'd want me to come, but he made me promise, said you'd been off-colour and someone should keep an eye on you."

"It was nothing," Celine told her. "Max can stop feeling responsible for me. I really don't need anyone fussing over me."

"Shall I go?"

"Oh, Nancy, of course not! Come into the kitchen and have a cup of tea."

It was one thing to tell Max she was prepared to cut his family out of her life, it was another altogether to snub a woman who'd been a second mother to her.

Over the tea ten minutes later Nancy said, "All the same, you have been avoiding us. You do know that no matter what happens, you'll always be part of our family?"

"Thank you," Celine said huskily. "Only we can't turn back the clock, Nancy—or make it stand still. Max and I aren't a couple anymore. If you want to visit me, you and the rest of the family are very welcome. But I won't come to your house."

Nancy nodded sadly. "I understand, dear." She sighed and said on an exasperated note, "Oh, I could *shake* my son! Doesn't he realise what he's giving up?"

"He thinks it's worth it," Celine said.

"Worth all this upset and heartache?" Nancy shook her head. "The trouble with Max is that he sets himself such high standards. Any man might fall for a younger woman, be flattered that she's interested, and even have a brief affair. But Max simply can't conceive of being the victim of an infatuation. It has to be something more important that could make *him* stray. Something worth breaking up a perfectly good marriage for!"

Celine had said something similar, she recalled, when Max first told her that he was in love with Kate.

"Have you *seen* the girl?" Nancy asked her.

"We've met a couple of times."

"She's not even his type!" his mother wailed. "I mean—that dolly?"

"Kate's a colleague of his," Celine reminded her. "Hardly a dolly."

"She looks like one," Nancy snorted.

"She's certainly very pretty."

"I would have thought Max had more sense than to be bowled over by a pretty face."

"Nancy—he loves her. And she must care a lot for him."

"Are you defending her?"

"I'm just facing reality. Kate has given Max something that I've never been able to give him."

"What?" Nancy asked scornfully. Then, a look of horror on her face, she said, "She's not *pregnant?*"

"No," Celine said hurriedly, "not that I'm aware of, and I know Max wants to... to wait until they're married."

"Thank goodness for that! I'm having enough trouble adjusting to the idea of a new daughter-in-law without facing the prospect of a new grandchild, as well!"

"Wouldn't you like another grandchild?"

"Well, of course I would! I've always thought it a darned shame that you and Max hadn't—but I'm not sure that I want *hers!*"

"I expect you'll get used to the idea. It'll be Max's, too." Celine paused, afraid her voice would wobble and give her away. "Kate...must be something very special, Nancy, for Max to have fallen so hard for her."

"Hmm, she is to him, obviously. I tried to tell him everyone finds their marriage going a bit stale at times, we all look over the fence now and then to greener pastures, but good heavens, in my day our marriage vows meant something! We didn't go hopping into bed with everyone who looked temporarily more exciting than our own partner. Sometimes the temptation wasn't easy to resist, but in the end it was worth it. What would have happened to my family—to *Max*—if I'd run off with—"

"With my father?" Celine enquired gently as Nancy broke off abruptly, her face flushing.

Nancy looked astounded. "He told you?"

"He didn't say you were the woman, but I guessed."

"Oh, Celine." Nancy's face showed remembered anguish. "I've felt so guilty about that, all these years. Your mother was my best friend in all the world."

"Dad says she knew."

Nancy nodded, her eyes filling with tears. "I know she did. But the only hint she ever gave, the only thing she ever said was, 'I'm glad it was you, Nancy.' I still don't know if she meant that she'd trusted me not to take him away from her, or..." Nancy made a helpless little gesture with her hands.

"Maybe she meant that she was glad it was someone worth loving," Celine suggested. "That he wasn't wasting all that emotion on someone...cheap or mediocre."

Nancy wiped her eyes. "Thank you. But I know we hurt her dreadfully—and now my son is doing the same thing to her daughter."

* * *

Michelle phoned the following weekend. "We're visiting Mum and Dad. Can I come round and see you?"

Celine's hesitation was only momentary. She'd already succumbed to Nancy. Was she going to tell her oldest friend point-blank that she didn't want to see her? Michelle had done nothing to deserve that. "Just one thing," she said, "I'd rather not discuss Max."

"Okay," Michelle answered. "It's just me—I'm leaving the kids with Tony."

True to her word, she refrained from mentioning Max, and after an initial awkwardness they were back on their old footing. When Michelle had gone Celine found herself humming a tune from their teenage days, when they'd been crazy about the same pop music and had plastered their bedroom walls with pictures of the musicians.

The office project was coming along nicely, and both Celine and Roland were pleased with its progress. He had given Celine a space on the premises and furnished it for her with a desk, a large table, some filing cabinets and a couple of chairs. She was able to check every step as the plans took shape about her. She had already been booked for another commission and was becoming confident she could earn her living doing interior design.

Once a week she collected her father and brought him home for a meal, and at other times she would visit him for an hour or two. He seemed to be making friends, and his garden was already showing the fruits of his loving labour.

Her own garden took up a good deal of what leisure time Celine had. The weather was cool now, and she found the physical work therapeutic, and although she sometimes got the husky teenage boy who did the lawns to help with heavy tasks like digging, or trimming trees, she enjoyed the fresh air and the feeling of accomplishment.

Several of the trees that needed their branches cut back to let light and air through to the smaller plants had been planted as mere saplings by her and Max when they'd first built the house. The climbers whose faded blooms littered the lawn and paths had once been single, delicate tendrils that she'd trained to wind up the supports Max had fixed for them. Some of the shrubs they'd put in together needed severe pruning because they'd grown overlarge and greedy for space, and a few had become sickly or died and had to be rooted out.

She hadn't seen Max for weeks. She told herself that she was learning to live without him, making a new life for herself. But they were empty assurances. All the time that she was keeping herself busy and interested, talking and walking and working, she felt like a hollow puppet. Her mind jerked the strings and made her appear lifelike, even animated, but inside there was a gaping hole where her heart ought to be.

Then one Sunday when she was in the garden she looked up from weeding around a rose bed and saw him standing only feet away. "Max!" She started to get up, and he stepped forward, holding out his hand.

Celine shook her head. "I'm all dirty." She pulled off her gardening gloves and dropped them with the trowel into the barrow where she'd been tossing the weeds.

"You're looking well," he said.

She had no makeup on and her hair was carelessly tied back, several strands escaping round her face. She wore a baggy, ancient shirt of her father's over faded old jeans with ripped and dirty knees, and her shoes were caked with dirt. "Thanks," she said dryly.

He had lost weight, she thought, regarding him critically, and there was a look of strain about his eyes and mouth. "Is something wrong?" she asked him.

Max looked slightly surprised and shook his head. "No. You've done a lot of clearing here. Not all by yourself, I hope?"

"Most of it. I had help with the trees and stuff. Would you like a drink or something?"

"Thanks. I'd love a beer." The weather wasn't as muggy as it had been in summer, but today the sun had shone all day.

"On the terrace?" she suggested as they made for the house. "I'll just have a wash and bring it out."

"I can get it. What do you want yourself?"

Celine hesitated. "Oh, a lime and tonic, thanks."

"No gin?"

"No gin," she confirmed, shucking off her shoes at the back door.

Inside she ran up the stairs, leaving Max in the kitchen. She quickly washed her face and hands and combed her hair out, retying it neatly. Looking at the old shirt and jeans, she grimaced, and went to inspect her wardrobe, biting her bottom lip thoughtfully. She changed into a clean pair of loose cotton pants, but the shirt would have to do, she decided. Max probably wouldn't notice what she was wearing. He didn't care anymore, she reminded herself brutally.

But he'd said she looked well. He had noticed that much. She peered into the mirror, wondering if she looked any different from last time he'd seen her. Perhaps her face was a little fuller? She took out a lipstick and, deriding herself for the vain effort, applied a swipe of colour, blotting most of it off.

When she came out of the house Max was lounging in one of the chairs on the terrace, a can of beer beside him and a tall glass set waiting for her.

He watched her as she walked to the table and sat down. "Thanks," she said, picking up the glass. "Cheers."

He returned the salute with a faint, preoccupied smile.

Celine sipped her drink, wondering when he would tell her why he was here. But the first thing he said was, "I saw Ted the other day."

"Where?"

"I just dropped in to say hello to him. He seems happy."

"Yes, I think he is." It had been kind of Max to stop by.

"He seemed to think that his being here might have led to our break-up."

Distressed, she said, "Is he still worrying about that? I told him he had nothing to do with it."

"I told him the same thing." He traced a circle on the tabletop with his beer can. "Are you still seeing Roland Jackson?"

"Sometimes," she said cautiously.

Without looking up, he nodded. "My mother says she's been to visit you a few times, and Michelle, too." He looked up. "I want to thank you for that."

Celine shrugged. "Your family isn't easily brushed off."

"They would have known if they weren't welcome."

There was silence for several minutes, and she finished her drink. "What are you doing here, Max?" she asked finally. "Why did you come?"

"I wanted to...to be sure you're okay."

"I am. You don't have to keep reassuring yourself of my well-being. Give that overactive conscience of yours a rest. It isn't the nineteenth century anymore, and women have more to fill their lives with than marriage and families. It's sad that our marriage didn't last, it upset me considerably for a while, but there's no point in mourning forever about something that can't be mended. There are other things in life—in my life. The best thing you can do for me is leave me alone and let me get on with it."

The beer can bent and crackled as his fingers tightened on it. "Is that what you really want?"

"I told you," she said, "I don't want your *friendship.*"

"You changed your mind about my family."

"I haven't changed my mind about you! You left me, Max. So don't—please—keep coming back and offering me half a loaf."

"All or nothing?"

"That's right."

He stood up and took two strides that brought him to the edge of the steps, then swung round, shoving his hands into the pockets of his trousers. "But it never was 'all,' was it? That was the problem with our marriage. We both settled for too little, right from the beginning."

"You were perfectly happy about that at the time."

"Were *you?*" he asked, his eyes finding hers with sudden brooding intensity. "Did I cheat you, Celine?"

"Cheat me?" Celine shook her head. "No! We were both absolutely honest with each other. I knew you couldn't give me what you'd given to Juliet."

"And you—?"

"I'd been burned once, and I didn't trust those feelings anymore. I didn't want to be 'in love' with anybody ever again. It clouds your judgement and it doesn't last. What we had was a much better foundation for marriage. At least that's what I thought then. We knew each other so well."

"Too well, maybe," Max said.

"Well, apparently not," she said tartly. "I never imagined that you'd—that this would happen to us."

"Neither did I." He had his hands deep into his pockets. "And I realise now what a very shaky foundation our marriage really had. We didn't expect much, did we? So we didn't get much."

"That's unfair and untrue." He still had the power to wound her, put her on the defensive. "We had something *good*. But you didn't value it."

"What we had was a close and loving friendship," he insisted. "That's what I wanted to salvage from all this. You're the one who insisted on throwing *that* away along with the other. Is it to punish me? You weren't in love with me on our wedding day, Celine." It was a blunt statement of fact.

"Nor you with me."

"True," he agreed coolly. "Are you in love with me now?"

The question was totally unexpected, like a stone hurled into a smooth pool. She felt the first impact with stunned surprise, then ripples of outraged shock began to spread throughout her body. She stood up, unable to sit any longer. Her head buzzed with tension, and her palms were damp as she clenched her fingers. "You have no right to ask me that!" she snapped.

"No right at all," Max agreed, his voice flat, level. "But I'm...curious. *Are you?*"

He sounded like an inquisitor. What did he want from her? The final humiliation of admitting that not a day went by that she didn't think of him, long to have him at her side, smiling at her as he made some wry remark, or putting a casual arm about her shoulders, or simply brushing his lips across her cheek as he left for work; that every night she lay in their bed torturing herself with the remembrance of what they'd shared; that when she found one of his socks that had fallen down behind the drier she'd held it to her face for a moment while the tears welled in her eyes? That every time she saw him she experienced a leap of her pulses for sheer joy, before the grief of knowing that he didn't want her stilled them? That she had to steal herself to hide her instinctive yearning for his touch every time he came near? That minutes ago, sitting two feet away from him, watching the way his hand encircled a cold beer can, the way his throat tautened when he raised the can to his lips, the way his hair grew on his neck, and the faint sheen of sweat on his upper lip, she'd been almost faint with wanting him? Even now she had a mad urge to hurl herself into his arms and beg him to come back to her on any terms at all.

And then, blessedly, a wave of anger swamped the tide of desire. *"You have a bloody nerve!"* she said. Discovering that she still held her empty glass in her hand, she recklessly hurled it at him, not even knowing what she'd done until it hit him on the chest as he sidestepped, too late to dodge it. And then two things happened. The glass fell and smashed to pieces on the tiles, and Max missed his footing on the edge of the terrace and went sprawling down the steps to land heavily beside the pool.

"Max!" Heedless of the broken shards and her bare feet, Celine plunged down the steps after him, but even as she made to kneel at his side he was getting up, his face thunderous, brows low over his eyes and the sculpted contours of his mouth drawn into an angry line.

"Max?" Half crouched beside him, she instinctively drew back, not realising how close to the pool's edge she was until she felt herself falling and then the water closing over her head.

She hadn't had time to take a breath, and she surfaced, gasping.

"Here." Max was standing above her, his hand extended.

Shaking water from her eyes, she grabbed the hand and was instantly hauled up. Her feet had barely touched the tiles before he released her hand and gripped her with both hands on her wet hair, his fingers at her nape and his thumbs on her cheeks, tilting her head, and then his mouth was on hers in a kiss that knew no mercy.

Astonishment held her rigid for a few seconds. But her mouth obeyed his silent, savage insistence, and parted for him.

The kiss became deeper, searching her very soul, making her heart pound and her veins catch fire. She was burning up despite the water that soaked her clothes and dripped down her neck and pasted wet tendrils of hair to her face. She shivered, but not because she was cold, and clutched at Max's shoulders, a muffled, astonished sound coming from her throat.

His hands left her face and swept to her waist, hauling her against him, hard. She went willingly, wanting him closer, so close that they would never part again.

And then, with an abrupt movement that would have unbalanced her again if his hands hadn't now been tightly clamped on her upper arms, he pushed her away, with the strangest expression of bafflement overlaid on the flush of angry passion, and his eyes lowered to the sodden shirt wetly moulded to her body.

Lowering her head, she brought her hands protectively to her stomach. She heard the distinct sound of Max's teeth coming suddenly together, and returned her eyes to him as he swallowed, and his face drained of colour.

"My God," he said, his voice hoarse and unnatural. "You're *pregnant!*"

## Chapter 12

"Yes," she said. Pointless denying it. She was still able to hide it under loose clothing, but he'd been holding her so close there was no way he could have missed the changes in her body.

Max shook his head as if to clear it. *"Now?"* he said, echoing her own initial disbelief.

"It needn't concern you." Celine brushed a dripping tendril of hair from her face with trembling fingers. She had known she'd have to tell him sometime, he'd find out, anyway. But today she wasn't prepared, didn't have the words ready. One thing she was determined on; she was not going to use this as a lever to bring Max back. Worse than knowing he had left her would be the knowledge that he'd returned from a sense of duty. "I ... think you'd better go," she said. "I need to get changed."

He was so stunned that he appeared unable to move from the spot where he stood. Celine had turned and walked up the steps, avoiding the broken glass, leaving a trail of water on the tiles, before he spoke again.

"Who does it concern, then?" he asked.

Celine turned. Now he came slowly up to the terrace and stood looking down at her, his face still pale. "Roland Jackson? Is he looking after you?"

Unprepared for the conclusion he was jumping to, she stalled. "He's . . . been very good to me." It was true. Since the day he'd whisked her off to the doctor, Roland had been anxious that she didn't overwork and that she ate regularly and well. A couple of times he'd persuaded her to eat out with him again. His unobtrusive pampering was balm to her wounded spirit. It was nice to think that someone cared, but she'd meticulously kept the relationship on a superficial level. She didn't want him to think she was likely to develop any deeper feelings.

"Have you seen a doctor?" Max asked. "Are you all right? It's a bit late to be having a first baby, isn't it?"

Her mouth curled wryly. "Yes, I've seen a doctor, and I'm on iron and calcium and having regular checkups. He said in view of my age, it's especially important that any problems are seen early. But I feel okay, just a bit tired sometimes."

"That fall into the pool—is it likely to—?"

Celine shook her head. "I'm not hurt, just wet and uncomfortable. It won't have done any harm. Please go now, Max. When I've changed I'll probably have a rest."

He still looked like a man who'd been recently pole-axed. "If you're sure that's what you want."

"I'm sure."

She had to think about this. Could she let him think that the baby was someone else's? It seemed wrong, and yet she dreaded telling him the truth. She needed time to consider all the implications. . . .

*You've had three months to think about it,* her conscience told her sternly as she trudged up the stairs after Max had reluctantly departed. And she still didn't know how to break it to him.

She had a warm shower, hoping it would soothe some of the turmoil from her thoughts. Her wardrobe yielded very few things that fitted these days. She slipped on a shirtwaister dress and removed the belt, revelling in the freedom from constriction. She'd have to go shopping for some maternity clothes. Soon there would be no hiding the fact of her pregnancy, and she badly needed some appropriate clothing. She couldn't help a small thrill of excitement at the thought.

She saw the shock on Roland's face on the day that the new offices were opened with a celebratory buffet lunch, and was smitten with conscience—perhaps she should have prepared him for this.

"Yes," she said quietly at his questioning look. "I'm going to have a baby."

He nodded. "I see." Although his next question confirmed that he didn't. "You've reconciled with your husband?"

Celine shook her head. "It's not quite like that."

There were people all around, but the level of voices was so high that, standing in a corner by the buffet table, they might have been alone. Roland said, "You're going through with it, though? The pregnancy?"

"Yes!" She'd never thought of anything else. "At least I'll have—"

"His child." Roland nodded. "You still love him, don't you?"

Apologetically, she met his kind brown eyes. "I don't think I'll ever stop."

He touched her arm. "Let me get you a drink." Looking down again at the bulge under her loose dress, he added, "Lemonade?"

Celine smiled. "Thanks, yes."

Now that the project was finished, Roland had no excuses to keep seeing her, and he didn't offer any more invitations. She missed him a little, but mostly she was relieved. He was too nice a man to hurt, and she knew he'd been on the verge of setting himself up for it. She hoped he'd find the woman he was looking for, someone whose heart was free to give him the love that he deserved.

*  *  *

She wasn't going to be able to keep her secret from Nancy, she knew. The next time the older woman came round, Celine said, "I have something to tell you." Today she wore a flowing cotton shirt over a pair of specially cut pants, and her condition wasn't so readily obvious. They were sitting as usual at the kitchen table, with cups of coffee and a plate of biscuits.

"Go ahead," Nancy said. "It's about time."

"You know? Did Max...?" Somehow she'd been sure that Max wouldn't mention it.

Nancy shook her head. "I guessed. I'm going to be a grandmother again, right? What I don't understand is why you and Max are still living apart."

"He...he doesn't know."

"But you just said..." Nancy's brow wrinkled in puzzlement.

"He thinks it's someone else's baby, not his."

For a moment Nancy was speechless. "But, Celine, dear! It is his—isn't it?"

"Yes, of course!" To her own surprise, Celine felt scalding tears fill her eyes and spill onto her cheeks. "Oh, I'm sorry! I didn't mean to do this."

Nancy got up and came round the table to put a soothing arm about her. "Have a good cry. You probably need it."

When it was over and Celine had wiped her flushed face with a paper towel, Nancy sat down again. "Did you have a fight about it?" she asked.

"Nothing like that. He just assumed..."

"And you didn't put him right? Why?"

"Because I'm afraid he might decide he should come back to me."

"Hmm. You don't think that might be a good thing?"

"Not if it's because of this. That's why...I have to ask you not to tell him, Nancy. Please."

Nancy looked slightly confused, but said only, "I'm glad you've told *me.*"

"It didn't seem fair to deprive you of your grandchild."

Looking her in the eye, Nancy asked, "Is it fair to deprive Max of his son or daughter?"

Celine looked back at her rather helplessly. "It's all such a mess!" she said. "Max doesn't want my child—our child—now. He's looking forward to having a family with Kate. Don't you see what it will do to him if he finds out now that...that I'm having his baby?" She shuddered, imagining Max torn between his love for Kate and his sense of right. Trapped into returning to her, he'd have to resent the fact, and what sort of marriage would they have then? "Maybe it won't matter once he's married to Kate," she said. "Maybe then we can tell him."

Nancy sighed. "It *is* a muddle, isn't it? But I can't help thinking that he ought to know, Celine. It just doesn't seem right."

"Nothing does."

"I have to agree with that. Oh, if only that wretched girl had never caught his eye!"

"Don't you like her?"

"She's nice enough, I suppose. I felt sorry for her more than anything. Max brought her round a couple of times when Michelle and her family were home with us, and we tried to welcome her for his sake. But...I think she felt awkward. The girls wanted to know where Auntie Celine was, of course, although Michelle had tried to explain. And Kate's obviously not used to children. She didn't know how to talk to them. She probably didn't want to come back."

"I'm sure when you get to know her better, things will be easier," Celine said with an effort at fairness.

Nancy looked at her curiously. "Maybe."

At first Celine had been afraid to start preparing for the advent of a baby, feeling it was tempting fate, but as the weeks went by and she began to be sure that the small fluttery sensations in her abdomen were not just wind, and her doctor continued to be pleased with her progress, she started to think seriously about what was going to be needed.

Max's study had remained empty and closed ever since he'd removed his things. One day she flung the door wide and walked in, deliberately appraising the room. "Perfect," she said to herself. She had taken another commission, for the house of a friend of Roland's, but now that the weather was often rather too wintry for gardening she still had time to spare. She would spend it on turning this room into a baby's room, eradicating the memory of when it had been Max's exclusive domain.

The cot would go in the corner by the window, and she'd need a changing table, maybe a low chair. The wallpaper was too neutral for a child's room. She'd get something patterned, bright. The books she'd been reading said that babies needed visual stimulation from birth....

She had just had her five-month checkup when the phone rang one evening and Max's voice said urgently, "Can I come over? I want to talk to you."

"You're talking to me now."

"I need to see you."

He sounded very tense, and she said, "What's wrong?"

"That's what I want to talk to you about. Are you free now?"

"Yes," she said hesitantly. She'd been fooling herself that she was getting over him, managing her life admirably without him. At the sound of his voice something within her went molten—hot and liquefied. If just speaking to him on the phone still did this to her, how would she feel seeing him face-to-face?

As she put down the receiver she experienced a ridiculous leap of hope. Maybe it hadn't worked out after all with Kate. Perhaps Max realised that he was making a mistake, and was going to tell her it was over.

Ruthlessly squashing such futile fantasies, she spent the next twenty minutes trying to relax and achieve a serene, unflappable mood.

When the bell burred she forced herself to walk calmly across the hallway and open the door.

She stepped back to let him in, but he didn't immediately enter. His eyes examined her face, lifting slightly to her hair, which she'd twisted into a new, sophisticated style, and then he shifted his gaze to the gracefully flowing fine rose wool dress that was gathered lightly under her breasts for extra fullness. "You look . . . wonderful," he said slowly.

"Thank you." She felt herself flush. The unexpected compliment appeared sincere.

In the lounge she offered him a drink that he refused. She sat on the sofa, expecting him to take one of the armchairs, but instead he remained standing, looking taut and almost brooding, his stance full of some tangible tension.

Finally she said, "What did you want to see me about?"

She saw his eyes wander again to the evidence of her pregnancy, then he dragged them away. "I saw—" He stopped and cleared his throat. "I met your friend Roland at a function I had to attend this afternoon. One of our clients unveiled a new computer database that they hope will revolutionise the business world, and invited half of Auckland to come and see a demo of the programme."

"I see." So far she didn't, and he seemed for once to be having trouble coming to the point.

"Do you?" His glance was almost hostile. "Did you know Roland has a fiancée?"

"If he has, it's recent," Celine said evenly. "But I'm glad for him."

He let out a breath. "Are you?" He sounded caustic now. "Even though you're supposedly having his baby?"

She moistened her lips with her tongue. "I'm not," she said, "having Roland's baby."

"No, you're not, are you?" The rigidly controlled temper that she realised was the cause of his tension began to show through. "But you deliberately allowed me to think so."

A little angry herself, she said, "You can think what you want to. It's nothing to do with you."

His eyes narrowed suddenly. "What the devil does that mean?"

"Just what I said. I told you, it's not your concern."

"No? So, how much sleeping around have you done since we parted, Celine? Do you even know who the father is?"

Celine stood up, her face flaming. "Whether I do or not, it's none of your business! You were the one who walked out, remember? You don't give a damn about me, or my baby. *My* baby, Max. That's all you need to know. I'm not asking you to pay maintenance, or have anything to do with it—or me."

His lips went tight for a moment. "How far on are you?" he demanded. Looking her over again, he added with deadly accuracy, "Five months?"

She didn't answer, but he must have read something in her face. "I'm right, aren't I?"

"What if you are? It doesn't prove anything."

"Five months ago you and I made love."

"Did we?" Still smarting from his brutal suggestion, she said caustically, "I must have forgotten to mark the date. Among so many, it slipped my mind."

"You know I didn't mean that. I was being sarcastic."

"You were being damned offensive!"

"All right. So I was. You don't think it's offensive to give me the impression that some other man fathered my child?"

"I didn't! You assumed..."

"For God's sake, Celine! For twelve years I wasn't able to give you a child. What the hell did you expect me to think, when you're running around with another man and suddenly you're pregnant! Of course I assumed—and you just didn't bother to disabuse me."

Her hands clenched. "You seemed quite happy with the explanation you'd worked out for yourself."

He took a step towards her, his jaw thrust forward. "Happy? Do you think I was *happy* to think you were carrying Jackson's baby?"

"It let you out," she accused him.

*"Of what?"*

"Responsibility for it—for me. It's all right, Max. I can handle this. I'm sure Kate can give you a family. She's young and healthy, and no doubt she'll be delighted to have your babies.''

Furiously, he said, "Leave Kate out of this! This is between you and me, Celine.''

"Oh, no!'' Vehemently, Celine shook her head. "You brought her into the equation. You can't just leave her out when it suits you. You and I are *separated,* Max. We have no obligations anymore to each other.''

"I have an obligation to my child.''

"I'm absolving you! We don't need you, Max. Go back to Kate.''

She thought he was about to shout at her, but instead he clamped his jaw tight for a moment, checking what he'd been about to say. "Is that what you would really like me to do?'' His voice was quiet now, his face very serious.

Celine swallowed. This was one of the hardest things she'd ever done. "I don't want you here, Max.'' *Not this way,* her heart cried. *Not out of guilt and a sense of obligation.*

His expression was bleak. "I can't go back to Kate,'' he said flatly. "That's over.''

## Chapter 13

"Over?" For a tiny, infinitesimal moment her whole being blazed with hope. Sternly, she quelled it.

Over. But he *loved* Kate. He'd given up everything for her.

Behind the rigidity of his expression she could see stark pain. "Oh, Max!" she said, her arms instinctively going out to him. "I'm so sorry!"

A ripple of shock passed over his face. He didn't walk into her offered arms, instead taking both her hands in a strong grip. "You're sorry?" he said in a strange voice. His eyes probed hers.

"Of course," she said in soft distress. She looked down at his hands holding hers. He didn't want her embrace. He still wanted Kate, and Celine was no substitute. "You must be feeling dreadful."

"It...wasn't easy," he admitted, his voice sinking almost to a whisper. His thumbs absently caressed the backs of her hands, and then he released her, raising his eyes. "I can understand you not wanting me anymore, but the baby—that's not something any woman should have to face alone. I let you down badly, Celine. At least let me try to make some amends. Don't children need two parents? You've always believed so.''

''What do you want?'' she asked him, on a breath of despair.

''To be allowed a part in our child's future. I want to help with the expenses—people say babies cost a lot. And anything else that you need. And . . . I know this may be asking too much but . . . if you can bear it, I'd like to be there when he or she is born.''

In the early days when they'd been confident that once she'd stopped taking the pill conception would naturally follow, Celine had broached the subject of his presence in the delivery room. Max had grinned then and said, ''Try to keep me away! It'll be the highlight of our lives.''

Did she want him there, now? ''Yes,'' she said, thinking aloud. ''Yes, all right.''

''Thank you.'' The rigidity of his shoulders relaxed slightly. ''If there's anything you want,'' he repeated, ''anything I can do for you—or for the baby, you will let me know?''

She hesitated, then spread her hands. ''I'll let you know.''

He'd wrecked their marriage, and now he'd lost Kate. It had all been for nothing. He must feel that the baby was the only thing he had left—and Celine had the power to deny him that. She knew that she couldn't do it.

Taking a quick breath, she said, ''Are you sure it's all over, between you and Kate?''

''Yes,'' he said curtly, his face closing. ''There's no doubt of it.''

She felt a tight ache about her heart for him. If he was suffering half as much as she had since he'd told her their marriage was over, he must be in agony.

The only way to deal with that kind of heartbreak was to keep your life so full of other things that the ever-present pain couldn't completely swamp you. Maybe he needed lots of things to do.

She said, "I'm turning your old study into a room for the baby. This—" she put a hand on her front "—will make climbing ladders to hang wallpaper a bit difficult, and I suppose I shouldn't be painting the ceiling in my condition." Was she mad? she wondered, but went on steadily, not giving herself a chance to let doubts stifle her instinct. "You can help if you like."

He could have paid a professional to do the job, she knew. But his face instantly lightened. "I'd like that," he said. "Very much."

Neither of them suggested that Max move back into the house, but he spent a good deal of time there. Over several evenings they stripped the walls of the study, not talking much but working in silent partnership, and then Max painted the ceiling and they repapered the walls in a cheery nursery print, with Max doing the climbing and fixing under Celine's critical supervision.

One evening he arrived with a large parcel under his arm, and invited Celine to open it.

She unwrapped it in the kitchen and opened the box inside, revealing a mobile featuring a dozen felt clowns suspended from an umbrella-shaped awning that turned while a musical box fixed above it played a gay little tune.

"It's great," she said as the music slowed. She was holding the mobile up by one hand, watching the clowns revolve. "Where did you find it?"

"I was passing by a toyshop and they had one in the window. You said something about getting mobiles for him."

"*She'll* love it," Celine said.

Max's grin was the first spontaneous smile she'd seen since the night he'd told her his affair with Kate was finished. "Whichever," he conceded. "Do you care?"

Celine shook her head. "Not in the least. I just hope for a healthy baby."

A shadow crossed his face. "Is there any cause for concern?"

"None," she said firmly. "I'm being expertly monitored, and so far everything is going just as it should. Come on, let's hang this in the baby's room."

They went shopping together for a cot, and discovered a new model that rocked at the baby's slightest movement. "It imitates the movements of the mother's body that the baby's grown accustomed to in the womb," the saleswoman told them. "So a restless baby sort of rocks itself to sleep. It was invented by a New Zealand woman."

Intrigued, Max gave the cot a gentle shove and watched it sway. He turned to Celine. "What do you think?"

They bought it and he stowed it in the back of his big car, along with a large teddy bear he hadn't been able to resist, and a plastic baby bath. Celine had given up arguing about who was to pay for the baby's needs. Max was determined that those expenses were his department.

By tacit agreement they never mentioned Kate. Sometimes he looked grim, bleak and older than his years, and Celine's heart went out to him in sympathy, but at the same time she had to suppress a hard core of resentment that never quite went away. She didn't like to see Max suffer, but knowing he was suffering over another woman sometimes made her want to hit him.

That, and the fact that she knew if he took her in his arms she'd immediately melt like chocolate in the sun, made her edgy with him. There were times when she knew her voice held an acerbic note, and if he came near enough to touch her she'd stiffen and move away. She was damned if she would allow herself to be used as some kind of consolation prize, or as a substitute for Kate.

Not that he seemed to have any such idea, she admitted to herself, ruefully surveying her burgeoning figure. He didn't comment or appear to even notice her acute sensitivity to his nearness. Compared with Kate's youthful slimness she must be a very unattractive-looking package, anyway. He'd find it difficult now to close his eyes and imagine she was Kate.

In fact, Max was careful to avoid touching her. She wondered if the idea repulsed him.

In every other way he was attentive and thoughtful, a model father-to-be. He noticed if she was extra tired, and would leave early, urging her to rest. When he found her folding newly washed sheets and towels he made her sit down and finished the job himself. He wouldn't let her carry anything heavier than a cup and saucer, and would be at her side like a shot to relieve her of any burden. He got into the habit of making her a hot drink before he left, and one for himself, and they'd sit at the kitchen table together making quiet, desultory conversation. It was almost, Celine reflected wistfully, like being properly married again.

Except that after he'd collected up their cups and rinsed them, Max would say good night, smile at her casually and leave, while she went slowly up to bed alone.

Sometimes she wondered how he felt, encountering Kate every day at work. Did he experience the same exquisite torture that his almost nightly visits caused Celine? The same yearning for a small caress, an intimate word, a loving glance across a room? Celine hardly dared look directly at him these days for fear that he'd read that yearning in her eyes and turn away from it, embarrassed that he couldn't give her what she so desperately needed.

It seemed he'd give her anything else. She made an idle mention one night of a particular brand of hand cream she'd always used that had gone off the market. Two days later he handed her a box of half a dozen bottles. He'd found a shop that still had some and bought the entire stock. When she remarked that she'd like to own a copy of a book she'd borrowed from the library, he bought it for her the very next day. An idle reminiscence about his mother's delicious banana cake brought Nancy round for lunch, carrying a freshly baked sample. Celine laughed and said, "When did Max talk to you?"

"Last night." Nancy grinned. "I think he expected me to get up and bake it for you there and then."

"You were in bed? Oh, Nancy, I'm sorry!"

"Not your fault. I was reading, anyway. At least you have a craving for something reasonable, not chalk dust or strawberries with mayonnaise."

Celine grimaced at the bizarre combination. "It wasn't really a craving at all. I just mentioned how good your banana cake was. But I'm not turning it down, thanks."

"You're looking great."

"Like this?" She looked down.

"Max said it's like watching a rose come into full bloom."

Staring, Celine flushed. "M-Max said that?"

"Why so surprised? I gather he can hardly keep away from you." It was almost a question.

"From the baby," Celine said feebly. "He...he doesn't want to touch me, Nancy."

Nancy frowned. "Doesn't want to, or doesn't dare?" she asked bluntly. "Have you ever asked him? Or encouraged him to?"

"And set myself up for a brush-off?" Celine asked. "No, thanks." Not again.

Nancy regarded her thoughtfully. "It's understandable. Have you two...talked?"

Celine avoided her steady gaze. "We talk all the time," she mumbled. "Quite a lot."

"I mean, *really* talked. About your relationship. About what happened."

Celine shook her head. "He hasn't got over her, Nancy. Maybe he never will." She paused, then asked, "Has he talked to you?"

"Max is past the age of confiding in his mother. Never did, much, come to think of it. He always tended to bottle things up, even as a child. I don't know what's going on in his head—or his heart—these days." Nancy sighed. "I only know he's not happy."

That was obvious. "I know. Perhaps the baby will help."

"Perhaps it will help you both." Nancy leaned over and patted her hand. "I'd like to see you two together again, properly."

\* \* \*

"I should tell you, Celine," Max said that evening as they sat in the kitchen, "I won't be with the firm much longer."

"You're leaving?" For once she was surprised into looking directly at him.

"I've decided to set up my own practice. I've found an office downtown and I'm moving in next week." He seemed to be thinking something over. "I wondered," he said finally, "if you'd be interested in advising on the furnishings, perhaps some pictures. It's new, but very bare, very bland. I'll pay you, of course."

"I can't take payment from you! But I'd like to see it." Was he leaving to spare himself from seeing Kate every day? Fleetingly Celine wondered if the girl had taken up with someone else from the firm. That would be rubbing salt into Max's wounds.

"We could go down there tomorrow, if you like," Max offered. "I'll pick you up at lunchtime so you can see the place in daylight. Unless you've got something else to do?"

"Lunchtime's fine."

"We could have lunch afterwards in town. Okay?" His smile was almost anxious.

"That would be...nice."

She dressed carefully next day in her prettiest maternity dress, a soft dark blue, and when the doorbell rang she was applying perfume to her skin. Inspecting herself critically in the mirror she saw that her skin had a new bloom on it and her freshly washed hair shone. She must be one of those lucky women whom pregnancy suited.

Max glanced over her with evident approval but didn't comment as he opened the car door for her.

The office was spacious but as he'd said, bare and uninteresting. Celine looked about, made some preliminary suggestions and scribbled a few notes in a small book.

"You know my taste," Max told her. "I'll give you a free hand within my budget."

"You'd better come with me to choose your desk and chair," she suggested. "I think I know the best place to go for office furniture." That was something she'd learned from working for Roland.

"Sure," Max said. "Is it okay for you to be doing this? I don't want you doing anything you shouldn't." He glanced at her figure.

"It won't do me any harm. I'm not going to lift anything myself, just do the choosing."

"What about driving? I can take you wherever you need to go."

Celine shook her head. "That's not a problem. I need to put the seat back a bit further than I'm used to, that's all. Don't coddle me, Max."

He smiled and shrugged. "Okay, I'll try not to. But you must tell me if you need anything. Now—" he glanced at his watch "—there's a table waiting for us at the Southern Cross restaurant."

The table overlooked the harbour, where even on a wintry weekday some yachts had braved the elements, and a pale sun shone over the green-blue sea. The gentle slope of the island volcano, Rangitoto, obscured the horizon, and a huge passenger catamaran ploughed across the water on its way from the further island of Waiheke to the ferry terminal at the bottom of Queen Street, the heart of the city.

"Are you allowed champagne?" Max asked her as he took the wine list from the waiter.

"Maybe one glass," Celine said cautiously. "What are we celebrating? Your move to your own practice?"

"Among other things." He ordered a sparkling New Zealand wine, and when it came he said, "Let's drink to the baby, and . . . to whatever the future holds for us."

She could do that, she supposed. "And your new practice." Raising her glass, she looked up into his eyes and saw that they were dark and sombre.

She tasted the wine and set it down, staring at the tiny bubbles rising in the fluted glass.

Max put down his glass and opened the menu. "What would you like to eat?"

\* \* \*

When he left her back at the house after their leisurely lunch, he feathered a fleeting kiss across her cheek before turning away and striding back to his car.

Celine entered the house in something of a daze, to hear the phone ringing. Hurrying across the hall, she picked up the receiver. "Hello?"

"Celine—you sound puffed. Did I make you run?"

"Honoria! No, not really. Anything makes me puff these days."

"You're not that old!"

"Not old—pregnant."

There was a long pause at the other end. "Pregnant? *Pregnant!* That's wonderful! Isn't it? I mean...how— who? Last time we met you said Max had left. I take it this is not a virgin birth."

"It's a long story, Honoria."

"But I'm dying of curiosity now! How about lunch tomorrow at my place?"

"Well...all right." She could do some preliminary scouting round for furnishings for Max's office, perhaps gather some samples and catalogues, and then lunch with Honoria. In the afternoon if she wasn't too tired she could spend some time in her workroom sorting and planning. "What time, then?" she queried.

"How about twelve-thirty? And you've got to tell me all about it!"

She wouldn't be telling the whole story, Celine thought as she put down the phone five minutes later. But she didn't want Honoria getting the wrong idea.

She edited out some of the details, but ended up telling Honoria a good deal more than she'd intended. Perhaps she'd needed someone to confide in. Most of their close friends had some connection with Max's job or family or were people they'd both known since childhood. Only Honoria and Tom were outside that circle.

"And now he's back in your life because of the baby?" Honoria asked. "What about the bimbo?"

Celine gave a faint smile. "He says it's over."

"Do you believe him?"

"Honoria, he's shattered. He tries to hide it, but I can see he's hurting."

Honoria put down the coffee cup in her hand and gave her a long, disbelieving stare. "Celine, are you *sorry* for the guy?"

"I know how it feels," Celine confessed. "I wouldn't wish that kind of pain on anyone."

"You are too soft!" Honoria told her scornfully. "I made Tom crawl for bloody weeks! What are you going to do? Open your arms and say, 'Come home, darling—all is forgiven'?"

Celine gave a choked little laugh. "I've too much pride for that. And yet, if he ever wants it, I shouldn't let pride get in the way of... of a reconciliation, should I?"

"Why not? You're entitled. The rat lit out on you, remember? Left you high and dry."

"I know but—Max isn't a rat. He's a man who has a very strong sense of—of honour. That's why he couldn't lie to me and go on having an affair behind my back. It's why he's trying to do the right thing by the baby. By me, too, I suppose. And that's what I find so damned unacceptable. What I want is for him to *feel* the same way about me as he does about *her*. And that's crying for the moon."

Honoria said thoughtfully, "Correct me if I'm wrong, but you know, even on your honeymoon, you two didn't strike me as being madly in love. A couple of nice, down-to-earth kids, really fond of each other but—well, if there were stars in your eyes, I couldn't see them."

"You were right," Celine told her. "That's what was missing, what we thought we could do without. We were wrong, and Max realised it when he met Kate. I guess now it's too late for us."

"When did *you* realise it?" Honoria asked shrewdly.

Celine was silent for a while. "Not until he'd left me," she acknowledged. "And now I can't be satisfied with less. I guess that's pretty stupid."

"Not stupid. Tom and I started out with so many stars in our eyes we could barely see anything but each other. Then the kids came along, and life caught up with us, and we grew older—Tom got desperate, I got disillusioned. But you know, last week was our wedding anniversary. Tom bought me flowers and took me out to dinner, and I put on a pretty dress that I hadn't worn for ages. We talked. The sky was cloudy that night, but you know what? On our way home the stars came out. And I thought, yeah—sometimes you can't see them but the stars are always up there somewhere, aren't they?"

Max went shopping with her for his desk and office chair, and Celine chose curtain fabrics and the other furniture, presenting samples for his approval. She persuaded the curtain firm to do a rush job for him, and they both spent several hours the night before he opened for business arranging the furniture. All that remained was to empty the boxes stacked in one corner and place their contents on shelves and in filing cabinets.

"You don't need to do this," Max told her when she offered to help with that task. "Anyway, you shouldn't be lifting."

"Books and files! They're not heavy," Celine protested. "At least, not one by one. I can hand them to you, and then you can put them where they belong. Come on, the sooner we start, the sooner we'll finish." She knelt and began to strip the sealing tape from the first carton.

It was almost like being back in the days when they'd been planning the house together. Sometimes she almost forgot that they were living apart. Except that every night she returned to an empty, lonely house.

There had been a brief argument when Max asked her to present a bill for her work. At first she'd flatly refused to take money from him, but Max was at least as stubborn as she, and finally she'd said, "All right, I'll send you an account—"

"Good!"

"And I'll give the money to the Red Cross."

His eyes narrowed briefly, then he gave a short laugh. "You can do what you like with the money, of course," he said. "Can you afford to do that?" She'd finally persuaded him that she didn't need his help to pay her household expenses.

"Yes," she said crisply. The truth was that she had no further commissions in the offing, and had begun thinking of ways to trim her budget. Perhaps by dispensing with Alice's services; with only Celine in the house it scarcely needed so much cleaning.

"You might pass the word that I'm available for more work," she suggested. "I'm doing quite well, but word-of-mouth is the best advertising. I've had some cards printed—perhaps you can leave some in the reception area for me. Anyone who likes your decor might think of giving me a call."

"You don't want to take on too much," Max said, frowning.

"I want to make it my living," she explained.

"You mean work full-time?" The frown deepened. "You can't do that!"

Celine lifted her brows. "Can't?"

"Shouldn't!" Max amended. "You're expecting a baby."

Glancing down, Celine said, "I know. It doesn't mean I can't work. Most women do, these days, right up to the ninth month sometimes."

"You're not most mothers. You know you're at more risk than a younger woman."

"Very slightly," Celine agreed. "As long as I feel well and don't get too tired, my doctor is quite happy."

"Well, I'm not! There's no need for you to be working at all. You know I can afford to look after you adequately."

"I don't want you to," Celine told him. She needed to do all she could to forge a real career for herself and be as independent as possible before the baby arrived. Afterwards she'd have to fit her work around the baby's needs, of course. But she wasn't going to get into the habit of relying on Max.

"It's my child, too!" Max said. "I'm simply trying to protect it. And you."

"I promise," Celine assured him, "if the doctor advises me to stop working, I will. Okay?"

"Will you also promise to be honest with him?" Max demanded. "And to ask for my help if you need it?"

"All right." She sighed. "For the baby's sake, I promise. I wouldn't do anything to harm it, Max. Surely you can trust me on that?"

Celine had found a new serenity that she deduced was the result of her being pregnant. She refused to speculate on Max's motives or let herself think too far ahead. Both hurt and anger seemed emotions that were scarcely worth expending emotion on, and she floated through the days with her attention increasingly focused on the miracle within her body. Sometimes she felt that everything must finally resolve itself without any help from her. So what was the point of anguishing about it? And if, when this was all over, she didn't have Max, at least she'd have his child to lavish her love and care on. She didn't want to think further than that.

One morning there was a birthday card in the mail from Celine's older brother, and a parcel from Michelle. They were a couple of days early, she reflected, glancing at the calendar. She'd had so much on her mind that she'd totally forgotten the approaching date. Michelle's present was a selection of perfumed toiletries in small packs, ideal for taking with her to the maternity ward when she had the baby. She'd considered having a home birth, but her doctor said at her age it would be wiser to opt for hospital. Celine reflected that never before had she been so often reminded of her advanced years.

It was time she thought about preparing the case she was supposed to have ready. She'd find the list she'd been given and make a start on that today.

The following evening Max phoned. "Can I take you out for a birthday dinner tomorrow?" he asked.

"Did Michelle put you up to this," she asked, "or your mother?"

"Certainly not. When have I ever forgotten your birthday?"

Never, Celine had to admit. But she'd always suspected that the womenfolk in his family had something to do with it. She knew very well that her brother's wife kept a note of family birthdays and nudged him into sending cards at the appropriate times. Her father seldom remembered.

"Well?" Max was waiting for an answer.

"Thank you," she said. "Yes."

Her suspicion that his mother had reminded him was dissipated by Nancy's call the next morning, to wish her many happy returns and ask how she was going to celebrate.

Knowing the query was a preliminary to making sure she didn't spend the day alone and forgotten, Celine smiled to herself. "Max is taking me out," she reported.

Nancy tried to sound casually pleased, but it was fairly obvious that she was delighted.

When he arrived, Max was carrying a bouquet of roses, carnations and fairylike gypsophila, and a small gift-wrapped parcel.

She put the flowers into a vase and carried them back to the lounge where he was waiting, before opening the parcel.

Raising the lid of the velvet-covered box inside, she gasped. "Oh, Max! That's beautiful."

It was a silver filigree bracelet, intricately designed, with several small sapphires embedded in the pattern.

"I hope it fits."

It had a clasp and safety chain. Removing it carefully from its velvet bed, she opened the clasp before slipping the bracelet over her wrist, but had trouble fastening it one-handed.

Max said, "Let me."

She was on the sofa, and he sat down half facing her. She felt his fingers warm on her skin as he did up the clasp. And when he'd finished he took her hand in his, admiring the effect, then unexpectedly lifted her fingers to his lips before releasing her.

Immediately he stood up, thrusting his hands into the pockets of his dark suit. "Ready to go?"

"Yes." She wasn't sure her legs would carry her, because her knees were shaking. When she made to get up she almost fell back, but Max shot his hands out of his pockets and steadied her, holding her arms.

"Sorry," she said, staring at the knot of his tie. "I'm clumsy these days."

He let her go and stood back again. "It must feel odd, carrying that extra weight around."

"Well, it happens gradually, you know. I'm used to it now."

The restaurant he'd chosen was small and intimate. There were not many diners and they had a secluded corner to themselves. Celine felt almost shy, as though she were on a date with a stranger—a very attractive stranger. She found herself covertly watching Max as he ordered wine and studied the menu, spoke to the waiter and touched a lean masculine finger to the flowers in a crystal vase on the table.

"They're real," she said.

Max's eyes glinted as he looked up. "I'd have complained if they weren't. Tonight everything has to be the way you want it."

He knew she disliked artificial flowers. "Did you order them?" she asked him.

He shook his head. "No, but I figured a place like this ought to have real flowers."

"It looks expensive," she said.

"Only the best."

"I've never been here before." It was on the tip of her tongue to ask if he had, but she bit back the question. Perhaps she didn't want to know the answer.

The pause went on a fraction too long, and then he said quietly, "Neither have I. But it has a good reputation."

She smiled at him, a shade too warmly. Of course he wouldn't have brought her to a place he'd taken Kate to. Lightly, she said, "I'm sure it will live up to that."

There were few awkward moments after that. The conversation was mostly confined to the food, the plans for his new practice, and subjects that were in the news. Then he asked casually if she'd done any more design work, and she said equally casually that she'd two small projects going, and was hopeful they'd lead to larger ones.

Somehow they skated over the events of recent months. Gradually Celine relaxed, and when they left and he placed a hand on her waist as they returned to the car, it felt perfectly natural.

Her waist had expanded somewhat since the last time he'd laid a hand on it, she thought, reminding herself that he probably wasn't getting any charge out of touching her.

It had been a leisurely dinner and by the time they left it was quite late.

At the house he went up the steps with her and waited for her to unlock the door. "You're not nervous on your own?" he asked.

Celine shook her head. "Not since I got the burglar-proof locks." Wondering if he was obliquely hinting, she hesitated as the door swung open on the darkened entry. "Would you like to come in—for a while?"

"No," he said. "I'll go. Do you mind if I give you a birthday kiss first?"

She stayed mute and unmoving, and after a second or so he lifted his hand to her face and gently turned her to him. His fingers lay against her cheek, his thumb lightly caressing her lips until she couldn't help but part them. Then he tipped her head back further and, taking his time, bent his lips to hers.

# Chapter 14

The taste of his mouth was so familiar, and yet it was like the first time. Initially it was a soft, almost tentative touch, as light as his thumb had been, then it became firmer, teasing and coaxing. She stood quietly, hardly daring to breathe, all her concentration on the sensations he was creating, the subtle movements of his mouth on hers. She wanted to throw her arms about him and bind him to her, but this delicate, tender seduction of her mouth wove too fragile a spell to be recklessly broken.

Just when she felt she couldn't stand it any longer, Max abruptly raised his head and his hand fell away from her face. Celine blinked with the suddenness of it. His expression in the dimness was unreadable. "I hope that hasn't spoiled your evening," he said.

"No," she said. "It's been a lovely evening, Max. Thank you."

He seemed to pause, then he was stepping down to the path. "Go inside," he said. "You don't want to get cold, standing about out here."

* * *

It was the beginning of a new phase. She lived in a curious kind of limbo, hopeful and yet wary. Max believed that Kate didn't want him anymore, but if she changed her mind would he be able to resist? Would he even want to?

And yet he seemed now to be centring all his attention on Celine—her and their child. He phoned several times a week, and sometimes called in after work just to check that she was all right. He brought her flowers, and at weekends he'd take her to lunch and then drive to the top of Mount Eden or One Tree Hill to admire the views of the city, or make a leisurely trip on Tamaki Drive, winding along the edge of the harbour. He took her to a concert and a couple of films, and to supper afterwards. Twice they spent Sunday afternoon with his parents, who treated the occasion with rather careful nonchalance.

Nancy, Celine could see, was dying to ask what it all meant. But she didn't know any more than they. Sometimes she thought she saw a warmth in Max's eyes that gave her hope. Hope of what? she asked herself. That things would return to the way they'd been before?

That was an illusion, she knew. There was no way of wiping out the past; they would have to live with it. She didn't know if she could, or whether Max even wanted to. Perhaps all he was capable of giving her was this rather aloof kindness, a tepid affection left over from a lifetime of friendship and twelve years of marriage—and spurred by a guilty conscience. He had spent all his deeper emotions on Kate, who finally hadn't wanted him anymore.

Sometimes Max kissed her in an almost brotherly fashion, not holding her close but simply touching his lips briefly to hers. And sometimes his lips lingered, tantalised, tasted before he withdrew, his eyes quizzical or simply enigmatic.

At those times she thought he was waiting for her to respond, reciprocate. It should have been easy, because those kisses set her pulses racing and liquefied her bones, and yet something held her back.

She'd told Honoria that in wanting what she wanted she was crying for the moon. Shouldn't she grab what she could get, for fear of being left with nothing after all? But some stubborn core insisted that she couldn't be satisfied again with half a loaf. If she didn't have all of Max's heart, all of his passion, she wouldn't settle for the small part of it that he could offer her.

Celine had been attending antenatal sessions at the hospital. Some of the women had brought their partners along from the beginning, and the instructor had suggested that the father or another helper should accompany them whenever possible. "The father or a friend can help you through the early stages if they know what to do."

She knew that Max, too, ought to be prepared, as he wanted to be with her at the birth, but she'd been reluctant to involve him to that degree.

Then he brought the subject up himself. He'd called in after work, "Just to see if you need anything, check that you're okay," he said, and she'd offered him a cup of coffee.

"Are you going to classes or something?" he asked her. "Andrew and his wife are having another baby, and they've been practising for weeks."

"I'm attending classes," she told him, "every week."

"Don't they like the father along, too?"

"Yes, if possible. It . . . is supposed to help, if the father is planning to be there."

"You haven't changed your mind about that?"

Celine shook her head. "I haven't changed my mind." She hesitated, then took the plunge. "Do you want to come to the next session with me?"

Max collected her and they travelled to the hospital together. After that he never missed a session. They practised correct breathing, and he learned how to rub her back, firmly but not too hard, and what to expect when the time came. And how to change and feed and bath the baby after it arrived. Most of the class were first-time parents, all of them younger. "Just kids," Max commented ruefully one night as he drove Celine home. "I look at them and think they're too young to be parents."

"Some of them are only teenagers," Celine said. "That girl who comes with her mother, and the couple who sat in the corner tonight. We're old enough to be *their* parents."

"Don't remind me," Max begged. Sobering, he said, "We'll do a good job, though, won't we, Celine? There must be some advantages to having a bit more experience than most before starting our family."

A family. Were they a family? Celine asked herself, if she and Max weren't living together? What sort of family was that for a child? It wasn't what they'd planned when they'd talked about having children.

Max drew up by the house and got out to open her door. Nowadays he had to help her from the car. He held her arm as they walked up the steps. "Want some coffee?" she asked him. It had become a ritual.

"Thanks." He took her key and opened the door. He might as well have his own key, Celine reflected. In fact, maybe she should give him one, just in case. If she went into labour and found it difficult getting to the door...

As had happened before, he seemed to read her thoughts. "If anything goes wrong, does someone have a key to get in to you?"

"You know the doctor says—"

"Yes, you're fine, everything's progressing normally. I still lie awake at nights worrying about you."

He did? "There's no need. But I've been thinking—"

"Yes?" he said quickly.

"If you're going to be driving me to the hospital, perhaps you'd better keep a key."

"Thanks. Has it occurred to you that you should have someone in the house?" There was a slight pause before he said, "I could move in any time you like."

Celine couldn't answer him. One part of her wanted to leap at the chance, tell him yes, yes! Another part warned her to use caution. Did he mean this as a permanent thing, or would he move out again once the baby was born?

His voice roughening, he said, "I promise I won't bother you with unwanted attentions. I'll sleep in the spare room."

"For how long?" she asked at last.

"As long as you need me," Max answered.

What if she needed him forever? What if she could never bear to let him go again? And could she bear being in the same house but not in the same bed? Having a husband who wasn't a lover?

"Well," he said finally, "whatever you decide."

"I'll...think about it," she said. "Meantime you'd better keep this key."

The following weekend he took her to a wild, west coast beach where blustery winds savaged the waves into creamy crests and sent spiked spinifex seed-heads bowling along the sand.

At this time of the year the beaches were the domain of the hardy and the fanatic. Surfers in wetsuits sometimes braved the waves, avoiding the deceptive calms that signalled a rip that would drag them remorselessly out to sea, and fishermen cast dangerously from rocky outcrops where a rogue wave was likely to sweep them into oblivion.

Celine was content to stroll along the wide, smooth, black-streaked ironsands, and watch the pounding waves from the safety of the beach. The wind whipped her hair from its fastenings and lashed it across her cheeks. She leaned on Max's arm and when she looked up into his face he was grinning down at her.

They'd always liked this beach in rough weather. One year their two families had shared a holiday house here, and the children had spent two halcyon weeks running wild on the sand and about the rocks, exploring dark, damp caves and climbing cliffs, tumbling down sandhills, digging for shell-fish at low tide, and swimming and surfing under the watchful eyes of their parents and older siblings.

Max and Celine still remembered that time with nostalgia. Years later they'd talked of buying a place there and spending holidays in it with their own children. But the day they recalled to each other most vividly was the day of the storm, when the surf club life-savers had closed the beach to swimmers and there was nothing to do but stay huddled inside the house playing Scrabble and I Spy.

Max, who was twelve that year, had got restless. That afternoon, when the unseasonable rain stopped driving against the windowpanes, he'd grabbed a windproof jacket and said, "I'm going to the beach."

His parents looked doubtful, and the other children told him he was crazy, the wind was just *howling* out there, and it was sure to rain again.

But Celine had said, "I'm coming, too."

The adults argued, but even then Max had been possessed of a strong will and the ability to argue any point. In the end the parents gave them permission provided, they were warned, they stayed well away from the water. "Not even a toe!" Max's father had ordered sternly.

"They'll be okay," Celine heard Nancy say as they fought the door open. "Max won't do anything risky if Celine's with him. He always looks after the younger ones."

Max had been a very responsible boy. Sometimes Celine and Michelle had thought him too bossy, and roused his ire by disregarding his orders. But that day the height of the breakers, great curving walls of water thundering along the shore, and the driving wind awed her into obedience.

She'd staggered once or twice, nearly blown from her bare feet, her heels sinking into rain-soaked sand. Max had taken her hand then, and hauled her with him along the beach until they found a niche in the sandhills where they could sit in relative shelter and watch the hurling, ever-changing sea. They'd huddled together in the shallow hollow for so long, hypnotised by the power of the elements, that eventually the women sent their two fathers to find them.

Today wasn't so turbulent, but the waves were impressive and the wind forceful enough to make Celine gasp and tighten her grip on Max's arm to keep her balance.

"Are you okay?" he asked, looking down at her.

Celine nodded. "Fine." She felt singingly alive, her mind clear and her body, despite its increasing ungainliness, strong and fit. They walked for quite a long way, until they came on a huge driftwood log that lay at the foot of a curved cliff, creating an almost windless space on its lee side.

Max quirked an enquiring eyebrow. "Want to sit here for a while?"

She nodded, and eased herself down gingerly, a hand on her back.

"Is it aching?" he asked, coming down beside her.

"A bit stiff, that's all."

He knelt beside her. "Turn a bit and I'll see if I can ease it for you. Put those antenatal exercises into practice."

She shifted and he moved in closer, holding her between his thighs while he massaged her back with firm, rhythmic strokes. "Any good?"

"It's soothing, anyway. A bit lower?"

He went on rubbing until she said, "You must be getting tired. It's helped. Thanks."

He slid his arms about her from behind, under her breasts. His hands rested on the curve below, and she felt the baby protest.

Max caught his breath. "The little blighter packs a punch," he said. His cheek was against her ear. He moved his hands over her stomach. "Do you mind?"

"No." Max was touching her, wanting to touch her, wanting to feel their child in her womb. The baby kicked again and she gave a slight breathless laugh. "Did you feel that?"

"Yes." His voice was deep, husky. "Am I bothering him?" His hands ranged over her slowly, lightly stroking across and down until they met near her groin, cradling the round fullness as she sometimes did herself on days when the baby weighed heavily and she needed to temporarily ease the burden. Her own hands lay in her lap. She lifted them and put them over his, feeling the strength of his fingers.

Max said, "He seems awfully big. Are you nervous?"

"A bit." She wondered if he found her size ugly. "Some of it's water, you know, and the placenta. The doctor doesn't think it's a big baby." Her voice sounded strained. She had a sudden desire to bring his hands down lower, invite an intimate caress. Her face grew hot, and she clasped her fingers in her lap again, away from temptation. She tried to breathe normally, her eyes on the relentless breakers racing helter-skelter, one tumbling over the other on their way to the shore.

After a while Max's hands slid up again over her stomach, and stilled on the new fullness of her breasts.

She held her breath, turned her head slightly, leaning back, and heard him whisper, "Celine—" His breath wafted her hair against her temple, and then his lips pressed warmly on the skin just below her ear. Behind her at the apex of his thighs she felt his body stirring, and his hands tightened.

"Max—" She made to move, to twist around and face him, hampered by his arms and thighs and her own cumbersome body.

Max's hands fell abruptly away from her and he stood up, the wind catching his hair and blowing it across his eyes. "God!" he said. "I'm a crass bloody fool!"

"It's all right." Celine started to get up, her hand on the driftwood log.

"No, it's *not* all right!" Impatiently, he shoved at his hair, not looking at her. His gaze fixed on the tumult of the waves, he said, "Just wait for me, I'll be back in a minute."

He went striding towards the water, and as he neared it she called, *"Max!"* Surely he wouldn't be crazy enough to go in? The surf today was murderous, and he was fully dressed.

She struggled to her feet, and then saw that he'd halted near the edge of the waves, his back rigid, feet splayed apart. He stood there for a while, then swung aside, picked up a gnarled chunk of driftwood lying nearby with a hank of seaweed attached to it, and hurled it far out into the spreading waves.

Then he turned and came trudging back to her, his hands thrust into his pockets, head lowered. As he neared her he cast a fleeting glance at her face and said, "Don't look so worried. I wasn't planning to throw myself in."

She tried to smile, but he wasn't looking at her, anyway. He scooped up a large, broken shell from the sand and threw it as hard as he could in the direction of the water, and then said, "Are you ready to go?"

He held her hand on the way back, steadied her when she stumbled, and supported her as she staggered up the sandy slope to the carpark.

The car seemed closed and stuffy after the exhilarating, boisterous air of the beach. On the way home Max hardly spoke, answering her few remarks in absent monosyllables, his eyes fiercely concentrated on the road.

Celine's thoughts were buzzing round in her head. She had no idea what was going on in Max's mind. For a brief few seconds he'd been sexually aroused. But when she'd tried to show her willingness to respond he'd pushed himself away and seemed angry.

She thought back over the sequence of events. She'd been aroused herself, even before his caress became overtly sexual. Had he felt it when he touched her newly sensitive breasts, guessed it, perhaps, even before that? Was that *why* he'd touched her that way?

And then he hadn't, after all, been able to follow through.

Why? He couldn't have been imagining she was Kate, could he? Not when he'd been tracing the shape of her—the very pregnant shape of her—with such care and deliberation.

It was weeks—months—since he'd said that Kate and he were finished. Perhaps it was quite simple. He had presumably been celibate since then, and proximity to a woman— any woman—had sparked a natural bodily reaction. It hadn't been a personal response to Celine, but the random consequence of sexual deprivation, a reflex that didn't require any particular attraction, just a crude physical stimulus that had taken him unaware when she'd leaned back against him, inviting some kind of intimacy.

Outside the house, he pulled on the brake and sat staring moodily at the windscreen, his hands drumming on the steering wheel.

"Will you come in?" Celine asked, breaking into his reverie.

He turned his head, but she wondered if he'd heard her. "Oh, sorry," he muttered, and hurried to open his door, walking round the car to help her out.

"Will you come in?" she repeated as they reached the front door.

He looked at her rather searchingly. "Would you like me to?"

"I think we should talk."

The faintest tremor of expression showed in his eyes. He followed her silently into the house.

Celine made coffee, and instead of helping or taking over as he often did, Max leaned against the sink counter, his hands in his pockets, staring broodingly at the floor.

Celine placed two steaming cups on the table and said, "It's ready."

He looked up then. "Oh . . . thanks."

She sipped at hers tentatively while he sat absently stirring his. After a while she said, "You'll wear out the spoon."

"What?" Following her ironic gaze, he removed the spoon, placing it in the saucer. For a moment he watched the dark liquid, still swirling round in the cup, and then he picked the cup up and took two large gulps before clattering it back into the saucer.

His shoulders, hunched over the table, rose and fell on a deep breath. Looking up, he found her eyes on him. "You have every right to bawl me out," he said.

"What for?"

"What *for?*" He shook his head disbelievingly and returned his gaze to his cup. A hint of dark colour crept into his skin. "For that exhibition of gross insensitivity and lack of control. I really—" He paused to clear his throat of some obstruction. "It was unexpected. That's not much of an excuse, I admit. I should have known that if I touched you . . . all I can say is it wasn't meant to be . . . to be . . ."

Watching him floundering, Celine couldn't help but smile. "Sexual?" she supplied, and saw with amazement how his colour deepened further. "Max," she said, "I'm not some shy young virgin, you know. I do have a fair idea how a man's body works. You surely didn't think I was shocked? As a matter of fact,'' she added quite deliberately, ''I'd have to say I found your involuntary reaction rather...flattering.''

''Flattering?'' He looked up, disconcerted.

''Women in my interesting state don't attract too many admiring glances,'' she said. ''I feel like a bloated cow, unattractive and unappetising—''

''Unattractive?'' Max exclaimed. ''You're *beautiful!* Why do you suppose I've hardly been able to keep my hands off you all the while I've been—''

''Been what?'' Celine asked him curiously as he hesitated.

He seemed to be searching for the right word. ''Wooing you,'' he said finally. ''Courting you. Ever since I found out that it wasn't Roland Jackson's baby you were carrying.''

Celine felt a shiver run over her skin. She swallowed, finding her voice. ''Is that what you've been doing?''

''Didn't you—?'' Max started.

And then the doorbell rang.

They sat staring at each other, as though both of them were willing the caller to go away, hoping that if they didn't move or make a sound whoever it was would give up.

It rang again, imperatively.

''Your car's in the driveway,'' Celine said, resigned. ''I'll go and see who it is.'' She got up and reluctantly went out of the room and along to the entrance lobby, and opened the door to find Kate Payne standing on the porch.

# Chapter 15

Kate's blond curls had been pulled back and secured in a loose bun. She wore an anorak and jeans, and very little makeup. In spite of the more sophisticated hairstyle, Celine thought she looked younger than ever. At a casual glance she'd easily be taken for nineteen rather than twenty-five or twenty-six.

Her face was thinner than Celine recalled—perhaps that was the effect of the hairstyle. She stared at Celine, her cornflower blue eyes widening as they took in the loose dress and the unmistakable bulge it covered. Her mouth parted, her eyes went oddly blank, while all the colour suddenly left her face. One hand went out to clutch blindly at the door frame, and Celine grabbed her arm, leading her inside.

"Here, you'd better sit down," she said grimly, almost dragging the girl into the lounge to push her into the nearest chair. "Put your head between your knees," she advised. "I'll get you a glass of water."

Kate murmured something incoherent and the fair head lifted slightly, then sank.

"Just keep still," Celine said, and made for the kitchen. Max had finished his coffee. "Who is it?"

Celine took a glass and filled it before turning to reply. "Your girlfriend," she said. "Kate."

*"Kate?"* He stood up, scraping his chair back so fast that he had to grab it before it toppled. "What's *Kate* doing here?"

"Fainting, at the moment," Celine told him. A horrible thought struck her. "Max—could she be pregnant?"

It was his turn to go pale. "Oh, God, no!" he said. "No!"

She carried the water back to the other room, and knelt by Kate's side. "Get your head up slowly—not too fast—and see if you can drink some of this." Max had followed her and was standing by the door. Her look over Kate's head warned him not to come closer.

She was relieved to see that the girl had some colour back now. Obediently, Kate drank half the water, and said, "Thank you. I feel much better now." Her gaze lit on Celine's figure again as she handed back the glass, and she gave a small shiver.

Celine stood up, using a hand on the arm of the chair for leverage, and placed the glass carefully on a side table. "You'd better sit there for a while," she said. "Are you by any chance pregnant?"

Kate blinked at her in shock, then shook her head. "*No!* Definitely not!" Apparently the idea horrified her, too.

Relief flooded through Celine. "Was it me or Max you came to see?"

"You." Kate swallowed. "I s-saw Max's car outside, and nearly went away again. But I wanted to talk to you. I didn't think I could screw up the courage to try again."

Deliberately, Celine raised her eyes to Max, still standing in the doorway. Kate turned her head and her lips parted soundlessly.

Max strolled forward and said quietly, "Hello, Kate. I'm sorry you're not well."

Her luscious mouth trembled. "Are you?"

Watching Max, Celine saw his face contract, the brows coming together. "Why are you here?" he asked.

The girl's hands twisted together, then she looked down and clamped them in her lap. "I wanted to talk to your wife."

Max was standing between her and Celine.

Celine moved to one side and dropped into a chair. It didn't seem right for both of them to be looming over their unexpected visitor. She said, speaking to Kate, "Do you want him to go?"

Kate looked at her, then at Max, and gave a little shake of her head. "It doesn't matter now."

Max took a step back, bringing him nearer to Celine, almost beside her chair. "Kate, do you really think this is a good idea?" he asked.

She scarcely glanced at him, returning an intense gaze to Celine. "He told me you *couldn't* have babies," she announced baldly.

"Kate!" Max moved almost threateningly towards her.

Celine said, "Let her talk, Max."

"That's why he came back to you, isn't it? Because you'd got yourself pregnant!"

"I did have help," Celine remarked mildly.

"I suppose he was sleeping with you all along—all the time he was with me. You told me," she added, lifting stricken eyes to Max, "that you weren't! You said all that was over between you, even before you moved out!"

Max's face was still pale. He seemed almost to wince.

To Celine, Kate said, "I was going to ask you to let him go."

"Let him go?"

"Yes. I thought if I could talk to you, explain how much we love each other, try to make you understand—"

Max said roughly, "Kate, please—"

Her voice rose a fraction. "He *said* he loved me! He said you'd never been in love with him, anyway. And you were so cold and distant you'd hardly notice that he'd gone—"

"Really?" Was that what he'd thought?

"I didn't exactly—" Max interjected.

"That's what you meant!" Kate threw at him. Turning back to Celine, she went on, "And when he told you he was leaving, you laughed at him."

That was true, Celine thought. Hadn't Max recognised the desperation behind her bitter laughter, the near hysteria of it?

"He said you wouldn't make it hard for us because you didn't care enough. You never had."

Celine momentarily closed her eyes.

"But if you didn't care, why did you keep *holding* him?"

"I'm sorry," Celine said, "I don't understand."

"There was always something," Kate cried accusingly. "He was forever running after you, even your father! Why did *Max* have to help him shift to the old folks' home?"

"It's a flat, actually. Max volunteered—I didn't ask him to do it."

"Maybe not, but I bet you hinted."

Max swore. "This has gone far enough! Actually, Celine's perfectly right. She never asked me for a thing. Everything I've done for her was my idea. Pack it in, Kate. I don't know what you hoped to achieve—"

"I told you—your freedom!"

"From me," Celine supplied, her eyebrows lifting ironically as she looked at Max.

"Kate, I tried to explain to you," Max said, his brows coming heavily together. "It's not the way you think—"

"No," Kate said bleakly. "I didn't realise that she—that *your wife* held a trump card. That the woman you told me you *weren't sleeping with* was having your *baby*. Oh, God, I've been such a fool!" She put a hand over her eyes and turned away, gulping down a sob.

"If it makes any difference, it was only one time," Celine told her. "Neither of us planned it."

Max said, "Celine, you don't have to—"

"It's all right," she answered without looking at him. A long time ago, and even more so recently, she had been just as wrenchingly hurt and humiliated, felt just as betrayed as this girl was feeling now. "It wasn't premeditated," she assured Kate. "And he couldn't have foreseen that this would come of it."

Kate had managed to swallow her tears. "Did you?"

"Did I . . . ?" Celine was confused.

"Did you...*foresee* you'd get pregnant? Why *haven't* you had a baby in all those years? You're supposed to be unable to conceive, and then suddenly, bingo! One night and that's it?" Her voice rose in disbelief. "Max said you both wanted a family—but did *you?* Or were you secretly on the pill?"

Celine heard the hiss of Max's indrawn breath. "No, I wasn't," she answered quietly. "It just...happened." She couldn't really blame Kate for the suspicion in the tear-washed eyes. "Luck," she said. "I wasn't out to trap Max into coming back to me."

Patently unconvinced, Kate said insolently, "You are sure it's his?" Turning back to Max, she added, "You told me she had a boyfriend."

"*Stop it,* Kate!" Max's voice was harshly angry. "I know I've hurt you dreadfully," he said, "and I'm sorry for it. Whatever you want to throw at me, I probably deserve ten times over. But I can't and won't allow you to attack Celine, understand?"

Watching her face, Celine doubted that he'd ever spoken to Kate in that tone before. "But...you loved me!" the girl said with stubborn despair, fresh tears swimming in her eyes. "You *did!*"

Max raked a hand into his hair. "No," he said. "I thought I did, God forgive me. You're a beautiful, talented young woman, Kate, and for a while I let that dazzle me. First it was blind emotion, and then...I'm afraid it was partly a sense of indebtedness, because you'd...given your heart and...and yourself to me. Don't ever think I took that lightly... I'm very aware of what it meant to you."

He glanced fleetingly at Celine, and then looked back at the dazed, bewildered girl before him. "Please believe that it meant a great deal to me at the time." He took a long, unsteady breath. "*I* was the fool, Kate, not you. I wronged you, and I wronged my wife, who is the best friend I've ever had, and who didn't deserve it any more than you did. Through my stupid, blind selfishness I've hurt you both, abominably and unforgivably. There's no way I can make that up to you. I'm going to spend the rest of my life making it up to Celine, if she'll let me.''

He was still looking at Kate, not moving, but Celine felt as though he'd put his hand in hers. She watched Kate's tragic young face and felt a tug of compassion.

"I love you," Kate whispered despairingly.

Max's jaw clenched. Celine could see the willpower he was exerting not to turn away. "I'm sorry I'm not worthy of it, Kate. There'll be someone else one day who you'll love even more. Someone who is free to love you as you deserve, wholeheartedly. Of course," he added with a ghost of a wry smile, as she shook her head, "you can't imagine it right now. You don't think that you can ever feel as intensely again. But please don't shut your heart to the possibility. I did that, and it was the greatest mistake of my life.''

There was a fraught silence before Kate unlocked her tightly entwined hands and stood up. Her face was colourless, and her lips trembled, but her voice was steady and her chin high and firmly set. "I—I suppose I'd better go, then." She didn't look at either of them, her shoulders consciously straight as she walked to the door.

Celine got up and followed her. Kate paused in the doorway to look at Max, who hadn't moved. "Goodbye, Max."

"Goodbye, Katie," he said gently.

She bit her lower lip and walked to the front door.

Celine hurried forward and opened it for her. "Will you be all right?" she asked as Kate dashed a hand across her eyes. "Maybe you should have a cup of tea.''

Kate looked at her with dull surprise. "Tea? No. Thanks, I'm all right.''

Quelling an urge to take the girl in her arms and comfort her, Celine said, "Take care.''

"You're not really a cold person, are you?" Kate said slowly, making an unexpected discovery. "Do you love Max?''

"Yes. I do...rather desperately, I've discovered."

The smooth young throat moved as Kate swallowed down her tears. "I'm...sorry," she said, removing her wondering gaze from Celine's face. "I misunderstood."

"We all did," Celine told her, and watched her walk away down the drive without looking back.

Celine shut the door and leaned back against it, briefly closing her eyes.

As she opened them again Max came out of the lounge and looked across at her. "Are you okay?"

"Yes." She straightened and said, "I suppose my coffee's cold."

He looked disconcerted, as if he didn't at first know what she was talking about. Then he said, "I'll make you some fresh, if you like."

"Don't bother." She walked into the lounge and picked up the half-emptied water glass.

"I'll take that," Max said, removing it from her hand. "*And* make some fresh coffee. You look all in. Why don't you sit down and relax?"

She did feel tired now, drained of energy, of the ability even to think clearly. It had been an emotional quarter hour or so. As Max left the room she sank down on the sofa. Leaning back on the cushions, she closed her eyes again.

She didn't hear Max come into the room, but the aroma of hot coffee alerted her. She sat up and took the cup from him. He had made another for himself, too, and he sat in the chair she'd used before, regarding her perhaps a little warily through a faint mist of steam.

"I'm sorry about that," he said. "Kate..."

"It's all right. I've been through it myself. Poor girl. I remember thinking my world had ended."

"Do you ever think about Mike Parrish these days?"

Celine shook her head. "Hardly ever. A waste of youthful passion, that was." She turned her cup idly in her hands. "Do you still think about Juliet?"

"Occasionally. She's a rather nice memory, and I still feel a certain sadness that she died so young. But the hurt stopped a long time ago."

He took some coffee, then nursed the cup, his eyes unseeing as they gazed past her, a line between his brows.

"She'll be all right," Celine said softly. "Your Kate. She's young, and she's no weak-kneed wimp. It took courage to come here—and even more to leave with dignity."

He cast her a rueful smile. "How did you know what I was thinking?"

"It wasn't hard to guess. I expect you'll be thinking of her for some time to come."

She saw he meant to deny it, but couldn't. "I guess I will," he said finally. "That's a penance I'll have to bear."

"I think I'm glad it was her," she murmured.

"What?" He looked baffled.

"Nothing." There were things Celine wanted to ask him, but where could she start? Max seemed withdrawn, unapproachable. She felt as though she was groping through a dim room towards the light outside, not knowing what lay in her way ready to trip her and send her falling.

In the end all the questions remained unspoken. Max took the cups to the kitchen and then said, "You probably need an early night. Shall I make you something to eat before I go?"

Celine shook her head. She had the impression that he was anxious to leave.

Over the next few weeks Celine reminded herself time after time that Max had returned to her of his own free will, that he had been the one to break off with Kate, not the other way round as she'd first thought. But always she came to the same sticking point. He'd done it because of the baby.

Not for her sake, for the sake of their child. It shouldn't matter, but it did.

He'd told Kate he didn't love her, he'd only thought so. Was it true? Or had he decided that was the only way to thoroughly burn his boats, so that Kate wouldn't tempt him to break his resolution? That kind of ruthlessness was like him.

He'd expressed his sorrow for hurting both Kate and his wife—my best friend, he'd called Celine.

Wife, best friend—many women would be perfectly happy with that description. Why wasn't she?

Crying for the moon again.


Although the weather had improved and jonquils had started flowering in the garden, Celine tended to feel lethargic. When Max suggested dinner out one cool, blustery evening, she countered with an offer of dinner at home. "I'll light the fire," she said, "and we can eat in front of it."

They used to do that in the early days of their marriage, usually with a take-away meal, but over the years the habit had lapsed to an increasingly rare treat.

"Don't bother cooking," Max said. "I'll bring something. Do you have any preference?"

"Chicken," she said.

"Spicy, crumbed, Chinese, Indonesian?"

"Any kind. Not too spicy, though. The baby might object."

He brought crumbed chicken with chips and a couple of salads. The fire was crackling away, a neat pile of freshly chopped wood stacked on the hearth. "*You* didn't cut that, I hope?" Max said.

"I didn't even carry it," Celine told him. "The boy who does the lawns did it all for me."

Max divided the food and handed her a plate. He sat by the fire on the floor, but she chose a chair. These days if she sat on the floor she had difficulty hoisting herself to her feet again.

"Delicious," she said, her emptied plate on her knee.

"Want more?" There was still some left in the containers.

"No, that was plenty. Can you put some more wood on the fire?"

It had died down to a sluggish red glow. "Not yet. It's just right for—" Max rummaged among the discarded wrappers and boxes "—these."

"Marshmallows! Don't tempt me!"

"That's just what I'm about to do. Hang on, I'll find a skewer."

Five minutes later he presented her with a delicately browned marshmallow, working it off the skewer for her and popping it into her mouth, where it melted warmly on her tongue. "Mmm," she murmured, closing her eyes. "Perfect."

The next moment she felt his mouth on hers, his hands holding her shoulders as her lips parted in surprise.

This was no tentative, formal brushing of mouth against mouth. It was a full-blooded kiss of passion, controlled but fierce and demanding. Sudden heat leapt along her veins, and her hands touched his shirt, warmed by the fire, the fabric crisp under her fingers. She slid them up until her arms were about his neck, her head tipped back under his kiss.

Kneeling before her, he pulled her towards him, kissing her still more deeply, tasting the sweet marshmallow with his tongue. Her dress rucked up as her thighs enclosed his hips. His arms went round her and he edged her gently but purposefully off the chair, easing her down as he knelt back on his heels, so that she sat comfortably on his thighs, her back supported by the chair.

His arms tightened. The baby gave a strong, protesting kick, and they broke apart, laughing.

"Wrong position, I guess," Max said, patting her placatingly. He carefully moved to one side, his arm about her shoulders. Celine straightened her legs, and his longer ones stretched out beside them.

His lips nuzzled her ear. "Do you realise," he breathed against it, "that's the first time you've kissed me back since—well, for a very long time?"

Celine sighed. "I know." Her body was pleasantly tingling. She tilted her head, allowing his mouth to wander to the groove below her ear and linger there. "It's the first time you've kissed me properly for ages," she complained. Lately he seemed to have gone back to not touching her unless he had to, his goodbye kisses nothing more than a formality, a bare meeting of mouths.

Max's head went up so that he could look at her face. "Did you want me to?"

"Sometimes," she admitted. "That day on the beach that you were so embarrassed about—"

"But you were trying to wriggle away—"

"No, you idiot! I was trying to wriggle towards you—turn around and kiss you. It just was going to take a while, arranging this bulge, but you didn't wait."

"I thought I'd blown it, offended you. You'd been putting up with the odd good-night kiss, but you were hardly enthusiastic. I figured that my reaction that day had put you right off."

"It didn't. It turned me right on." But they hadn't been able to go on where they'd left off that day, because of Kate's advent. She said, "I kept wanting to return those kisses, but somehow...I just couldn't bring myself to."

"Yes?" His free hand began lightly massaging her distended figure. "You never actively refused, and I hoped that you liked them, but there was no reciprocation. I wondered if you were trying to punish me."

"Punish you?"

"I can't say I didn't deserve it." His hand momentarily stilled as he looked up at her, and then he resumed his slow stroking.

"It wasn't that," she said. "Only I wanted more."

His eyes questioned hers. "More lovemaking?"

"More loving. Passion. I don't mean in bed—I mean, we've never allowed ourselves to express all our feelings, never tried to get under the surface of each other, of our relationship. Oh, I know I'm being unreasonable. You didn't promise me anything more than what I had. But even if it's true that you're not in love with Kate anymore—"

He stopped what he was doing and raised both hands to her face, making her look at him. "What makes you say that?" His eyes were shadowed. "Do you think I could have been that cruel to her if it wasn't true?"

"If...you wanted to set her free, because your sense of responsibility had sent you back to me, and you were determined to stick by your decision." She met his eyes unflinchingly, prepared for more pain, but knowing she had to have the truth.

"I had to set her free, yes." Max dropped his hands to her shoulders, his eyes still holding hers. "It would be monstrously selfish and unfair to let her go on thinking that I loved her. She didn't get the message when I tried to do it kindly, so the only thing left was to be brutal. It made me feel like dirt, and I won't blame Kate if she hates me for the rest of her life. I'll carry the guilt of that for the rest of mine. But I wasn't lying to her, Celine. I was fighting for my life. I was ready to sacrifice Kate or anyone else for our marriage."

"What did you feel for her, Max?" Celine asked him quietly. "It was something pretty potent."

"Attraction, at the start," he said slowly, his hands leaving her. "Physical attraction, obviously. A middle-aged impulse, no doubt. And I liked her, too—her intelligence, her drive, her eagerness about her job. She still had a youthful freshness of outlook, an idealism about the practice of law that I'd more or less forgotten as I grew older."

"But that wasn't all."

"No, it wasn't all."

"A kind of loving, then?"

Perhaps he wanted to deny it, but in the end he bowed his head in brief acknowledgement. "I guess it was," he said. "Only it didn't last. She said once I was asking too much of her, and she was right. I suppose for a little while I projected onto her, wanted to find in her, all the things that I felt I'd missed."

"In our marriage?"

He picked up her left hand, looking down at her fingers, her wedding ring. "None of it was your fault."

"Some of it was," Celine acknowledged. "You were trying to give me signals that you weren't happy, and I ignored them, didn't I?"

"It seemed like that at the time but, as you pointed out, I had the kind of marriage I'd been willing to settle for. If suddenly it wasn't enough I had only myself to blame. And I wasn't miserable, you know. I just wanted—"

"Stars."

He looked slightly confused, and she explained, "Honoria says on our honeymoon there should have been stars in our eyes. And she didn't see any."

"I think I know what she means."

"That was what Kate gave you that I hadn't, wasn't it?" Celine asked wistfully.

"I guess. The trouble is, it was about all we had. We had a lot in common at work—I thought that the strong physical attraction and the fact that we could talk for hours, share ideas, stimulate each other's minds, enjoy each other's company, added up to love. I have to admit, the way Kate looked up to me as a mentor, in some ways even a role model, fed my ego. On her part there was an element of hero-worship, I'm afraid. I guess the thing I feel worst about is that I took unwitting advantage of that. Looking back, it wasn't fair."

"But it didn't occur to you at the time?"

Max made a wry face. "At the time I was too caught up in a muddle-headed romantic daze to think it through. Oh, hell, Celine! I shouldn't be telling you all this."

"I was very jealous." Perhaps he was right, but since he'd started talking of it, she discovered a dire need to hear more.

"Jealous?" His eyes searched her face. "I wondered, a couple of times. But you seemed so cool. Angry, of course, but I put that down to hurt pride. When you started advising me about Kate in that detached, clinical way, I thought, This woman doesn't give a damn. If you cared at all for me, in more than a mild fashion, I didn't see how you could be so... objective. The odd thing was, when it should have pleased me, it made me mad as hell."

"I wasn't always able to be objective. And at that particular time, if you recall, you'd just made love to me and then told me it was all a mistake that shouldn't have happened."

Max momentarily closed his eyes. "It was then," he said, opening them again, "that I became totally confused. We'd made wonderful love together, after the biggest fight of our lives—not barring when we were children—and I wanted nothing more than to take you back to bed and do it all over again. But by then I was committed to Kate. Making love to two women concurrently must be an all-time low for despicable behaviour.'' He gave a crack of laughter.

Staring, Celine said, ''What's funny?''

''It isn't, really. The fact is, after that night I couldn't... satisfy Kate. I guess I hated myself so much my mind put a halt to things. I wasn't able to perform.''

''Oh, Max! How embarrassing.'' She tried to look sympathetic, and she was, she *was,* she reminded herself, sinking her teeth into her lower lip.

He must have seen the suppressed laughter in her eyes. ''All right,'' he said. ''Crow if you want to. It wasn't funny at the time, I can assure you.''

''You mean after that you never...?''

He looked at her and glanced away. ''A couple of times I managed...but somehow it was never the same. And it didn't help that every time I saw *you,* my mind insisted on replaying that last time we'd been together, remembering how fantastic it was. I had to keep telling myself it couldn't have been that good.''

''Yes, it was,'' Celine told him.

''For you, too?'' His eyes lit briefly. ''I didn't dare to believe that.'' He sighed. ''You seemed to get more beautiful and more desirable every day, and it jolted me when I found that other men had noticed. You weren't the only one who was jealous. I despised myself for that, too. As you said, I'd given up the right to feel like that about you. I should have let you alone, left you free to make a life without me, and yet I found myself clutching at any excuse to see you.''

''So Kate wasn't imagining things?''

He shook his head. ''She had a right to complain. Every time I saw you, I'd remember how it had been, the things we both liked, the way we could share a joke without exchanging a word—I always had to explain, to Kate, and then she often didn't see it, or didn't think it funny. I kept recalling the stupidest little happenings and wanting to say, 'Do you remember...?' We'd shared so much for so long.''

''I thought that was part of the problem,'' Celine objected. ''Weren't you bored because you thought we knew all there was to know about each other, that there was nothing new for us?''

"Maybe," he conceded. "No, it wasn't that, exactly. I've always known that there were depths to you that I'd never explored—that maybe you didn't want me to." Giving her no chance to comment on that, he continued. "I'd remember what you were like at ten years old—at fifteen—at Kate's age. And then I found myself comparing, finding her less mature, less perceptive than you were even at twenty-five."

"We'd known each other a long time by then," Celine reminded him. A faint, fluttery hope fought with a confusion of other emotions. So he'd found Kate less than perfect, after all. But all that meant was that she'd been less good at reading him than Celine, who'd known him all her life.

"I know," Max agreed. "I knew I was doing her a gross injustice, and felt like a louse. The fault was in me. Why couldn't I accept her for what she was? Good God, I'd ditched my marriage, treated you appallingly and virtually estranged myself from my entire family because I was so sure I'd found in her exactly what I wanted, what I'd been subconsciously searching for. And when it began turning sour, there was no one to blame but myself."

Celine bit her tongue. There was no arguing with that. But she restrained her natural impulse to rub salt in his wounds. Max was doing a fair job of beating himself; he didn't need her help.

"I was going crazy," he said, "falling in love with my own wife—my estranged wife!"

*Falling in love?* Celine's head jerked up at that, her eyes painfully fixed on his face.

His voice had lowered, and he didn't meet her eyes. "I kept thinking of you—wondering what you were doing, who you were with. In the end I had to tell Kate I'd made a horrible mistake. That it was all over. And after what I hoped was the minimum decent interval I came to find out if there was any hope you'd have me back, and discovered you were pregnant, as I thought, to another man—and even though

I thoroughly deserved it, that was the worst—*worst*—time of my entire life.''

He raised his eyes then and, catching her arrested expression, he frowned. "What is it? What's the matter?"

"You..." Her voice cracked, and she started again. "You broke off with Kate *before* you knew I was pregnant?"

"You didn't know that? I'm sure I said—"

Vehemently, Celine shook her head. "I assumed you'd done it because of the baby. Heavens, that's why I tried to keep it a secret from you that you were the father! I didn't want you back out of duty or conscience. I couldn't *bear* it!"

Max grabbed both her hands in his. "The baby—once I knew it was mine—was a bonus. What *I* couldn't bear was the thought that I'd thrown away everything we had, and everything we might have had in the future, for a mirage, a false emotion that hadn't lasted."

"Your mother said you couldn't conceive of being the victim of an infatuation, that you'd have to believe it was something more important."

Reluctantly, he seemed to think about this. "Maybe she's right. I guess I'm an arrogant bastard—I didn't want to see myself as just another married man involved in an extramarital affair. And then Kate—I knew it wasn't a trivial thing for her, and I couldn't just walk away. So I persuaded myself I had to be serious about her. A way, I suppose, of retaining some self-respect. Being in love was my excuse for what I'd done to her—and to you."

In a funny way she could understand that. She'd done some pretty strange things, too, in her attempts to retain her self-respect. "Our problem was," she told him, "that for twelve years we short-changed each other, skating over the surface of our emotions, never allowing them to go too deep. Because we'd loved once and found that it hurt when things didn't work for us."

"You're damned right," Max agreed. "It wasn't true that I had used up all my capacity for romantic love on Juliet. I'd just slammed those feelings away and locked them up because I couldn't face the prospect of that kind of grief again.

But when I thought I'd lost you, through my own stupid fault, I discovered how deep my feelings for you really were. Much deeper and much truer than I'd ever realised.''

"And it wasn't true, either, that Mike had taken all the romance from my life. I was just scared that I'd give myself, my heart, all over again to someone who didn't really want it.''

"I practically told you I didn't want it when I asked you to marry me,'' Max recalled. "I'm sorry, Celine. Sorry for the years we've wasted.''

"They weren't wasted. All these years that love has been building up, layer by layer. Even if the stars don't always shine, they're still in the sky.''

"I guess we never saw them before because we didn't believe in them.'' He lifted her hands and kissed them one by one, almost reverently.

That was one thing Kate had done for him, she supposed. He'd been shaken out of his conviction that falling in love was a once-in-a-lifetime thing. She decided that the next time, and the next and the next forever after, it was going to be with her.

A little hiss came from the fire, and Max said, "I'll put on some more wood.''

"If you like, but—''

"But?'' Poised over the woodpile, he looked at her inquiringly.

"I think I'd be more comfortable in bed.''

"I guess so.''

She saw he was uncertain of her meaning. "Help me up and take me to bed,'' she said.

When he slid into the bed beside her, he said, "What do your baby books say about star-gazing?''

"They say it's easy if you adopt the right position.''

"Sure it's allowable at this stage?'' He took her hand again and began nibbling at her fingers with his lips.

"I'm sure.''

He put his other hand on the hump under the bed-clothes. "I love this, I'll miss it when it's gone. It's such a round, smooth, feminine shape. Quintessentially, prime-vally female.''

Celine turned her head and kissed him.

"Is it okay to touch you here?" he asked her, his hand tentatively on her breast.

"Okay? It's wonderful." She manoeuvred herself into a more comfortable position.

"What about here?" he whispered, his hand wandering.

"Mmm, bliss."

Max shifted, trying to fit himself around her. "We're going to have to learn a whole lot of new techniques."

"Sorry."

"Not at all. It's exciting, don't you think?" he asked her as his hand found a new place to nestle.

Celine gasped. "That is!"

Some little time later he said, "Can you—no."

Stifling a laugh, Celine murmured, "Maybe we could—umph! They *say* this is possible! Hand me a pillow, would you?"

"Better?" she asked him when she'd settled herself again.

His tongue circled her ear. "Ah, yes. Is it comfortable for you, like this?"

"It's—it's more than comfortable. Oh, Max—"

He laughed softly. "I'm glad you like it. I do, too. I'll make it last if I can, but I've waited so long for this—"

"So have I . . . I want . . . Oh, yes! *That!*"

The stars came down out of the sky and burst around them, and much, much later, as he lay at her side with his hand resting lightly against the sphere that housed their baby, she said, "And the moon, too."

"What?" Max's eyes gleamed at her in the darkness.

"Never mind," she said, drifting into a euphoric, weightless sleep. "No more crying . . ."

# Chapter 16

"What are we going to call her?" Max gave his little finger to his new daughter, and watched entranced as she curled her small hand about it. "Do you want to name her for your mother?"

"I don't know. Do you think she looks like an Elizabeth?"

"Beth, maybe."

"What about Bethel?"

"Mmm. She could shorten it if she wants to."

"You don't mind that it's a girl, do you?" Celine asked. "She could be the only one."

"Mind? I'm over the moon, haven't you noticed? And she's definitely the only one!"

Celine laughed. "It wasn't that bad!"

"I never want to go through that again!"

"*You* don't?"

"I don't want to see *you* do it again. I was scared stiff for you."

"It was hard work, but worth it." Celine looked down at the baby, who had relinquished her father's finger and was gazing up at her mother while she tried to stuff her hand into her mouth.

"God, I love you!" Max said, his eyes on Celine's smiling face.

Celine looked up, her eyes reciprocating, and he leaned across to kiss her, his lips lingering.

The baby opened its mouth and wailed, limbs flailing inside its wrapping.

Max sat back. "I thought she'd stop making our love-life difficult once she was born."

"She's hungry." Celine began unbuttoning her gown.

Fascinated, Max watched the baby nuzzle impatiently at her breast and begin to drink.

After a while he said, "Do you mind if I hold you while you do that?"

"It might be a bit tricky." There was amusement in her eyes.

"I've learned a thing or two in the last couple of months," he said, and walked to the other side of the bed to hitch himself up on it and seat himself behind her. His arms came round under hers, cradling both her and the baby, and his cheek was against her temple. "Do you know I find this incredibly sexy," he whispered in her ear.

"Max!"

"Have I shocked you? It's okay, I know I have to be patient, and I will be, for as long as you need. Promise. But I can dream." He turned his head a little and kissed her temple, then slid his lips to her ear and gently caught the soft lobe in his teeth.

Celine moved her head, and he lifted his. "Sorry."

But she turned her face to him and said, "I dream, too. You won't have long to wait, Max. Kiss me."

Max obliged, with barely restrained passion, while their daughter, oblivious to what was going on above her downy head, continued to get on with the important business of life.

\* \* \* \* \*

Get Ready to be Swept Away by
Silhouette's Spring Collection

# Abduction *&* Seduction

These passion-filled stories explore both the dangerous
desires of men and the seductive powers of women.
Written by three of our most celebrated authors, they are
sure to capture your hearts.

### Diana Palmer
Brings us a spin-off of her Long, Tall Texans series

### Joan Johnston
Crafts a beguiling Western romance

### Rebecca Brandewyne
*New York Times* bestselling author
makes a smashing contemporary debut

Available in March at your favorite retail outlet.

ABSED

**MONTANA**™
*Mavericks*

Stories that capture living and loving
beneath the Big Sky, where legends live
on...and mystery lingers.

This February, the plot thickens with

### WAY OF THE WOLF
### by Rebecca Daniels

Raeanne Martin had always been secretly drawn to
the mysterious Rafe "Wolf Boy" Rawlings. Now they
battled by day on opposite sides of a murder trial.
But by night, Raeanne fought an even tougher battle
for Rafe's love.

Don't miss a minute of the loving as the passion
continues with:

> **THE LAW IS NO LADY**
> by Helen R. Myers (March)
>
> **FATHER FOUND**
> by Laurie Paige (April)
>
> **BABY WANTED**
> by Cathie Linz (May)
> and many more!

Only from **V** *Silhouette*® where passion lives.
™

**HEARTBREAKERS**

Hot on the heels of **American Heroes** comes Silhouette Intimate Moments' latest and greatest lineup of men: **Heartbreakers**. They know who they are—and *who* they want. And they're out to steal your heart.

RITA award-winning author Emilie Richards kicks off the series in March 1995 with *Duncan's Lady*, IM #625. Duncan Sinclair believed in hard facts, cold reality and his daughter's love. Then sprightly Mara MacTavish challenged his beliefs—and hardened heart—with her magical allure.

In April *New York Times* bestseller Nora Roberts sends hell-raiser Rafe MacKade home in *The Return of Rafe MacKade*, IM #631. Rafe had always gotten what he wanted—until Regan Bishop came to town. She resisted his rugged charm and seething sensuality, but it was only a matter of time....

Don't miss these first two **Heartbreakers**, from two stellar authors, found only in—

INTIMATE MOMENTS®
Silhouette®

# Southern Knights

Join Marilyn Pappano in March 1995 as her **Southern Knights** series draws to a dramatic close with *A Man Like Smith*, IM #626.

Federal prosecutor Smith Kendricks was on a manhunt. His prey: crime boss Jimmy Falcone. But when his quest for justice led to ace reporter Jolie Wade, he found himself desiring both her privileged information—and the woman herself....

Don't miss the explosive conclusion to the **Southern Knights** miniseries, only in—

KNIGHT3

# EXTRA! EXTRA! READ ALL ABOUT...
## MORE ROMANCE
## MORE SUSPENSE
## MORE INTIMATE MOMENTS

Join us in February 1995 when Silhouette Intimate Moments introduces the first title in a whole new program: INTIMATE MOMENTS EXTRA. These breakthrough, innovative novels by your favorite category writers will come out every few months, beginning with Karen Leabo's *Into Thin Air*, IM #619.

Pregnant teenagers had been disappearing without a trace, and Detectives Caroline Triece and Austin Lomax were called in for heavy-duty damage control...because now the missing girls were turning up dead.

In May, Merline Lovelace offers *Night of the Jaguar*, and other INTIMATE MOMENTS EXTRA novels will follow throughout 1995, only in—

INTIMATE MOMENTS® Silhouette®